# SIGNATURES AND SACRAMENTS

**By the same author:**

*A Journey of Ascent: A Family Saga,* Book Guild Publishing, 2012

# SIGNATURES AND SACRAMENTS

*A Family Story From London's Past*

Best wishes
Andy P. Weller

Book Guild Publishing
Sussex, England

First published in Great Britain in 2013 by
The Book Guild Ltd
Pavilion View
19 New Road
Brighton, BN1 1UF

The characters are based upon real people.

Typesetting in Baskerville by
Nat-Type, Cheshire

Printed in Great Britain by
CPI Group (UK) Ltd, Croydon, CR0 4YY

A catalogue record for this book is available from
The British Library.

ISBN 978 1 84624 800 9

# Contents

# Acknowledgements

As with my first book, *A Journey of Ascent: A Family Saga* (Book Guild, 2012), I am grateful to the Library Services of the London Borough of Hillingdon for locating and supplying a range of books I requested to aid my research in support of the telling of these stories.

# *Prologue*

Josephus Clout came to Clerkenwell as a boy of twelve looking for work and was taken on as an apprentice bookbinder. He followed the same path taken by his uncle who had previously left the Kentish countryside looking for work. Josephus was a man of faith. He carried the same old Hebrew name as his father, a name deliberately chosen as a sign to others of faith and religious awareness.

Josephus was an ancient Jewish historian who was born just a few years after Jesus was crucified. Josephus wrote about Jesus but also about Jesus' brother James, John the Baptist, Pontius Pilate and the Sadducees and the Sanhedrin and the high priests of the Temple who played such a large part in Jesus being brought to trial and then executed on the cross.

What appealed to Christian scholars through the ages is that Josephus, a Jew, described Jesus in terms of being 'the Christ'. Yet many serious Christian scholars questioned whether a Jew would ever make such a statement about Jesus being the Messiah. Then there were others all too happy and willing to accept this as evidence for their faith from someone that lived so soon after their Lord Jesus was crucified on the cross.

Our Josephus' church and his beliefs in God and the Scripture were fundamental to his very existence and being. He was a constant member of the congregation at his beloved Wren-built church of St James's close by Piccadilly. Whether you were sitting or standing in the main body of the church or you were up in the galleries, as many as two thousand souls could clearly hear the preacher's lesson and address.

Clerkenwell was famed for bookbinding and printing but also for brewing and distilling. Indeed, Cannon's Brewery in St John Street was one of the largest breweries in the country. With the arrival of Italian immigrants, the area also gained a reputation for watch-making and glassblowing.

We pick up the story when Josephus has been married to his second wife, Elizabeth, for some eighteen years. Their relationship is based upon companionship though there is a degree of affection. Neither seems to need or to require the intimacy of the marital bed, as a consequence of both their nature and character and no doubt their deep-seated religious beliefs that physical desires should be suppressed unless with the specific intent of creating new life.

Nine years separate their ages. Elizabeth Clear was but seventeen when she accepted Josephus' proposition of marriage. Elizabeth was both willing and pleased to commit herself to someone of good character and of sound moral and religious fortitude. She knew also that her potential husband had a respectable trade and steady income. Many young women of her age and from such an ordinary background and station in life would aspire to such a circumstance. Elizabeth also accepted that Josephus was seeking a wife so soon after the loss of his first wife, also named Elizabeth, because he needed someone to tend and care for his young daughter, Mary Kezia. She accepted that this was to be her lot in life.

Kezia is also a traditional Hebrew name and is found in the Old Testament as one of the fair daughters of Job. Josephus decided upon the names of Mary and Kezia both as a sign of his faith and family tradition and to display his knowledge of Scripture to all those who were acquainted with the word of God.

It was to be some three years into their marriage when Josephus and Elizabeth were to have their one and only child. He was baptised as William Frederick in honour of His Majesty King George William Frederick (King George III).

Now let the story begin.

# Timeline

*King or Queen*

George III (1760–1820)

George IV (1820–1830)
William IV (1830–1837)

Queen Victoria (1837–1901)

*Notable events*

1776 US independence

1789 outbreak of French revolution
1805 Battle of Trafalgar
1815 Battle of Waterloo
1833 Slavery abolished in the British Empire

1845–1849 Irish potato famine
1854–1856 Crimean War
1861 Charles Dickens completes *Great Expectations* in book form
1865 Bazelgette completes London's sewage system; *Alice in Wonderland* published

# THE PRINCIPAL CHARACTERS

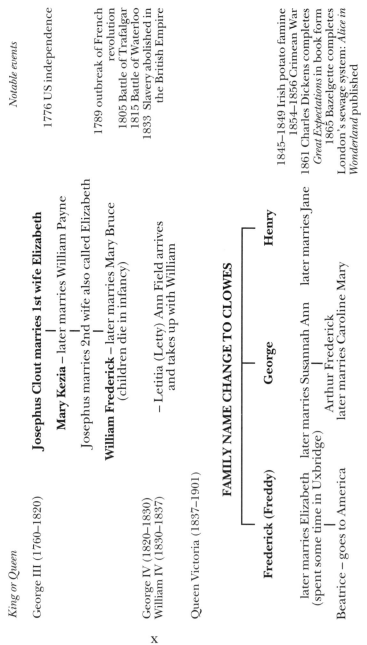

**Josephus Clout marries 1st wife Elizabeth**

**Mary Kezia** – later marries William Payne

Josephus marries 2nd wife also called Elizabeth

**William Frederick** – later marries Mary Bruce (children die in infancy)

– Letitia (Letty) Ann Field arrives and takes up with William

# FAMILY NAME CHANGE TO CLOWES

**Frederick (Freddy)**     **George**     **Henry**

later marries Elizabeth  later marries Susannah Ann  later marries Jane
(spent some time in Uxbridge)

Arthur Frederick
later marries Caroline Mary

Beatrice – goes to America

# THE FAMILY OF ARTHUR AND CAROLINE MARY

Arthur – later marries Edith

Christopher

Caroline (Carrie)

Phil (Aetherius Virgilius Augustine) – later marries Grace

Hilda Faith

Aidan Finian Cuthbert Chad

Gregory Alban Ambrose Bede

Elsie (Althea Ethelreda Monica)

Twins: Benedict Theodore Laud Charles and
Scholastica Theodora Helena

1885 professional football legalised

1894 Tower Bridge opens to traffic

1899–1902 Boer War

Edward VII (1901–1910)

1908 Ford start production
of motor cars

1914–1918 The Great War (WWI)

George V 1910–1936

1921 signing of the Anglo–Irish Treaty that in turn leads to the establishment of the Republic of Ireland

# SIGNATURES

# Part I

# The House of Detention

# Chapter 1

'Gotcha! You think you can steal off of me, do you, old man? I've had enough of you vagrants and idlers taking advantage of me. Send the whole lot of you to the colonies, that's what I say.' Then, turning to his lad helper, he adds:

'Thomas, off to the Watch House with you and bring back a constable.'

'I've seen this man about, Mr Preston. I'm not so sure he is a vagrant and his appearance suggests he is perhaps not such a person, Sir,' answers Thomas.

'He was trying to steal from me and that is enough cause for him to be up before the magistrates. Now get on your way to the Watch House. I'll detain him here. Doesn't look as though he is capable of causing me any more trouble.'

About an hour later Thomas returns with the constable to apprehend and take away the thief, who by this time is sitting quietly upon a box in a seemingly distressed and confused state of mind.

After some coaxing, the constable gets the thief to give his name so that Mr Preston will know who he is to testify against when a case comes up for trial. The constable then leads the thief away to be charged and detained.

Thomas hears the name 'Josephus Clout' and remembers that he has seen this man coming in and out of the bookbinder's premises that he passes when visiting his parents at home.

Thomas is convinced that what has taken place is more than a case of a vagrant or an idler lifting another person's property. Above all, the thief seemed genuinely confused and the quality of his dress showed that he lived in a manner that was certainly better than Thomas' own situation. Thomas decides that someone needs to know what has taken place. Somewhat unusual, it may be thought, for a lad of such age to show such maturity, but Thomas Field makes discreet enquiries at the bookbinding establishment. He finds out where this Josephus Clout lives.

It is as a consequence of this young man's actions that Josephus' wife Elizabeth and daughter Mary Kezia call upon Mr Preston. They hope to appeal to his Christian spirit and charity and not to press for a harsh criminal penalty.

Upon leaving Mr Preston's premises, Mary spots young Thomas Field returning, she supposes, from some sort of errand on Preston's behalf. Mary approaches him.

'We should have asked your name when you came to tell us about what had happened to my father. We were too distraught. Please tell me now.'

'Thomas, Miss. Thomas Field.'

'Well, Thomas, we are grateful to you and at least we have had the chance to talk to Mr Preston and to appeal to his Christian nature. How long have you been working for Mr Preston and how old are you, Thomas? Does Mr Preston treat you kindly?'

'I have been here some four or five months, Miss. I am coming on for eight years of age and I run errands for Mr Preston and do some small deliveries and he lets me sleep in there beneath the counter.'

Thomas points inside, beyond where the stall juts out into the street.

'He can bark at me sometimes, Miss, but I have no reason to complain. My father, mother and my brothers and sisters have fairly recently come to London from the country as there is no work to be had there. We are seven in all and we just have the one room, so it's best for me and best for them that I can sleep and stay here and at least we have a few more pennies coming our way.'

'When you are a bit older, Thomas Field, you can seek out my brother William Clout at the bookbinder's in Sheep Conduit Street. I know you know it well because that's where you found out where we live. Now if you have a mind to it, he may be able to set you up to learn about bookbinding. It is an honourable trade for any working boy and man to be in and you will do better than if you stayed with Mr Preston. We will then be able to repay your kindness to us.'

'Thank you, Miss. Thank you very much. I think I would like that.'

For the first time since his family left the open spaces and fresh feel of Frimley, young Thomas Field feels that he has something to smile about. In the meantime, however, he would continue to try and work hard and to keep Mr Preston satisfied with his efforts.

# Chapter 2

Mary Kezia has been with her family as a housekeeper and governess for some seven months before the arrest and detention of her father. Mary has always envisaged that she would not need to seek employment and that she would have a comfortable life at home until such time as she married and married well. Mary is not what you would call a pretty girl but she is far from being unattractive. Her shapely figure and her long, reddish-brown hair often encourage a gentleman or a man to glance in her direction a second time. She is also quite tall and this adds to her bearing.

Sometime ago the reality of her family's situation dawned upon her and Mary had to accept that her father was not going to be able to continue working for much longer and that she would have to become more responsible for her own upkeep and well-being.

Mary is an intelligent and well-read young woman. However, given the relatively few opportunities for a young woman such as her, she settles upon seeking a position as a governess or a housekeeper–governess. At least this would give her a station better than and higher than other persons entering into service below stairs. Even so, through her employment she now finds herself placed in a particular social category and this will determine her whole future. Apart from the company of the children in her care, hers is a rather lonely existence in the household. She is not one of the servants and yet she is not one of the family either. Although Mary and the cook, Mrs Crompton, have a reasonable relationship, it would not be proper for Mary to take her meals below stairs. Mary therefore takes her meals alone in her room. In the evenings she has nothing to do for entertainment other than to read.

Mary has heard bad things about how some of these so-called 'middle-' or 'professional-class' families treat their servants and staff. She considers herself fortunate. Her family is decent and they are honourable in the way in which they behave towards their servants. Mary is treated in a courteous and reasonable fashion. Those less fortunate than herself, particularly girls and young women from the country, are all too often mistreated and abused.

Mrs Crompton is a widow who has known more comfortable times but now finds that she needs employment as a cook in order to be able to keep herself. The housemaid-cum-parlour maid Susan completes the servant side of the household. Susan is a conscientious and hard-working girl who also fully appreciates her good fortune in finding such a good family to work for.

The master of the house in Baker Street is by profession a manager of a branch bank. The mistress, some ten years younger than her husband, has a kind and gentle disposition, although she is somewhat reserved in as much as she receives visits from only two or three persons who are clearly her close friends.

Mary has the impression that Mrs Carlton neither needs nor seeks a wide social circle. Yet, being a good and loyal wife, she attends and hosts any events in support of her husband and with apparent good grace. When the Carltons entertain in numbers, agency staff are brought in. It is important to show that they can organise and hold successful social gatherings.

The son, James, is nearly seven years old and his sister, Charlotte, is almost two years younger. Before the children got very much older a private tutor will be engaged. Eventually, as is the way of things, James will be sent away to board at school. Mary therefore wonders just for how much longer her services will be required.

The arrest and detention of her father and now the up-and-coming trial presents Mary with a dilemma. Should she keep quiet and hope that her employer did not get to hear about things, or should she volunteer the information and hope that she will be able to retain her position. Mary has to decide quickly. Too many people are all too eager to spread gossip and to exaggerate the circumstances whilst they are about it. Mary decides to speak to Mrs Carlton after the children have completed breakfast and the master has left for his business.

As is the custom, Mary knocks on the morning-room door before entering but does not need to wait for a response.

'If it please, Madam, may I talk to you about a sensitive and personal matter and a situation that I feel that both you and the master should be aware of?'

Mrs Carlton looks up from her correspondence and personal papers that she has been attending to at her desk. She has a puzzled look upon her face as Mary has only ever spoken to her before in relation to matters affecting the running of the household or the care of the children.

'Miss Clout, by all means. You do indeed look troubled. Would you care to sit down?'

'That is kind of you, Madam, but I prefer to stand, thank you very much. There is something that has happened that I feel I should tell you about. It is in relation to my father, Madam. As you will recall from our interview, my father has for many years now been engaged as a bookbinder and as a journeyman he has been responsible for the training of his apprentices. You will also recall that not only is he highly respected within his profession but also within his church.'

Mrs Carlton nods her head but retains the puzzled look on her face as she wonders where this conversation is leading to.

'Well, Madam, what I have not told you is that of late my father's health has somewhat deteriorated. Particularly at times like this in this cold and damp weather he has the tendency to lose some of the mobility in his hands. This means that he is now spending more time bringing on his apprentices than actually partaking in his profession. My father is a proud and independent person, Madam. He misses the practical aspects of his work and feels shame that his hands will no longer do his bidding. I am sure that this affliction has been preying on his mind for some considerable time.' Mary hesitates a moment before continuing.

'We have noticed another change in him. There are times when he becomes withdrawn and of late there is even about him a sense of confusion. We have a fear that someday soon he may lose his wits altogether.' Again she hesitates.

'What I have to tell you now, Madam, does not come easy. The news I have may give you cause to consider whether you still wish to keep me in your employment. You know just how cold and severe this weather has been of late. Nevertheless, my father's income and that of my brother, who you will remember is also a bookbinder, together with what I send home from my earnings, enables my family to live in a degree of comfort. We certainly have enough to house ourselves and to keep ourselves warm.

'Well, we think that my father's ... confusion gave him cause to behave in an irrational and unnecessary manner. On his way from work to home we think that the sight of coal and lighting materials besides a can of oil besides a merchant's stall excited him. In his confused state of mind we think that he was convinced that such things were needed for his and our security and warmth. His hands were in such a poor and pitiful condition at that time, Madam, that he could hardly pick the items up, let alone take them away, but this is what he tried to do and to do so without paying.

'My father was detained by the merchant in question and his boy was sent to the Watch House to fetch a constable. As a consequence, my father is now held in the Clerkenwell House of Detention and will remain there until he comes up in front of the magistrate sometime after Christmas ... charged with larceny.' Mary's voice falters but she gathers herself together.

'I value and enjoy my engagement here, Madam, especially with the children. My father has been a good and honest man all his life – his church and his beliefs are the cornerstone of his character. His illness has caused him to act in this strange way and now he is to be considered a criminal. All I can ask, Madam, is that you do not judge either my father or me too harshly.'

After a few moments of silence Mrs Carlton finds her words.

'These are indeed most serious and grave tidings. I must speak of this to my husband when he returns this evening. You must wait to hear what we decide. I, certainly, will not press for your dismissal – indeed, I have been much pleased with the way in which you go about your duties and your care for the children. We will speak on this matter later.'

For the remainder of the day there is nothing more that Mary can do other than to go about her duties as normal. Her concerns swing between the fate of her father and, to a lesser extent, what decision the master and the mistress will arrive at. For now Mary will say nothing of this to either Mrs

11

Crompton and certainly not to Susan. There will be time enough for that later.

It is not in fact until the following morning that Mary is spoken to by Mrs Carlton. The interview is very brief.

'My husband and I have discussed the matter, Miss Clout. You may remain with us.'

Mary is left with the impression that perhaps the master has needed to be brought around to Mrs Carlton's thinking. Perhaps his position as a branch bank manager makes him less receptive to having her stay on in the house. Now is the time for Mary to tell things to Mrs Crompton and to Susan before others have the opportunity.

# Chapter 3

Will has fallen in love with Mary Elizabeth Bruce – his 'Sweet Mary' and the friend of his sister, Mary Kezia. Their coming together has been somewhat contrived with the assistance of Will's sister. The girls – now young women – have known each other for a number of years. The two Marys used to visit each other's houses. Will was obviously a few years younger than his half-sister and her friend, but then, as Will turned from a boy into a young man, it became clear to his sister that Will was starting to take an interest in her attractive friend.

Will would often enquire of his sister when Mary was next coming for Sunday tea. Will's sister then started to arrange things so that whenever Mary Elizabeth called it was at a time when Will was expected to be at home. When outings were arranged Mary would try and bring Will with her. Will's interest appeared to be reciprocated and whether or not it was because Mary Elizabeth was becoming worried that she had yet to find a husband, Will did not care. He knew what and whom he wanted and Will took to attending Mary

Elizabeth's church rather than his customary own place of worship.

Then came the sad turn of events about his father and Will has realised that he needs to break the news to Mary. It is a bitterly cold December morning and the north wind is enough to cut a soul in half. The sky is dark with heavy low clouds and during the service driving sleet has started to fall. After the service Will pulls on Mary Elizabeth's coat sleeve, indicating that he wants them to remain behind in the church.

'Mary, my dearest. I have some difficult and distressing news to tell you that may give you cause to ask for us to bring to an end our understanding. Come, let's sit down over there so we that might not be noticed so easily.'

Even in the relative gloom of the church Will can see Mary's face change and drain of all colour. He feels her body stiffen.

'What is it? Do you not love me after all?' Mary says in a soft and pleading voice.

'Of course I do, you silly goose, but things have happened and you and your family may want no more association with us Clouts any more. There is no easy way to tell you this, Mary. You know that my father is prone at times to confusion and that the problems he has with not being able to use his hands and work has been making his mental condition worse?

'Now steel yourself, Mary, against what I have to say. My father, whilst in such a confused state of mind, has been caught in the act of trying to steal a few pieces of coal and some oil and paper. The constable was sent for and my father is now being held at the House of Detention in Clerkenwell. He will come up before the magistrate in a few weeks' time and, although we are to engage a lawyer to make a special pleading, it is certain that he will be sentenced to more time in gaol. With all this shame and disgrace I must now offer you the chance to break away from me. You will, of course, also need to take into account what your family thinks about all this.'

'Oh your poor father!' is the first thing that Mary can say. 'This must be terrible not just for him but for your mother and Mary and of course for you, my love. No matter what happens, Will, I want to be your wife and for us to be together. As for my father and mother, well if they should now rail against us being married then I shall remind them about the black sheep in *our* family.'

'My dear! You humble me with your answer. Then we shall go on as planned. It will still take some time for me to continue to progress as a bookbinder and to build up some savings but as soon as we can I promise that we will be wed.'

# Chapter 4

For a little over four weeks now, including over Christmas, Josephus Clout has been detained in Clerkenwell prison, also known as the House of Detention, the normal place where persons are kept before their appearance and trial before the magistrates.

Above the main door to the prison there hangs in relief a grotesque face with an open screaming mouth, sunken eyes and matted hair. The image is intended to represent a prisoner's despair.

Once inside the body of the House of Detention, prisoners are faced with iron steps that then lead them down into a world of damp labyrinthine tunnels and corridors and to the miserable, dark, dank and dingy underground cells.

The constant sound of dripping cold water from above onto the damp, cold stone floor adds further to the chill and terror felt by all. The whole fabric and feel of the House of Detention are enough to unnerve any man and indeed they have had such an effect upon the hapless Josephus. The distress and fear caused by such conditions is even worse for the children who are also detained in this dreadful place. Their crying and wailing greatly affects Josephus' already shattered nerves and troubled mind.

Whoever finds themselves in this godforsaken place soon becomes aware of the expectation that at some time or another they will encounter the shadowy figure of a lady's ghost wandering the grim and dark underground passages. It is said that such were the depths of this lady's despair that her grief and torment has become imprinted into the very bricks and mortar of the place.

It is the seventeenth of January and Josephus has been taken from the House of Detention and now comes before Magistrate McKinnon, Justice of the Peace, at the Middlesex Sessions in Clerkenwell.

This being the first time Josephus finds himself on the wrong side of the law he is fearful of his fate. He is completely overawed by his surroundings: by the size of the building and the holding dungeon cells where he has spent the night in preparation for his trial. The ornate grandeur of the courtroom makes him yet more ill at ease. Josephus has only seen such splendour before where it should be: in the House of God. Josephus Clout is now standing in the dock and Magistrate McKinnon begins the proceedings.

'Josephus Clout, of the parish of St James, Westminster, you stand charged of larceny to the effect that on the thirteenth of December 1809 you did steal the goods and chattels of one John Preston, the goods in question being four pieces of coal to the value of three pence, half a pint of oil to the value of three pence and twenty sheets of paper to the value of three pence.'

'I see before me the unusual prospect of a prisoner in my court that has a friend to represent him. Who are you are, Sir, and why are you here?'

'I represent the prisoner in this matter, Your Honour, and I am Francis Thane, attorney-at-law. If it please Your Honour, the prisoner openly admits his guilt and not wishing to be a burden upon the Court's, and of course your, time, he places himself at your mercy, Your Honour. My reason for being here, Your Honour, is to offer a special pleading on the prisoner's behalf. The family has found the necessary funds to engage me in this matter and this, I think, is an indication of their warm affection for this man and their deep concern for his fate. So, if it please Your Honour, before passing judgement may I just say a few words about the circumstances that have led the prisoner to be standing before you today?'

Magistrate McKinnon nods his head and waves his hand in a somewhat uninterested manner to indicate that Thane may proceed.

'Josephus Clout has led an industrious, sober and productive life to date but now at the age of fifty-three, and with his hands being in such poor condition, he finds that he is unable to work at his exacting trade as a bookbinder when the weather is cold or wet. That said, Your Honour, he has continued to be engaged as a journeyman educating and bringing on his apprentices. Furthermore, added to the difficulty with his hands, he is a man, like others of his age, who can be affected badly with the confusion and loss of wits that can befall older people.

'The prisoner has previously led a good, sober and godly life, regularly attending church and being a good provider to his wife and two children who are now themselves respectable adults making their own way in the world. The prisoner is much ashamed that he now finds himself before this court for wrongfully stealing those things. In his confused state he merely intended to take the items home to provide fuel and heat for his family when they were very well capable of providing such things themselves through payment received for their own hard work and efforts. This happened, Your Honour, at a time of the year when the prisoner finds it is beyond him to use his hands to good effect and when his balance of his mind is more than usually affected. Indeed, his hands were in such a condition that he could hardly pick up the items that he is charged with attempting to steal.'

Magistrate McKinnon stops taking his occasional notes and looks up.

'Coming upon hard times is no excuse for stealing another man's property and any person can claim a temporary loss of their wits and reasoning. The rule of law and good public order and respect for property must be maintained. On far too many occasions I find thieves before me claiming hardship as a justification for their crime.'

The magistrate looks directly at Josephus Clout. 'Your attorney has spoken of your previous good character and it is to your credit that you admit your guilt in this matter. I take into account your age and your occasional temporary infirmity and I also note that you have supported your family to date and regularly attended church.'

'Mr Thane, how and where do the prisoner's family members have employment?'

'Your Honour, the son is a bookbinder and the daughter a housekeeper-governess.'

The magistrate speaks again.

'Josephus Clout, in such cases as yours I would normally consider a sentence that would serve both as an appropriate punishment for this crime and as a deterrent. I would include in my consideration the prospect of deportation or imprisonment for some considerable period of time…'

Josephus Clout grips as best he can the rail to the dock and closes his eyes in anticipation of what may come in the way of a sentence.

'… Is the victim of this crime, Mr John Preston, here today?'

17

Preston stands and steps forward.

'I am indeed here, Sir.'

'Is there anything you wish to say before I pass sentence?' McKinnon asks.

'I was able to recover the goods in question before the prisoner could make his escape. I was most angry at that time and had no hesitation in sending for the constable. However, since then I have had time to ponder on the matter. It was indeed a pitiful sight to see the prisoner trying to take hold of the goods when his hands clearly would not do his bidding and it does appear that the prisoner was at that time in a somewhat confused state of mind. I am also a Christian man, Your Honour, and now having both reflected upon the incident, and also being aware of the prisoner's previous good, sober and Christian character, I do not press for a severe punishment nor do I wish to speak against the special pleading.'

The trial has already taken a full five minutes and Magistrate McKinnon decides that it is time to draw proceedings to a close.

'Very well. Josephus Clout, I have heard what has been said in your favour and especially that the victim of your crime does not seek for severe punishment to be imposed. I am mindful also of your age and apparent infirmity. I do not see you either as a danger to society or a threat to peace and good public order and for all these reasons I am prepared to limit your punishment to a further one month's imprisonment, to be undertaken at His Majesty's pleasure at Coldbath Fields Prison.'

Upon these words Josephus Clout is taken down from the dock to begin his sentence.

# Chapter 5

On the morning of his release Elizabeth awaits her husband at the gates of Coldbath Fields Prison. Not so long ago, before the prison was built, the place had a rural aspect. From this elevation it was possible to look down upon the City of London, the walls of which were no more than half a mile away, and to see the ebb and flow of the slow-running river Thames. Upon this site, despite the large rubbish heap located nearby, people used to come and take waters from the healing spring from which the prison would later take its name. The rubbish heap was removed and the prison was built in its stead. A channel runs under the prison carrying the spring waters – now polluted by the nearby insanitary habitations – and forms the sole water supply for the prison.

Josephus had always been a thin man with rather gaunt features. Even so, his incarceration has brought about a dramatic transformation in his appearance. His skin has the look of parchment stretched over his bones and that parchment-like complexion is in turn covered in places by sores and scab marks. His eyes are sunken, not so unlike those in that terrible face above that gate at the House of Detention. Added to which there is also a distinct yellow-black discolouration all around his sunken eye sockets. As he walks – or rather shuffles – towards his wife to greet her it seems as though he has now taken on a pronounced stoop.

'Oh Josephus! The sooner we get you home the better. As cold as it is, let's just take our time, as I am sure you are not used to walking. Then I shall make for you a warming hot drink and maybe a little something to eat for it looks as though you have hardly eaten for a month. Did you not receive any of the food I sent through for you?'

Josephus just shrugs.

'Well, I have a nice broth from a sheep's head waiting for you and your favourite of a rabbit stew with a suet-pastry crust. I have taken new lodgings just a mile or more away in Upper Rathbone Place. The rooms are better suited to our needs and, although more modest, we remain comfortable and respectable.'

Josephus merely grunts again as they continue on their journey home in almost complete silence. Every now and then they have to stop and rest for a while either because Josephus starts to feel dizzy or because he breaks into a coughing fit. This coughing is something he can thank prison for. To Elizabeth, her husband seems a broken man and indeed he is. Prison has had its desired effect in the breaking of this man's spirit.

Josephus slumps into the chair by the small range and Elizabeth puts a blanket around his shoulders and then she soon gets a full fire burning by adding more coal to the remaining embers from the fire that she had stoked up before going to meet her husband at the prison gates.

As Josephus' hands are too unsteady she helps to feed Josephus some of the now-reheated broth and particularly the bits of meat that have fallen off the sheep's head during the cooking. It is then that she notices that Josephus has lost even more of his teeth. After finishing the broth Elizabeth asks, 'You've lost some more teeth, I see. How did that come about?'

'First one and then another just worked loose. I had no choice but to keep on wiggling them until I could get my fingers around them and pull them out. There's one there now right at the back that hurts so much when I bite on it.'

This is the most that Josephus has spoken since he and Elizabeth were reunited at the prison gates.

'Well, you'll have to try and eat on the other side of your mouth. The stew is nearly warmed through again so once you've eaten go lie down in our own bed. We'll have to go to the tooth-puller when you have had a good night's rest.'

'No. Waste of money! You'll just have to put some twine around the bad'un and tie it around the door handle and then kick the door shut. I saw my uncle do that when I first came to London and moved in with him.'

Elizabeth does not press Josephus to tell of his experiences but over the coming weeks she slowly builds in her own mind some sort of picture of the conditions he has endured.

The House of Correction at Coldbath Fields holds men, women and children on short sentences of anything up to two years. Not so long ago many prisoners now sent to Coldbath Prison would have been sent to Newgate to await their execution or transportation for offences no more serious than the theft of property worth more than five shillings.

Evidently, three categories of prisoners are kept at Coldbath Fields Prison. Felons, such as convicted petty thieves like Josephus, misdemeanants, those being persons who have committed offences of a lesser nature than felony, and lastly debtors. The magistrates administer the prison themselves and ensure that the regime is strict. Silence is rigorously enforced, through what is known as 'The Silent System', which is meant to ensure that prisoners are both able to contemplate their crimes and prevented from communicating amongst themselves and so contaminating each other with evil thoughts and ideas. Josephus has hardly spoken a word to anyone in over a month. Never a great talker, Josephus speaks even less after his ordeal.

In consideration of his age and poor physical condition, Josephus was spared the ordeal of the treadmill. The treadmill is used as a means to either grind grain or to work the water pump. On other occasions, the treadmill is disengaged from grain grinding or operating the water pump and is just used as a means of making the prisoners undertake a futile task as a means of 'improving' their

21

character. Prisoners at Coldbath work the treadmill for as much as six hours at a time with no break or respite. The treadmill is located in a gallery above one end of the exercise yard. While down below prisoners and vagrants are compelled by the guards to walk aimlessly back and forth, up in the gallery up to a dozen men are lined up along the length of the treadmill, or the tread-wheel as it is sometimes called, to perform their six-hour stints.

The men up in the gallery face onto the exercise yard with a handrail to grip. They then step on one of the lengthways slats of wood on the treadmill, causing the whole contraption to move until the next slat of wood comes into play and so on and so on for hours at a time. In the summer there is no respite from the heat of the sun. In the winter there is little shelter from the wind and the rain. Even in the worst of the weather the men wear just their own meagre clothing. Come rain, wind or shine they are always hungry and dreadfully tired. The only time of respite is on Sunday when prisoners are compelled to go to the prison chapel and hear long sermons and exhortations to repent their sins.

Josephus was also excused, owing to the useless condition of his hands, the hard labour of 'picking oakum' – the pulling apart of fibres from tarry ropes so that they could be reused. Prisoners designated to this task sit in long rows on wooden benches for hours on end arduously picking away at the ropes whilst maintaining utmost silence. The overseer on the raised platform before them, dressed in his long coat and top hat and wielding his big stick, together with the other thuggish guards, makes sure that there are no slackers and absolutely no talking.

Just ten years previous to Josephus' incarceration, the poet Samuel Taylor Coleridge in his poem 'The Devil's Thoughts' wrote the following lines of verse that conjure up only too well the awful desperation of the inmates at Coldfields:

*As he went through Cold-Bath Fields he saw*
*A solitary cell;*
*And the Devil was pleased, for it gave him a hint*
*For improving his prisons in Hell.*

# Chapter 6

This Sunday, as with the Sunday before, Will has not joined his betrothed, Mary Elizabeth, at her church. Will wishes not to stray too far from home so he reverts to attending the service at his own local church to offer up his prayers. Mary has instead agreed to visit Will at the house later in the day.

Will and Mary are now properly engaged. They are to be married next February at her church of St Margaret's in Westminster, this being the church that sits to the side of Westminster Abbey and the church where Mary was baptised.

Josephus' death is now expected someday soon. The cough that he brought home with him from his time in prison has continued to get worse. His body has never recovered from his ordeal and his dementia has worsened over the last six months to the extent that he now needs constant care and attention. The worst thing of all is that Josephus' spirit is shattered and, despite his faith, he has lost the will to carry on. If this is what the point of prisons is, then they work. They work very well indeed.

'Mother,' says Will, 'why don't you take some air? You have tended Father constantly and if you wrap up warm I am sure that a break will do you some good. He is asleep now anyway and Mary and I can look out for him.'

His mother is looking tired and drawn. She merely nods, picks up her heavy woollen shawl and her bonnet and closes the door behind her without saying a word.

'We can't leave your mother to fend for herself, Will. It won't be long now before your father leaves us. Your mother will either have to come and live with us after we are married or go and live with her brother and his family.'

A few days later Will rushes home from work after what has been a dull and then rainy November day and evening. Will's half-sister, Mary Kezia, had been granted leave and permission by her mistress, Mrs Carlton, to attend her father. Mary Kezia has heard that his life is surely very soon coming to a close. On this last night, with all his family around him, Josephus seems to know that those whom he loves and those who love him are at his bedside. A few days later at St James's church in Piccadilly, the church that he has loved so much and where he married both his wives and where Will was baptised, Josephus at the fine age of fifty-five is taken for his funeral and committal service.

# **Chapter 7**

*Some years earlier…*

Josephus is a bookbinder journeyman and he takes under his charge and trains apprentices. It has been, therefore, almost a foregone conclusion that Will would follow his father into the same trade.

It is William's first day at work where he is to study and undertake his apprenticeship under the guidance of his father.

'Will, what I am going to show you now as we walk around the workshop is how by hand we make up a notebook intended for a fine gentleman or lady or a professional person with discerning tastes. This is but a small part of our work but this will be enough to show, in part at least, our – and eventually *your –* purpose here.

'We are sometimes commissioned to produce bindings for legal documents that lawyers and advocates may then find it easier to refer to. Other professions also come to us seeking a similar service.

'Once you have grasped the principles of what we are about here, I will explain what we are doing across the way there.' Josephus points to the adjacent building. 'They bind books in a manner that is quicker, say with the use of adhesive and no sewing or stitching, and therefore less expensive. However, while this may suit the more popular side of the market, it is vastly inferior to the traditional methods we use here.

'You will learn, Will, each step in the process of hand bookbinding and how to use the bookbinder's tools and then, if you show the temperament and aptitude, you may eventually be entrusted with the rebinding of books, some of which are old and valuable. I have made my living from this trade and I expect no less from you, Will. However, if all else fails then you will find yourself across the way there doing less skilful and less rewarding work. And expect no special favours or treatment from me. You are here to learn and learn you will, otherwise you will be out!'

Holding up in turn three types of notebooks each of a different character and nature, Josephus embarks on his first imparting of knowledge and training to his son.

'The key and watchwords in this business, Will, are accuracy, patience and care.

'Accuracy in measuring is essential at each and every stage of the process. Even when to the eye things look to be true and square you must measure and check again to ensure that they are! Otherwise all your work is wasted. Materials cost money and time wasted also costs money. If you waste money or time, then your wages will be reduced accordingly. Notice how quiet it is here? There is no time for gossiping and everyone is concentrating on what they are doing. This is serious business for serious people.'

Josephus then begins to walk with Will around the workshop pointing out the various stages of work.

'To start with, we need to create the notebook pages and to this end we have to prepare and cut the paper to the required uniform size and in the required amount. You will see here how Jim, having previously done all his measuring, is now placing his carpenter's square along the top edge of those sheets of paper and in a second or so you will see him drawing a sharp knife down the side of the square. He will repeat this squaring process until he is sure that each of the corners is true. To get the best results we only do this with three or four sheets of paper at a time. Any more than this increases the chances of getting uneven edges or ending up with torn corners.

'After that each individual sheet needs to be folded – without using too much pressure, otherwise the paper may crease – in such a way that the sides are in line with each other. Now you will find out that there are various methods of folding, each method having its own place depending on what we are seeking to achieve. Over time it will become apparent to you which method to use and when.

'Now then, a number of folded sheets, usually around four or five, then come together in gatherings that are called "signatures". The more signatures of lesser bulk then the stronger the eventual binding of the book will become. Now we call them signatures because after each folding and gathering of sheets a mark or a signature is made on the back edge next to the fold in the gathering. Then when we are sure that every signature is in the right order and complete – you see, Will, some people might commission us to include maps or pictures in their book – then we can look towards sewing the component parts of the book together.

'How we go about the sewing process depends on the size

and weight of the book. A small slim book may require only two ¼-inch tapes, an average-sized book perhaps two ⅜-inch tapes, but a very large book could have up to four ½-inch tapes. You can see here that Susan – don't worry about names, you'll get to know everyone all in good time! – Susan has decided on two tapes and has pencil marks already drawn across the backs of the signatures to guide where the tapes will be positioned. The tapes have the purpose of supporting the weight of the soon-to-be-sewn signatures as well as holding them securely to the boards that will form the stiff outer covering of the book.

'When it comes to the sewing up of the book this is when both nimble and supple hands and skill and care and patience are required. I have found that women and girls take more easily to such work as they tend to have smaller hands. Even if they do take to the various stages of bookbinding, they will not be considered in the same way as us men and will not be taken on as apprentices. For that and for other obvious reasons they do not deserve a man's wage.

'You can see on the bench over there what is a bookbinder's sewing frame. Bookbinders have been using this sort of sewing frame back to the time of the ancients and I suspect no better equipment will ever be found. Learning this part of our art will take you some considerable time to perfect. Sewing through the folds of the signatures is necessary not only to secure the tapes but this allows the reader to turn the pages freely and for the book to open flat. Never, never, though, should a book be mistreated in such a way as by leaving it open face down on a table or any other such surface.

'We now come to what is known as attaching the mull and it looks as though Jenny is just about to do this. The mull is a strip of cloth that is wider than the now-sewn signatures but not as wide as the length of the strips. The mull is glued to the back of the sewn signatures and to the tapes both to reinforce the backbone of the book and to provide a means for adding the boards. The boards themselves, as you would have observed before, are bigger overall than the sewn signatures. What is left then is to cover the boards and the spine of the book so as to protect the sewn signatures themselves and to hide the signs of sewing. Cloth or paper or even leather can be used for this purpose with the material turned over on the inside of the cover boards. Then all that is left from the binding point of view is for two end sheets to be pasted on the inside of the cover boards so as to hide the tapes and the overlapping mull and the signs of the turned-in book covering.

'Some books, such as leather-bound notebooks, are left as they are. Others may have handwritten or printed labels pasted upon them, and our more discerning client may look for more ornate lettering – sometimes in gold leaf – thereby adding to and finishing off the presentation of the book.

'So, this is your future now, Will. Take to it if you can.'

Will indeed took quite naturally to his father's trade. That is not to say that he found the work easy, particularly some of the aspects of sewing, but he had the disciplines, patience and ability to make this his vocation. He also did not want to let himself or his father down by falling short of expectations.

In those days a bookbinder's income, even that of a journeyman, was at best adequate for a man or a family of moderate tastes and desires. The living, though, was good enough to escape resorting to the slum dwellings, such as those in St Giles and the notorious area nearby known as Seven Dials. For regular work and regular pay could enable a person to be considered as being of a deserving and dependable nature and therefore suitable as a tenant in property of an 'improved nature'.

# Part II

# Will's Time

# Chapter 1

William Frederick Clout – known as Will – is married to his beloved Mary Elizabeth Bruce on a bitterly cold February day. It is such a shame because Mary looks so grand in her new blue dress as blue as the bluest of summer skies and in her matching blue bonnet.

'You look wonderful, my love. You must have saved and saved to buy such a dress,' said Will as soon as his bride removed her overcoat inside the rather cold church. 'You make the rest of us look so shabby.'

After the brief ceremony they are all buttoned and wrapped up so well that no one would be able to tell what they are wearing underneath their layers of outdoor clothes.

The previous month had been deceptively mild with a fog that had lasted a week. Then as February and the wedding day approached it became so cold as to cause the river Thames to freeze over. A number of either brave or foolish people ventured out on the ice without any mishap. Along the riverbanks there are a number of waterman's stairs where, at high-tide, passengers wait to be ferried along or across the river. At low tide the sloping causeways are used to embark and disembark passengers and goods. The ice between Blackfriars and Three Crane Stairs, including the stretch in front of St Paul's, is thick enough for much sport and entertainment to be had.

'Oh Will. We must all go down onto the ice. It shall be such great fun!' pleads Mary.

'Indeed we shall, dearest. We may never see the like of it again and what a way to celebrate and to add memories to our wedding day.'

The wedding party is small, comprising the bride and groom and, on Will's side of the family, his mother Elizabeth and his half-sister Mary Kezia, together with his uncle and his wife, who had agreed to take Elizabeth to live with them. On the bride's side of the family are her parents, Robert and Sarah Bruce, but no others. And so the happy couple and their families set off from Westminster and make their way down to the frozen stretch of the river where all the fun and enjoyment is to be had. They are not to be disappointed.

Stalls have been set up running down the middle of the ice and some clever wit has come up with the name of 'The City Road' for this frozen thoroughfare. All manner of things can be found and bought – from warming hot drinks, some laced with alcohol despite the lack of a licence, to all sorts of souvenirs created by the likes of potters and by printers who have even set up their presses on the thick ice.

Mary Elizabeth's face is a picture. Her wedding day is indeed proving to be a memorable one.

'Will!! Look, look! They are roasting a sheep on the ice. Lapland mutton – how wonderful! We must try some.'

And of course they all do, using their fingers despite the grease from the meat sticking to their hands and to their faces as they eat. Robert Bruce looks the worst for he has a thick beard that soon becomes messy despite the annoying attentions of his wife to unsuccessfully wipe it clean.

After finishing their mutton and wiping their hands as best they can they continue their stroll down 'The City Road'. Mary Elizabeth looks at the souvenirs including the plates and mugs whose labels proclaim 'Bought on the Thames' and '1814 Frost Fair'. The daylight is beginning to fade when she makes one last plea.

'Oh Will! The donkeys! Let me ride on a donkey! What a thing to tell our children that their mother rode on the Thames on the back of a donkey!'

Will has to pay a little extra so that Mary comes to the head of the queue but he feels this of little consequence given the occasion and the obvious delight and enjoyment it gives his bride. Soon after, the members of the wedding party are to go their own separate ways and Will and Mary are to return to their new home for the first time and to start their married life together. This though is not before one more surprise for the bride.

'Mary, look over there. An artist doing sketches, I think. Let him do a sketch of you, then in the years ahead every time we look at it the sketch will bring back memories of today and how bonnie you look.'

'Will Clout! I do declare, you have the softest and kindest heart of any man that I have ever known. Mind you, apart from my father, you are just about the only man I have known so don't get too carried away by that!'

And the company all burst into laughter.

By the following week, as it becomes slightly warmer and the snow turns first to sleet and then to rain, the ice on the river starts to disappear and with it the never-to-be-seen-again 'City Road'.

Married life suits Will very well and he is happily in love. Mary Elizabeth also finds deep contentment and thrives on the love and contentment that Will has brought to her. Just over a year after they are wed, Will and Mary are blessed with their first child: a daughter who is to be given her mother's names – another Mary Elizabeth.

# Chapter 2

Mary Kezia is in the habit of walking on her own around the edge of Green Park on her Sunday afternoons off and when the weather is not too inclement. Mary knows that Regent's Park is closer and beautifully laid out with sweeping terrace crescents and a fine lake but entry to the public – as, indeed, is the case with Green Park – is forbidden and little can be seen of the park from the public streets. But at least in the case of Green Park it is possible more easily to admire things through the railings from the surrounding streets even if access is denied.

Every time Mary goes for her walk she recalls the magnificent fireworks display that was set inside the compound of the park itself just two years before and the disaster that attended it.

The display, so Mary read at that time, was intended to mark one hundred years of the Hanoverian dynasty. One hundred years previously back in 1714 Queen Anne had died. The Queen had survived her own children and someone had to be found to take the throne. Mary knew very little about history and when she saw an item in the papers she was most intrigued. Of course, she, just like any other Protestant, still had deep suspicions about the Catholics and feared the influence of Rome should a Catholic monarch return to the throne of Britain. What Mary did not know until she read it in the newspaper was the details of why we had invited a foreign prince who spoke German and not English to take the British Crown.

Britain had laws about who could succeed to the throne. Mary learnt from the newspaper that it was to do with the Act of Settlement that prohibited Catholics from coming to the throne. That was why the foreign prince was invited to take the throne. The Catholic Stuarts and their supporters in Scotland, aided by those dastardly French, had tried later to rebel twice in Scotland to restore a Catholic to the throne of Britain.

When Mary first started on her walks around the perimeter of the park she was able to see quite clearly the vast ornamental temple known as the Temple of Concord, erected to celebrate the centennial celebration. The fireworks display, trumpeted as 'The Prince Regent's Gala', came with a bigger bang than expected. Some of the fireworks explosives were stored in the Temple of Concord and a stray missile caused the whole edifice to explode. Mary saw it all as she was in the large crowd that had come to see what they could of the display. When the building exploded it was with a sound the likes of which she had never heard anything to compare with in all her young life.

Some of the satirical pamphlets circulating at the time made great fun of this accident. Mary still has a copy of one of them in her box of mementos. In Mary's own copy it is recalled that exactly the same thing had happened before, back in the year 1749, before even the time Mary's father, Josephus, had been born, when the then Temple of Peace, erected to commemorate the end of the Austrian War of Succession, came to the same unfortunate end during a fireworks display.

Mary is distracted on this particular Sunday afternoon as she is becoming more and more concerned about the security of her position as a governess. She does not notice until she gets back to her room at her employer's house that she no longer has possession of her purse. Has she just dropped it or has she been the victim of a pickpocket? She is normally so careful to keep her things close to her as pickpockets both young and old are a constant hazard.

Her purse contained but a shilling and a few coppers but this is still an amount of money to be much missed. She also had a letter from Caroline, a cousin that she has not seen for many years, to which she intended to respond later that evening. Mary values the purse, although it is not of any great worth in itself, as it had been a present from her now sister-in-law from back in the days when they were friends growing up together. Mary goes to bed that evening feeling rather low and resigned to her loss.

Sometime ago Mary has flaunted convention and changed to having her meals below stairs rather than take them on her own. Late in the afternoon on the Saturday following when Mary lost her purse, and as Mary, Mrs Compton and Susan are settling themselves to take tea, there is a knock on the kitchen door. Other than tradesmen – and none were expected at this hour on a Saturday – callers seldom come to visit them below stairs. For a moment the three of them look at each other and then the knocking is repeated. It is Mary who gets up to see who it might be.

She opens the door to a smartly dressed man of around thirty who immediately removes his hat to her.

'Yes' is all that Mary says.

'Forgive me, Miss, I do not wish to intrude. I was just wondering if a Miss Mary K. Clout resides here.'

'I am Miss Clout. I do not believe, Sir, that we are acquainted. May I ask what your business here is?'

'Last Sunday afternoon, whilst I was taking some air in the proximity of Green Park, I saw a lad throw something into the side of the street where there was still a puddle of water from the rain a few days back. Would you have by any chance have been in the area of Green Park last Sunday and did you perhaps lose some property?'

'I was indeed talking a walk around the edge of Green Park as I do when I can and when the weather is fair. I did indeed lose a purse together with a sum of money and a letter that I intended to respond to later that day. Have you by any chance come across my lost purse, Sir?'

The man takes out a purse from his pocket and offers it to Mary.

'What money there is I'm afraid has gone but apparently the thief had no interest in either the purse or the letter. I took the liberty at glancing at the address and so have been able to return the property to its rightful owner. I am much relieved that I have accomplished this.'

'You have indeed achieved your objective and I am both most grateful and indeed pleasantly surprised to have my purse returned to me. It is of some sentimental value. Have you come far, may I ask, Sir?'

'I have lodgings in Marylebone.'

'Not so far then but still some distance out of your way. You are most kind, Sir. Unfortunately I cannot invite you into the house to offer you a cup of tea out of consideration for my mistress's concerns about strangers not being allowed into the house.'

'I apologise for not introducing myself before, Miss Clout. I am William Payne. I am a widower for some little standing and my business is that of an upholsterer. May I ask, Miss Clout, if perhaps you are likely to be in the area of Green Park again soon? If so, I wonder if I may prevail upon you to take afternoon tea with me? I would welcome some company and conversation.'

'I am grateful for your trouble, Mr Payne, and for your boldness, for that also gives me cause to be as equally bold and to agree to your suggestion. Would three o'clock the Sunday after tomorrow be convenient?'

'It is indeed convenient, Miss Clout, and I look forward to meeting you then. Good day to you.'

'Good day to you, Mr Payne.'

Mary tries to hide the smile on her face as she returns to the others seated around the kitchen table. They had clearly heard all that was said and warmly congratulated her on her new 'beau'. Mary waved their congratulations aside – she has so little opportunity to meet with anyone and she was impressed with Mr Payne's kindness and consideration – what could she do other than to accept his kind invitation? Over the next few days, however, Mary reflects on whether or not she had been too hasty and a little foolish to have accepted an invitation from someone she does not know and someone she has not been introduced to.

On the appointed Sunday Mary Kezia and William Payne hold their rendezvous. The conversation is easy between them, but stays strictly within the boundaries of what is appropriate between strangers. They decide to meet again and this soon becomes their habit on Sunday afternoons.

After several months as autumn advances, and the opportunities for walking out become more limited owing to the weather, Mary decides that she could do a lot worse than William Payne. Who else is likely to come along anyway? Would she find anyone with better security or prospects?

# Chapter 3

Will and Mary Elizabeth are getting ready to leave their rooms in Castle Street, fairly adjacent to the Castle Tavern, for St James's church in Piccadilly for their daughter's baptism. As Will knows all too well from his religious instruction and church teachings, this event will be for baby Mary Elizabeth the first of the seven sacred sacraments to be received by this the first child of a new generation in the family.

Their walk will take them down Holborn, with its heavy congestion of coaches and other traffic, and past the large number of coaching inns and taverns such as The Greyhound, The Crown, The Bell and The Black Bull. They will pass along the way splendid timber-framed frontages including that of the Staple Inn, previously one of the nine Inns of Chancery that originally performed the role as preparatory schools for entrants to the four Inns of Court. The Staple Inn's reputation nowadays though is as a social club and as a provider of accommodation for those in the legal profession not entitled to enter the Inns of Court.

Their route will then take on a more hazardous nature, for the area of St Giles is one of the most overcrowded, squalid and insanitary places in London. The slums of The Rookery are the worst and many Irish immigrants are forced to live there. The Irish never get the good jobs and are often paid less than their English counterparts. Low incomes, large families, overcrowded lodgings, with three, four or even five families living in one room, and poor sanitary conditions all lead to high rates of both infant mortality and people dying before their time.

Local legend suggested that this was where the first outbreak of the Great Plague broke out some 150 years before. Those people unfortunate enough to have nowhere else to go or be other than St Giles suffered the most from the ravages of the plague in 1665. St Giles remains even now the site of the most utter deprivation and poverty and the haunt of the worst sorts of murderers, villains, rogues and scoundrels. As old slum dwellings nearby are demolished to make way for new developments, even more people cram into the area of St Giles, adding to the heaving mass of pitiful humanity. Still, the worst of the place can be avoided by staying to the northern edges.

After negotiating the neighbourhood of St Giles, Will then leads his family through the small, crowded and somewhat foul-smelling streets and lanes of Soho. Soho, though, is beginning to change its character as writers and entertainers decide to take up residence there and small entertainment events such as one or two-man shows and with rooms providing a small stage for lesser performers not engaged in the likes of music halls or theatres. With Soho behind them, it is then just a short way on to the church for the celebration of baptism and a small family reunion. It is a proud and happy mother and father that make their way back home to Castle Street on a cold and grey March afternoon.

Hopes, as always with those not in the most desperate of states, tend to be raised as a New Year beckons and people look forward to good fortune, hopes are particularly raised given the defeat of the Old Enemy and the knowledge that Napoleon is out of harm's way on that remote piece of rock in the Atlantic Ocean known as St Helena. The year 1816 disappoints and brings to too many families personal tragedy. Winter seems to drag on for ever and the coming of spring is late. The news circulates that, when there has previously been a violent and wild volcanic eruption on the other side of the world, poor weather has always followed. It is now common knowledge in London and elsewhere that there has indeed been a volcanic eruption in the East Indies the previous year and this has to be blamed for the appalling weather. Most people have little idea where the East Indies are, only that it is a long way away and takes many, many months to get there by ship.

As everyone looks forward to the eventual arrival of spring and hoped-for improvements in the weather, soon to be followed by a fair summer, such hopes were dashed. Stories are doing the rounds of there being snowdrifts in northern Europe in the middle of July. England is battered by rainstorms and food is becoming more scarce. And, whenever things are in short supply, there comes the high food prices that the poor cannot afford pay.

The poor relief system both in town and in the country is under severe pressure but things soon become even worse. Typhus breaks out first in Ireland, already so badly hit by the food shortages and consequent famine. It is said later that up to 100,000 people perish in Ireland. Typhus then moves to England and to London.

The infant Mary Elizabeth is one of those that perish. The baby's mother is beside herself with grief and Will is at a loss about what to do. He fears that Mary is about to lose her mind. One practical thing Will can do is to find for them new accommodation away from the memories of the rooms where they had nursed their lost child. A move to Clerkenwell would take Will closer to his work, although they are not that far from his place of employment as it is. Will hopes that the change will help the start for Mary to repair her mind and slowly overcome her loss and grief and that Mary will once more feel like becoming a wife again. As things are Mary shuns any contact with her husband.

Will goes to work, comes home to a not enjoyable home life and goes to work again the following morning. Will even starts to miss some Sunday church attendances as he struggles to manage the loss of his daughter virtually on his own, unable to share his grief even with his wife. His church fails to bring any comfort.

The one celebration in the family was that Mary Kezia and William Payne decide to take the plunge and to get wed. This follows shortly after Mary finally loses her position with the Carltons. Mr Carlton has become manager of a more substantial branch of the bank and with that comes the expectation that he will undertake more elaborate and frequent entertaining and this requires a new house and staff. In any event there is no longer a need for a governess now that the children are older.

Will is delighted when he is asked to be a witness to the wedding ceremony at St Marylebone. The afternoon and evening before the wedding the two Marys meet up for some last-minute shopping and to find some diversion that may lift Mary's spirits as it is the first time that Mary has attempted to socialise since the loss of her daughter.

'Mary dear,' says Mary Kezia, 'this is the first time we have been out together in such a long time. I know how hard it has been for you to bear your loss but today it has been so good to see you smile again. You are young and still have plenty of time to have more children. Will has been hard hit, as well you know, and he has had the added worry of seeing how badly you have been affected. Can you not find it in your heart to share your grief and to comfort each other? Can you not use my wedding tomorrow as an occasion for you to restore your marriage? You were so much in love! Do you not think it is time to try and come out of yourself and to try and bring some joy back into each other's lives?'

41

Their conversation continues for some considerable time and it is the first time that Mary Elizabeth has spoken to anyone about the loss of her daughter.

After the wedding and the afternoon celebrations, Will and Mary return home in good spirits and, for the first time since losing little Mary, Will and Mary spend the night together as husband and wife. As if in answer to Will's prayers, and almost exactly nine months after they have rekindled their marriage, Mary gives birth to a son who is to be baptised with his father's names – William Frederick. On this occasion they break with the family tradition and choose to hold the baptism in the now-nearer church of St George in Bloomsbury, a relatively new parish carved out of the existing parish of St Giles. The church of St George has been built not just because of the swelling numbers of the population in St Giles but because St Giles is not a place where the gentry or refined people are expected to venture into. Will also hopes that, by choosing a different church, memories of the baptism of their lost daughter will not be stirred.

The more local and accessible church in any event is far from being unimpressive. It cuts a fine scene with its stepped tower topped by a statue of King George I in Roman dress flanked by fighting lions and a unicorn. Steps lead up from street level to the impressive frontage – a ten-columned Greek-style portico. It is the first time Mary has been in a church since her child's funeral.

Now with an infant son there seems to be a feeling that the family is complete again and it seems as if the sadness and deep depression have at last been lifted from Mary.

The infant William Frederick – soon to be given the nickname of 'Billy Boy' – is a noisy child from the outset. He often cries for long periods and cannot be comforted. At times he is a trial of endurance for his parents. At first, Will puts it down to his imagination that the baby's head seems to be getting larger and that the baby's body does not seem to be growing at the same rate. He thinks also that the child is gradually spending less time at his mother's breast. Mary denies anything of the sort. Then the infant's character seems to change. He becomes less aware of movement around him and when Will waves his hand in front of the baby's face he seems not to react at all.

Is the child blind? Will asks himself. What is wrong with his skin? It looks so thin and shiny.

One Sunday morning Will awakes slightly later than normal as he does not have to go to work. Mary is already up but the room is unusually quiet. Mary is sitting in the chair by the crib rocking herself back and forth. She seems to be holding the infant tight to herself. Will gets up and approaches Mary, but she turns away from him and clings the infant yet more tightly to her. Things are clearly not right with the child. Will decides that he must go for a doctor. Fortunately, there is a doctor just a few doors away, further down in Duke Street.

Despite the relatively early hour and it being a Sunday, the good doctor, clutching his medical bag, comes back with Will after some ten minutes. It takes quite some time and gentle coaxing from both Will and the doctor to encourage Mary to let go of the infant. The doctor seems to undertake a thorough examination with his hands and does not even open his medical bag. He then lays the sickly child back down in his crib. The doctor then gently steers Will by the arm to the other end of the room.

'Have you seen such a condition with infants in your family before now?' the doctor asks.

'Why no!' says Will. 'Our first child perished from the typhus some two years back but that was nothing like this.'

'What about your brothers or sisters or their children or those of your wife's family?'

'I have a half-sister, that is all, and she has yet to produce children. My wife has never spoken of such matters. Why do you ask?'

'I fear that the child has a condition called water on the brain. I have seen it before on various occasions and it is sometimes a condition that appears in the same family.'

'What can be done?' pleads Will.

'Prayer is the only remedy I can offer and even if the babe is to survive he will never live a full life. He seems to be already blinded by his affliction and the brain is no doubt damaged by what has happened. If you give me three shillings now for my attendance, then I will prepare a solution for your wife that may make it easier for her to sleep as I doubt that your child will survive for very much longer.'

This tragedy that follows sends Mary back into a black mood of depression and despair. Will's faith is harshly challenged again and he all but gives up his church attendance. He suffers the loss of the son that has shared his name to an even greater extent than the loss of their daughter. Will has nowhere or no one to turn to for comfort or solace. He is a man and is expected to behave like a man. Will's home life is once again empty and he finds that he is no longer certain of his feelings towards his wife.

Will starts to ponder on whether he should seek female companionship elsewhere. Then he dismisses the thought almost immediately. He is certainly not like one of those toffs who can afford a second house to keep a mistress and he certainly is not going to risk the pox by picking up a girl or a woman off the street. No! He will have to carry this burden in the hope that Mary will eventually come back from her despair and will then feel like being a full and proper wife again.

# Chapter 4

It is two years since Will and Mary Elizabeth's son has died and, apart from the most perfunctory of kisses or walking arm in arm when they go out for a stroll, there has been no intimacy in the marriage.

Then Mary Kezia breaks the news that she is expecting her first baby at last after five years of marriage, and not through want of hoping to start a family. It is like someone has pulled a lever. Mary Elizabeth wants to try again for another baby and Will just cannot believe his good fortune that, little more than six months after Mary Kezia and William have their first child, to Mary Elizabeth and Will is born a daughter, their third child. They call her Eliza, a shortening of Mary's middle name, Elizabeth.

There is joy in the Clout household once again and there is a light behind Mary's eyes. The two families make the point of meeting one fine Sunday afternoon to take a halfway ride on the new horse-drawn omnibus. It is almost impossible to join the omnibus along its route as it is often already filled with passengers. Then there is the added difficulty of trying to catch the coachman's attention so that he can try and bring the omnibus to a halt in the road amongst all the other traffic. Will therefore suggests a walk to the terminus next to the Bank of England, so that they may board at the beginning of the route and then alight halfway down the route, so as not to be too far from Will's home and a welcome cup of tea, before William and Mary make their own way back home.

Will is now coming to the top of his trade and is now considered to be a journeyman in his own right and he also, just like his father before him, has started taking on the training of apprentices. Things could not be better and the lack of dramatic domestic events is very much welcome. A cause of more joy and celebration is that Mary Kezia and his brother-in-law William are expecting their second child – to be born just after the New Year. Will has found his faith again and has not failed once to attend church on Sunday since his wife told him that she was expecting their third child. Will could not ask for anything more than what he now has.

# Chapter 5

Winter has come early, with snow falling in London as early as October, and as winter advances into the New Year the Thames ices over again, although not to the same extent as during that equally bitterly cold snap ten years previously when Will and Mary were married and celebrated their wedding at the Thames Frost Fair. They say that the new London Bridge allows the water in the river to flow more swiftly and for that reason another frost fair is unlikely to ever happen again.

Spring comes early and by May it is unbearably hot. There is little ventilation in their rooms and even with the small windows open the air hardly stirs at all. The odour from the street does not encourage the opening of windows on days when it is hot and there is little or no breeze. Mary Elizabeth finds herself taking young Eliza in the pram for a walk around the edges of Regent's Park where the gentry continue to build their villas and big houses on what was once farmland with attendant cottages. Although again not accessible to the likes of Mary, she sometimes walks further north to the fringes of Primrose Hill in the hope of catching something of a cooler breeze. She does so enjoy the view of looking down on London and the City and being away from everything and everybody down there.

It is so warm in the house at nights that it is often difficult to sleep. More often than not, Will arises and leaves for work not feeling rested at all. One of the first things Will always does when he gets up is to look into the cot where his daughter lies but on this particular morning she does not look right. Will puts the back of his hand to her little cheek and she feels cold and clammy.

'Surely not again!' he shouts.

For the third time they suffer the unbearable loss of a child and the doctor says that there is no obvious answer to why she has perished during the night.

Mary is inconsolable. By the time of the funeral she is close to emotional and physical ruin. Mary needs to be supported lest she collapse during the service. Having been absent for two days after the burial service, Will has to return to work. Mary Kezia has her own children and cares to attend to but promises to visit as often as she can.

Will comes home from work some two or three days later expecting to find his wife at home. Where could she be? Will then notices that some of her things are not there but there is no note. Mary has said nothing about visiting her parents but then she has said nothing since the day of the funeral. Fearing for her state of mind, and given that it is already almost nightfall, Will has no choice but to make his way all the way over to Lambeth. This is where Mary's parents now find themselves, following a serious change for the worse in their circumstances that means they can afford no better accommodation than the two rooms they rent for four shillings a week. They let one of these rooms to two labourers who pay between them two shillings a week, thus halving the costs of the accommodation.

The streets and the bridge across the river are less crowded at this time in the evening and the way is clear of the cattle that are driven routinely every day into the city to the various holding pens and unlicensed abattoirs to be slaughtered. Each night boys and men with carts come to clear the roadways of the muck from the passing horses and cattle to sell as fertilizer. Needless to say, in the increasing dark Will often finds he had trodden in stuff he wishes he could have avoided.

Will takes the wrong turning a couple of times when he is on the other side of the river. He seldom has cause to make his way there and the cuts and the alleys are even more confusing in the twilight.

The place where his parents-in-law live is in darkness. Candles cost money. It does not take too long to get a response to his knocking and calling out. The door opens slightly.

'Is Mary with you? She seems to have taken some of her things but not all of them and she gave no word and left no note. Is she here?'

'No, Will. We have not seen her since your poor child's burial service,' answers Robert Bruce.

'I fear for both her mind and for her safety. Since the loss of Eliza I have not been able to get a word out of her. In fact, she seems hardly to notice that I am in the same room as her.'

'Would she be with your sister and her husband?'

'I don't know. That is where I must go next as she knows no one else and has nowhere else to go.'

'The church clock sounded ten o'clock not so long ago. I doubt if they are still up in Marylebone and in any case you won't make it there tonight. Why not rest here and leave first thing in the morning? There is a chair that you can sleep in.'

'No! I must go and look for her. If she does come to you, send word to me as soon as you can. If she is not with my sister, and I know it is a waste of time, I shall nevertheless enquire at the Watch House. I must be on my way. Goodnight.'

Will has to come back on himself to get across the river as no waterman is working at this time of the night. It is coming on midnight by the time Will reaches Marylebone. It takes some considerable time and effort to rouse anyone before William Payne eventually calls from the other side of the door.

'Who is it? What do you want? Do you know what time of the night it is?'

'It's Will. Is Mary with you?'

There is the sound of bolts moving and then the door opens.

'Will! Come in, do. No, Mary is not here. Come and tell me what has happened.'

Will stays the night in Marylebone, although he is all set for returning home in the hope that Mary might be there. After barely any sleep at all, and before William and his sister are about, Will returns home but there is no sign of his wife.

Will picks up the sketch taken of Mary on their wedding day and he goes to the Watch House and, in vain he knows, makes enquiries and asks what could be done. The indifferent constable on the desk takes the briefest of notes but offers no helpful advice or assistance. All Will can do for now is to return home and to continue to go to work and just hope that Mary will turn up.

In the following weeks Will spends hours after work and on Saturday afternoons and all day on Sundays walking the streets in the hope that he will spot Mary. The weeks change into months and for almost a year Will continues walking around London and the City, venturing into some of the most gruesome, stinking and outright dangerous of places, sometimes showing passers-by the sketch taken of his wife. All in vain. It is as if his wife has disappeared into thin air. Will's journeys even take him south of the river into Southwark, Lambeth and even as far down as Brixton.

Then one night, as he is walking exhausted back through St Giles towards home, he tries one more time to intercept another passing stranger outside a shop that is still open and where there is light enough from the oil lamps to be able to see.

'Have you seen my wife?'

As Will starts to unfold the now somewhat crumpled sketch, a fist comes flying out of nowhere, followed by another, and Will finds himself on the ground being kicked around the head and face as he tries to cover his face with his hands. No one intervenes and no one cares. It is none of their business. Much dazed, Will starts to pick himself off the ground. He looks around for the sketch of Mary but it is not to be seen. Cut, grazed, bleeding and in some considerable pain, Will staggers back to his empty rooms and a night with hardly any sleep. The next morning he is stiff and aching and one eye has almost completely closed up. *No work today, that's for sure,* Will says to himself.

In fact, Will is unable to attend work for the next three days and when he does he is still very stiff and sore and his eye remains almost completely closed. Lying there on the bed he once shared with his wife Will has plenty of time to reflect. He remembers the ups and downs of their marriage. The joy of their wedding day and the times leading up to the birth of their first daughter, Mary Elizabeth. The pain of their losses and how Mary changed from being a caring loving wife and mother to the extent that Will feared that she would lose her mind and how shamefully he had begun to question his love for her. Mary's mind must be shattered now beyond all hope and Will has a deep dread of what might have befallen her. Is she dead or had something worse befallen her? There are some ruthless and dastardly men that run girls and women for their living.

Will also has another thing to ponder over and to feel ashamed about. He has and had questioned his faith in God on more than one occasion and his church attendance has once again become sporadic.

It is no consolation but Will finally admits that he has done all that he can. His wife Mary is lost to him and, even if he were to find her, would she be completely mad and he a stranger to her?

# Chapter 6

'Why should it be like this?' Will tells his sister, Mary Kezia. 'All I do is go to work, come home to an empty room and go to sleep, and there are some nights when I need a few ales to enable me to do that. I go to church on Sundays, well sometimes anyway. I come and visit you and William and the children every other Sunday. That is something I look forward to but there has to be more to life than this. Mary has been gone for some three years now and no word of where she went or what has happened to her. She could still be alive or she could be dead. We just don't know. I don't know where I stand,' says Will.

'I do not know the law and when a man can say he is no longer married if that is what you are aiming at, Will. I know you, Will. I saw you born and grow up into a fine man and marry my best friend and have a family of your own. I have seen you in all sorts of circumstances and all sorts of moods and states of mind. I can tell what you are thinking and can read you like one of those books you are so busy binding. I probably know you better than you know yourself, Will Clout! Now something is afoot, otherwise you would not be talking to me like this. Are you going to tell me or does your big sister have to drag it out of you? Is there someone you have taken a fancy to? Is that it?'

'Ha! I'm not sure I should come here anymore for it is impossible to hide anything from you or to keep a secret. You remember Thomas Field, the lad who came to us after father's arrest? Well, I am pleased to say that he has turned out to be a steady and hard worker and sometime ago he came to me and asked if there is any possibility of finding work for his sister. I said that I was prepared to have a look at her and if I liked what I saw and she showed some flair for the work I might be able to put a word in for her. Letitia Ann, that's her name. Even her name sounds beautiful and when she came to me I was immediately struck by her appearance, her demeanour and even by the way she speaks with her soft country tones. Not that we are allowed to talk much at work, that is. We just grab the opportunity whenever we can, though what with me instructing her that does provide additional opportunities for us to talk to each other.' He smiled, before continuing.

'Well, I decided to test her on the sewing of the signatures. She has just the sort of nimble hand required for the stitching of signatures and she is neat and methodical about her work and listens well to my instructions. She has such beauty that at times I find my gaze drawn towards her. She must have noticed my attention being drawn to her and she would often smile back as much as to say "I know you are looking at me and I don't mind." Well, after quite some time of this we started to talk about things other than her work. I know she's a woman of no education – indeed, I don't think she can even print her own name – but she is nonetheless such an engaging young woman.'

'And how old is this vision of beauty, Will?' Mary Kezia teases.

'She is some twenty years younger than me but she does not seem to mind that.'

'Ha! She probably thinks you are a good catch and she does not know about Mary and your lost babies, I would suspect.'

'But she does, Mary! She does. I have told her everything and she does not seem disturbed by these events.'

'Will! When and how do you have the time and opportunity to talk to her like this. Have you no sense of reason, no shame in telling a stranger all your secrets?'

'I have fallen for Letty and that's the truth of it, sister! If I could have her for my wife I would jump at it tomorrow. As for the when and the how, you have, as always, got the better of me. We have been seeing each other secretly, although I am sure that her brother Thomas is aware of what is growing between us.'

'Will, this is dangerous. London is far from being a virtuous place but you could still destroy a young woman's reputation. Have a mind to what you are doing and what others may say against both of you, not to mention those pious creatures your church.'

'As I have said, sister, she knows of my past and background so I will not be asking her without her knowing everything.'

'Asking her what, Will? You can't be asking her to marry you! You can't! Not as things stand at the moment.'

'I know that but, if I find new lodgings away from where I am at present, then most people will just assume that we are a married couple. First things first though. I have to ask her if she is willing to risk all and to take up with me.'

'You have not put this proposition to her yet then?'

Will shakes his head.

'Then let me talk to William when he comes back. He should not be much longer now. William is a man for convention but if he agrees, would you be willing to bring this young woman to Sunday lunch so that I can judge her for myself before you ask her anything more? You have been alone too long, Will, and I want to make my own assessment before you commit to going any further. If you have set your mind on this affair, then I expect nothing I could say will matter but at least let me come to my own conclusions. Will you do that, Will. Will you do that for me?'

'I shall see if Letty agrees to your invitation though I see no reason why she should not. How about next Sunday then?'

'You are in a hurry, Will! You are obviously smitten by this young woman. Then next Sunday it is.'

'The next Sunday it is then,' Will echoes, beaming back at his sister. 'Now enough of this. How are things with you and the family and why is William taking so long to be at home on a Sunday?'

Some ten minutes later the door opens and in walks William Payne wearing a rather grim face.

'William, what is it? You look so serious and it is unlike you to be late for your Sunday meal.'

'I do apologise, my dear, and my apologies to you, too, Will. We got into such a discussion that I lost all track of time.'

'What was so important to cause this, I wonder?' Mary responds.

'All sorts. I don't know what the world is coming to. The upshot is that all the fabrics we use are going to become more expensive. The market is difficult enough as it is and people won't pay more for their furnishings. It seems that last week those damned fools in Parliament have made some new laws about children working. Children indeed! I'd hardly call someone between the ages of eleven and eighteen a child.'

Seeing puzzled looks on their faces, he continues.

'Let me explain. It now means that anyone between the age of eleven and eighteen and working in textiles can work no more than twelve hours a day. Then a child between the ages of nine and eleven can only work up to eight hours a day and no child under nine is allowed to work at all! I am telling you the cost of my textiles will go through the roof. Children get paid just a fraction of what men or even women get paid. The next thing you know they will be telling us that we can't have children working for us at all. Don't the fools realise that some of these kids bring in the only money that their families have. Don't they realise that these kids would be back in the workhouse if it wasn't for the likes of me and others giving them work? We'll be driven out of business – that's what will happen, you mark my words.'

'I won't having you talking that way over the table, William Payne,' his wife scolded. 'Not on a Sunday and not when we have Will coming to see us. Now just wash up and sit down. We're all hungry through having to wait for you. Now let that be the end of it.'

'You're getting to look more and more like a pudding, Mary. How much longer to go now?' asks Will.

'Looking like a pudding, am I, Will Clout?! You'll be wearing yours in a minute.'

William returns looking more fresh-faced after washing with the jug and basin of water situated on the table in the bedroom.

'Has Mary told you that we are thinking of moving from here, Will? With another on the way, I'd like to find somewhere better to raise our children.'

'Just a minute ago you were all doom and gloom about being driven out of business and now you are talking about finding somewhere else to live. You can't have it both ways.'

'Perhaps you're right, Will, and perhaps we will wait a little longer but it would be nice if we can find somewhere better to live and where there's some fresh air.'

# Chapter 7

Will returns to work the following Monday feeling rather strange. In fact, he is somewhat earlier than he needs to be. Anxious, nervous ... he is not quite certain how he feels. *Am I actually feeling scared?* Will asks himself. Then he gets cross with himself for being in such a state. He then sees Letitia coming into the yard from the street and he feels all the more jittery. Will looks up from his work as Letitia moves towards her bench. She smiles back and Will no longer feels scared. It's now or never and before too many people arrive, he decides, and he then starts to walk over towards his desire.

'Letty, please will you come with me to take lunch with my sister and her family next Sunday?' he says in a rush.

'And good morning to you, Will. My, it seems as though you wanted to get that out of the way quickly. Lunch with your sister and your family next Sunday, you say. Now a girl may come to a conclusion that you have some design upon her with such an invitation. Is it perhaps that you have some sort of design on me, Will Clout?' she teases with a grin and looking Will in the eye.

'I … I … well, I …' Will tails off.

'Oh for heaven's sake, Will Clout! You should have worked things out by now. Yes. I'll come and meet your sister and I hope we become friends but I need to know for certain what the lie of the land is between us. You never know, I might have other offers to think about, so you had better make up your mind and make up your mind quickly.'

'Other offers? What other offers? I don't think I could bear it if you were to take up with someone else, Letty.'

'There are no others, you ninny. I just wish you would make up your mind and ask me if you want me to come and be with you or not, because I'm not for walking around the edges of things for much longer.'

'You are so forward, Letty. Is everyone like you where you come from?'

'One hard lesson we have learnt, Will, is that if you sit around just waiting for things to happen or for something to turn up you either starve or you end up in the workhouse.'

The following Sunday Will meets with Letty and together they make their way to Marylebone. A short while after they arrive, and before they sit down to lunch, the two men, Will and William, each open a bottle of beer. This provides Mary with the opportunity to have her own conversation with Letty.

'You come from Frimley, you say. I have never heard of it, Letty. Tell me about it and tell me about your family,' asks Mary.

'There is little to tell of Frimley. It is just fields where things are grown. There is a windmill and the river Blackwater nearby and coaches stop there on the way to and from

London and Portsmouth – not for long, mind you, just long enough for there to be a change of horses at The White Hart. The canal passes quite nearby as well. It seems that Frimley is just a place for people and things to be passing through and passing by.

'It was always difficult to find work save when it was time to sow or to harvest. Then they got machines to sow the seeds and machines to thresh and winnow the corn so there was even less work to go round. We were about to lose our home so we had no choice but to come to London. I can't say I like it here much. I much prefer the country but we need to feed ourselves and now I have met Will! I feel that my luck and my fortune have changed all for the better.'

The two men continue to pass the time over their beer before the meal comes to the table. Will still feels the need to say grace before they start to eat.

After they have eaten and passed an hour or so in pleasant conversation, it is time to leave. Once out on the street, Letty puts her arm through Will's.

'Do you think I passed the test then, Will.'

'What makes you think that this afternoon was all about a test?'

'I may be a simple girl from the country but I am not *that* simple. Now is there something you want to ask me or not?'

'I have become so incredibly fond of you, Letty. In fact, I think I have fallen for you completely. For all the reasons you know, and as much as I want to, I cannot ask you to marry me. What I want more than anything else is to be with you. Will you risk all, Letty? Will you come and be my wife in all but name?'

'You have never shown me where you live, Will. Why don't you do that now? And Will, there is no need for you to walk me home tonight. Now does that give you your answer?'

The walk back to Duke Street seems to take an age. Perhaps owing to anticipation and a degree of nervousness or perhaps just because they felt that there is little to say now they were about to move their relationship to a different level, they continue mostly in silence. Just the odd word, with Letty asking, 'Are we nearly there yet?' or 'I have no idea where we are – how much further, Will?'

No sooner Will has closed the door behind them they are in an embrace and kissing. When Will eases Letty's dress off from her shoulders and it falls to the floor he finds her to be even more beautiful than he had ever imagined.

The following morning they leave Duke Street together for the first time to get to work. That evening Letty returns to her squalid shared room in St Giles to collect her belongings, few that they are, and her limited amount of clothes. She then makes her way back to Duke Street. That night is to be as passionate as the night before.

# Chapter 8

News spreads fast throughout London and the City, even in those areas where the flames and smoke are obscured by the tightly packed buildings, that Parliament is ablaze. It is October and the nights are drawing in. The moment Will and Letty finish work they go to join the crowds watching the spectacle of the Palace of Westminster on fire.

By the time Will and Letty find a vantage spot the fire has already passed its peak but the size of the blaze is still considerable. Will allows himself a smile.

'I wonder how William Payne feels now after Parliament banned children or restricted the hours they can work in the mills? Is he laughing to himself now?'

'What are you talking about, Will?'

'No matter, my love. No matter – it is just something silly he said when I was with them a few weeks back.'

Two days after the event, when the facts start to become known, Will takes the unusual step of buying a newspaper – he will save it for many years to come. His own copy of *The Times* dated 18 October 1834. 'The Greatest Conflagration since the Great Fire of London' trumpeted The Thunderer'. Blame for the fire is placed on the shoulders of Richard Whibley, the Clerk of Works. He was evidently under instruction to finally end an archaic way of keeping records, such as financial transactions, by marking notches on bits of wood called tallies. These bits of wood were of no use or worth and could easily have been used by the poor as firewood or burnt outside on a bonfire. Whibley, however, was a man of rigid reason and protocol. The sticks had to be burnt in private and he did not want to light a bonfire as this might annoy the neighbours. The newspaper reported that Whibley therefore decided to instruct two workmen to burn the tally sticks in the under-floor furnaces used to heat the House of Lords.

The men had been seen all day throwing large bundles of the sticks into the furnace with little regard for the dangers of overheating and damage to the flues from the ensuing intensity of the flames. With their working day coming to a close the workmen went about their task with even more vigour. It was thought that as a consequence the lining of the flues collapsed and as the brickwork heated up the wooden joists supporting the stone floor to the chamber above caught light. When the flooring collapsed, the flames spread quickly through the remainder of the building.

'I bet they won't be offering him another job then,' Will says of Whibley after reading the report to Letty.

# Chapter 9

Will and Letty settle down to a domestic life in Duke Street. With Letty now quite obviously very advanced in her pregnancy there are things to be decided and things to arrange.

'Letty, we must decide on what we are going to call the baby and where to have the baptism. The child must be baptised but we are unwed and I do not want to see the child described as "baseborn". We will have to take the baptism away from here to some place where we are not known,' says Will.

'Can we get the baby baptised away from here? I always thought such things should be done either where a baby is born or where people lived. What do you want to do about the naming?'

'If we have a boy I want a child to take my own name.'

'No, Will! I am not having that. That will invite bad luck with you having already lost a son with that name. Besides that it makes me feel as though you just want me to have your babies and a boy that will take your name. We have to agree on something else should we have a boy. Now if we have a daughter, then that is different. You always said how pretty you find my name so if we have a daughter then she is to be called Letitia Ann. You still haven't told me what we can do about having the child baptised anyway.'

'I have heard that some people find it fashionable to go to Chiswick to get married and that the Reverend there is not one to ask too many questions and welcomes, shall we say, further contributions to his income. I am sure that he will take the same approach to baptisms if asked. Chiswick is not far from Ealing so it could be a good time to meet with Mary and William again and to find out how they like their new surroundings.

'Now, as for the name of the boy, because I am certain we

are going to have a son, if you are against the name William Frederick how about Frederick William?'

Letitia laughed. 'Well, that's what I call a compromise.'

'As for ourselves,' Will continued, 'it's time we quit Duke Street. I know I said we would some time ago but let's do it now before the baby is born. I think it unlikely that we will have any problems, other than a slight twinge of our consciences, but if we declare that our child is the son of William Frederick and Letitia Ann Clout of Duke Street, no one in Chiswick would question that and we won't be here anymore anyway. As soon as the child is born, I can set about making the arrangements for the baptism.'

'It will be nice to see Mary again. I really liked her from the first time you took me to their house. I just hope the day is fine and we don't get a drenching sitting on the top of the coach. Now I have been on my feet all day and I need to lie down.'

It is indeed a baby boy that is born to Letty and a healthy boy at that. Will is able to get a letter to the Reverend at St Nicholas Church in Chiswick and the arrangements are made for the baptism to be held around midday on a Sunday shortly after the main Sunday morning service.

It is a fine spring day and Mary and William make their way from Ealing to the church on foot. For Will and Letty not the luxury of riding on top of one of the stages that run to Bath and Bristol but on the top of one of the more ordinary service coaches that undertake shorter routes to and from London itself. It is a short walk from where Will and Letty alight from the coach to the church that stands near to the river. Here in Chiswick the water seems so much cleaner than the foetid brown highway that runs through London and the City.

No questions are asked as Will sees Reverend Barker sign off and complete the details of the baptism in the parish register. Will and William are greatly attracted by the range of inns on offer in Chiswick, which is home to Fuller's Brewery, and choose The Bull's Head, which is situated close to the riverbank. The women are far less drawn to this amenity but submit to sitting across the way from the inn, and sharing the modest picnic they have brought with them whilst the men take on a more liquid diet.

'So how do you find living and working out this way, William?' asks Will.

'It has worked out very much for the better, Will. Mary and the two little children – well, one is still very much a baby really – are thriving and there is so much more room and space. The air is fresher and everything seems more clean and orderly and there are so many less people out this way yet I find no shortage of work. There is talk that within two years Mr Brunel will bring his railway from Paddington to the west through Ealing. That will be grand if for a special treat we can afford the fare to go on the train. Perhaps not back to London though but going westward. What is the point of London when we have quit the place? Sorry, Will! By that I did not mean to suggest that we would not wish to see you and Letty.

'Anyway, Will, the both of you seem to be thriving, too. Taking a younger woman does not appear to have done either of us any harm!'

They both break off into laughter and grin and nod furiously to each other and laugh again.

'I must say, though,' William adds, 'there are times when I think I am beginning to feel that my age is starting to catch up with me. What of you, Will? What of you and what are your plans?'

'I hope me and Letty go on to have a big family. After the bitter loss of my babies and Mary's disappearance, I want us to have lots of fine healthy children. Letty is a good woman and despite our difference in age we seem well matched. We did say before the baby arrived that we should move from Duke Street but we have yet to do so. Perhaps after our next child we will need a bigger and better place. Do you think we should have one more pint before we re-join the women?'

'Or even another to keep the first one company. Seems the best idea of the day to me.'

It is to be the last time they are to enjoy a drink together. Just three months later William keels over at his work and is severely paralysed down one side and loses his speech. Then just two days later he suffers another seizure and that is his end. For widows such as Mary Kezia who have married a man considerably older they find themselves in a situation where in all probability they are too old to remarry and yet have to find a way of sustaining themselves. Such things cannot be planned for. Unless the widow happens to have married a man of considerable substance, who could ensure that his wife and family would be provided for when the husband is gone, a widow's existence is likely to be a struggle even for one as intelligent as Mary. She cannot abandon her family so there was no prospect of her becoming a governess or housekeeper again. She decides that she will just have to swallow her pride, roll up her sleeves and find work charring and taking in laundry.

# Chapter 10

For some time Letty is able to continue to go to work with Will with young Freddy carried in a basket that also makes do as his crib. Letty's pay is less than before as she takes time out from stitching the signatures to either suckle the child or to change its diaper clout.

Since Freddy's birth Will has taken to smoking a pipe of tobacco in the evening after supper. One particular evening

Will and Letty are seated having a quiet moment when Letty breaks the comfortable silence.

'Every time I have to change Freddy it reminds me of just how common our name of Clout is, Will. It never worried me before, because really I am still called Field, but now it certainly does get to me particularly when I am up to my elbows in Freddy's diaper clouts!'

They laugh, but then Letty puts on a serious face.

'There's something else I have to tell you. I think I may be pregnant again.'

'Can you be sure?' asks Will.

'Fairly sure, I think. I've missed my last two months and that has only happened once before and that was when Freddy was on his way. Trouble is with you, Will Clout,' says Letty with a smile on her face again as she looks into his eyes, 'is that you like too much what goes on under the blankets. Not that I'm complaining, mind you. At this rate we are going to be a rather big family.'

As the months pass, Letty has the feeling that hers is no ordinary pregnancy. A call upon the doctor confirms that Letty is to expect twins. As the time approaches, the doctor, expecting payment of course, insists that he is called to attend and assist the delivery of what they hope will be a healthy set of twins.

The twins are considerate enough to decide to come into this world in the early evening when Will is at home and it is too early for the doctor to have retired for the night.

Letty is in labour for several hours and has suffered considerably by the time the second boy is delivered. The doctor announces that both the boys are well formed and in seemingly good health. As for the mother, despite her exhaustion, she is elated. The doctor suggests that, with a little rest and good care, Letty should soon be able to tend to the newborns and to their brother Freddy and to maintain the house if she takes things relatively easy. The doctor asks if someone can come and help Letty over the coming days.

Will dozes in the chair that night spending most of the time looking at Letty and the new additions to the family. As he tugs on his pipe he starts thinking of names for the boys. He knows that after years of prevarication the family now needs to move out from the relatively cramped quarters at Duke Street. As there is a new vicar down at St Giles, and Will has not attended there for a long time preferring his local church, Will decides that, rather than going back to Chiswick, they should chance their luck there in the hope that the fact that they are not married will go unnoticed. Anyway, with young Freddy with them as well, why should anyone question the marital status of the parents?

Will tends to Letty as best he can over the next couple of days and then he must return to work. The evening before he returns to his job Will and Letty talk about names for the boys.

'Well, Letty. We could do it so that you name one of the boys and I name the other or we give a name each to each of the boys. What do you think?'

'What is your thinking, Will?' Letty asks, knowing that he has already worked this out in his own mind.

'Well, why don't you give them the first name and I give them the second?'

'I have always liked the name Henry. It is such a strong manly name and how about George after our four kings? Henry for the first-born and George for the second, yet they look so alike I am still not sure which one is which. Do you think they look like you, Will?'

'Look like me? They look like no one at the moment. As for the names, that is fine by me, as long as Henry has the second name William and George the second name Frederick!!'

'You bugger, Will Clout!' Letty laughs, 'I have never known

a more determined man to ensure that his name lives on through his children.'

'But, my love, the King is named William Henry so Henry William is a grand name for a loyal British subject to give to his son. Then George Frederick is also a kingly name. It's just a coincidence that the second names coincide with mine.'

Letty laughs. 'So Henry William and George Frederick it is. We don't have to drag ourselves down to Chiswick again, do we?'

'No, my love, not to Chiswick. Leave it all to me and I will find us new accommodation this time, I promise.'

Mid-morning the following day Mary arrives to help out, though she together with her two children makes for a very crowded and noisy household. While Letty spends most of the next few days in bed nursing the twins and resting, Mary is able to do the fetching and carrying, catching up with the laundry, preparing the meals, attending to young Freddy and her own children, and generally keeping the place clean.

That first evening before getting ready to retire Will and Mary take the opportunity to catch up. Will has offered up his place besides Letty and he is to sleep in the chair.

'It is so good to see you, Mary, and I am grateful to you for coming over for a couple of days. How have you been coping?'

'William was such a kind and thoughtful husband and father. It is only now that he is gone that I realise just how much I love him. He worked so hard and always tried to do his best for us. I miss him dreadfully.'

Will just nods his head as he senses that Mary has had little opportunity to talk of her grief and her loss of her husband.

'He so much wanted a better life for us and to get us away from Marylebone and down to Ealing. I must do everything I can to keep us there, otherwise it will be a betrayal of all he tried to do for us. Things are not going to be easy but I am determined that we will make do. I can let out one or even the two rooms upstairs and we can all move into the downstairs. It should not be too bad for the three of us and I am sure there are many that would wish for a couple of rooms with just an adult and two young children in them. I have been making sure that Harriet and Henry have their reading and writing up to a good standard so that they are not disadvantaged in life later on. Harriet may well end up entering into service. This is not what I want for her but there are so few opportunities for girls. I was lucky that I found a position as a governess but I fear that Harriet will not be that fortunate. We will just have to wait and see.

'I have started to do some charring and taking washing in. I would much rather be doing some tuition but there does not seem much hope of that at the moment. Oh Will! What have things come to? Me becoming a washerwoman!'

Tears well up in the corner of her eyes and run down her cheek. Will gently brushes the tears away with his finger.

'Dear William, he doted on his children nearly as much as he loved me and now he will not see them grow and have children of their own.' Mary wiped her eyes determinedly. 'Look that's enough about me and my troubles. Now then, Will, tell me about what you and Letty are going to do now you have the twins?'

Mary stays one extra night and leaves for Ealing on the Sunday morning. Letty remains in a degree of discomfort but has regained some of her strength and vitality and is able to do most, if not all, of the chores and to attend to her enlarged family. Will makes arrangements for the twins to be baptised at St Giles and the following day, having rented a handcart, they move to slightly larger accommodation in Gilbert Street. Letty's brother Thomas provides an extra pair of willing hands.

# Chapter 11

Will and Letty, like many other Britons, are loyal to their King, even though their lives were seldom touched by whatever the King did or did not do. Parliament, on the other hand, could affect the lives of poor people considerably even though they had no say in what Parliament or parliamentarians did. The idea of suffrage and the freedom to elect parliamentarians never occurred to common men of the likes of Will.

King William had died. The common people had liked this King. He had served in the navy and some liked to call him the 'Sailor King'. He was sixty-four when he came to the throne. Will had read, mainly fairly respectful stories, about his association with the actress known as Mrs Jordan by whom he had nine children. Most of these children were given titles and the daughters were an integral part of the royal court so everything was out in the open. The problem was that the King had no surviving children from his marriage to the Queen. So, as far as the succession was concerned, when the King died after just seven years on the throne his title fell to his niece Victoria. As for the old King's Hanoverian title of Elector, that could not pass to the Princess Victoria upon her coronation. By the laws of the state of Hanover, the title of Elector must pass to a male successor back in Hanover and not to the Princess Victoria.

There was much talk of the succession to the throne of an eighteen-year-old young woman. The Clout household was no different from any other in the country.

'How will Britain fare in the world, Letty? Don't get me wrong. She is our Queen and sovereign and I will not have a word said against that, but I just wonder whether our standing as a nation abroad will be lessened by the fact that we have a queen and such a young queen at that. Let's hope that she is something like the old Queen Elizabeth all those years ago, with the exception, of course, that she marries and has children. We do not need nor want another virgin queen.'

'That's all that matters to you men, isn't it. Women are only here to have your babies and to cook and to clean up after you.'

'I doubt if the Princess and now our Queen does much in the way of cleaning and cooking,' Will interrupts.

Unperturbed, Letty continues. 'Oh, and you men are always trying your utmost to get us into your bed and you can take that smirk off your face, Will Clout. Well, I hope the young Queen makes a difference in this man's world.'

'You ready for bed yet, Letty my love?'

# Chapter 12

*Seven years later...*

Will and Letty have moved again as Will's steady income and employment allow them to move to more spacious accommodation for the expanding family. Freddy is now eight coming on to nine years old and showing already that he is a strong-willed and determined individual. The twins, Henry and George, are thriving six-year-olds but have different natures. Henry is more of an extrovert and is similar in some ways to his elder brother, Freddy. George, on the other hand, is of a quieter disposition yet will not let himself be pushed around by his two more assertive brothers. Many people comment though on how similar in feature they all are to their father.

There then is a gap of nearly four years in age between the twins and the baby, Charles Frederick – 'Charlie'. Letty hoped for and then lost the daughter she wanted and she tried hard not to let her bitter disappointment show. Letty did not want

Will to worry that she might go 'funny' like Will's wife Mary had. Letty's wishes are granted with the birth of a second set of twins, one a boy and the other a girl, who take the names of their parents, despite Letty's earlier worries of inviting bad luck in the case of the boy. In celebration of the birth of another set of twins, and perhaps also by way of making him feel better on insisting that his new son be called William Frederick, Will buys Letty a new bonnet – a bonnet that Letty is all too happy to sport as she thinks she is being fashionable.

Will is now fully at peace with his God. Having turned away from Him following the loss of his three children by Mary, and with her ensuing insanity and disappearance, Will slowly found his faith again and now he ensures that without fail he attends church every Sunday. He takes with him the three eldest boys to ensure the habit is instilled in them from an early age.

Will works hard and long hours to support his family. His love for Letty knows no bounds and he tries his utmost to save enough money to buy her special things when he can. This often makes Letty cross, if only for an instant, and she gently chides him, saying that the children would be better off with shoes or a new pair of breeches. Will one day thinks that he has found the perfect surprise present for Letty when he ventures down to the bird market at Seven Dials in St Giles. A bird in the cage he thinks will remind Letty of the countryside. Even better if the bird can sing.

'Oh no, Will, we cannot keep the poor creature. The bird needs to be free! If we keep it here in this tiny cage, it will surely perish. I know you mean to please me, Will, but there is no need for you to spend what little money we have to spare on me. If you really want to please me, come with me now to the edge of Regent's Park so we can let the creature fly free. Freddy can look out for the children for an hour if they stay inside. Then when we come back home you can show me tonight how much you love me in another way.'

Letty puts on her special bonnet and arm in arm they walk towards Regent's Park.

'You never talk much about home, Letty. Are you sure you don't miss the country at all? The closest I've ever been to the country is when we had Freddy baptised in Chiswick but it was so nice to be out there in the open.'

'You know the answer to that, my love. My life is here now, Will, with you and our children. As they say, 'you can't live on fresh air alone'. There are times when I miss the fresh air and the open space and the sound of birdsong and where the birds are free to do their singing.'

'Aye, and we have our children to show for it and two sets of twins. *Two* sets of twins! I have to pinch myself sometimes to see if it's true but then there are other times when the house is so full of children crying I know full well it *is* true. It is still a blessing, even if it is a noisy one!'

'Well, I am late again, Will, so perhaps our blessing is going to get even noisier.'

'Why, Letty, that is grand. Mind you, as soon as Freddy is old enough we are going to have to send him out to earn a few pennies. No more bonnets for a little while it seems and definitely no more birds in cages.'

Having reached the railings to the park, Letty holds open the door to the tiny cage. The bird flies off without any encouragement.

'There, Will, that's as good as a present to see the little birdie fly off and to be free again. Now, my love, let's get home and later we can see about my other present.'

Letty is indeed expecting again. Though tragedy is to strike fairly early on in the pregnancy. For no obvious reason, and the cause being a mystery to mother, father and the doctor attending, young William Frederick dies in his sleep just a few weeks after his second birthday. Will takes the loss of his namesake son badly. Letty tries her hardest to keep her grief to herself for the sake of the other children and not to add to her husband's sadness at the loss. Letty does though curse herself for agreeing to the name of William Frederick. It was indeed bad luck to have given the child the name of one before who also died so young.

# Part III
# Murder and Flight

# Chapter 1

Freddy had said nothing about him expecting to be late from work this evening and here we are in what must be the early hours of the morning and there is no sign of him. Even if he has been given a special and urgent commission to undertake, he should have been home hours ago. And if he were to work late or was delayed, she knows that either of his twin brothers would bring word to her for they all work together at the same bookbinder's. The same bookbinder's where she and Freddy had met.

Freddy is not one for the alehouses in the main because they did not have the money to spare. Has he been hurt? Has something bad happened to him. Maybe he has decided to go and see his mother but then he would not stay out all night.

'Oh my God,' she says to herself out loud. 'Don't say he's abandoned me and the baby.'

Elizabeth, or rather Lizzie as she is commonly known, spends the night in fits of worry, sometimes bursting into tears.

An unmarried mother and not yet nineteen. Cast out by her family and too young to marry without parental consent and with her and Freddy struggling to make ends meet. Only the previous night she had told Freddy that she thought she might be pregnant again.

'Oh please Lord, let him be safe and make him come back to me. What will I do without him!'

# Chapter 2

Freddy is about to turn the corner into one of the smaller alleys in The Rookery of St Giles. He is in a hurry to get home to Lizzie and his infant son that carries his own name. It is raining hard, otherwise he would not take this routing particularly after dark. There are cut-throats and villains that would not think twice about maiming or killing a stranger if there is the prospect of a shilling or more to be found on the victim's person. It is the sound of a woman's terrified scream that brings Freddy to a halt.

Freddy presses himself against the wall and risks a glance round the corner. It would have been far wiser to have turned on his heels and retrace his steps before finding another way home. Freddy sees three men, two of them with what look like big sticks or clubs raining blows on what seems to be the woman whose first scream had chilled Freddy to the bone.

'You are O'Rourke's whore and you belong to and you work for me!'

'Please no, stop it. I'll come back and work for you again, I promise.'

More blows come down on the poor woman.

'Too late, whore. You ran away from me and no whore has ever gotten away from O'Rourke. The others will soon understand that when I have finished with you. Right, Charlie, let's finish her off then everyone will know just why they should be afeared of us O'Rourkes.'

Heavy blows come crashing down on the unfortunate and moans soon give way to silence. The slightly smaller of the assailants bends down over the prone form of the woman.

'That's it, Pa. She's done for. Now let's get out of here before someone sees us.'

'No one has seen us, boy, and even if they did they will say nothing. We are the O'Rourkes.'

The three men then turn to leave the scene unaware that their actions have been watched. For a moment Freddy is rooted to the spot. He has of course heard of the O'Rourkes, but then who hasn't? What should he do next? he asks himself. Showing a bravery and determination that surprises himself Freddy decides to follow the killers to see where they end up. He must then go to the police in Holborn and tell them what he has seen and what he heard said. At the time the peril in which Freddy is placing himself and others does not occur to him. Freddy follows the men. After a few minutes the clubs or sticks the men had been using are thrown over a fence. Freddy notices the location and continues to follow them and eventually sees two of them go into The Flute where, judging by the reactions of others, the men are known.

Freddy then makes his way to the police station in Holborn. Within a minute of starting to give his account to the constable on the desk, Freddy is told to stay where he is while the constable fetches his sergeant. Within a few moments the sergeant comes out and beckons Freddy to follow him into a room beyond the desk. The sergeant closes the door behind him and tells Freddy to sit down. Pulling a paper and a pencil out from the drawer in the desk, the sergeant then looks up at Freddy.

'Now then. First start with your name and where you live, then tell me everything that you have seen and heard tonight.'

After a few minutes the sergeant interrupts.

'The O'Rourkes, is it? You heard their names and what they called each other?'

'Yes, and I followed them after to The Flute where I saw two of the men go inside. The other, the one with the crooked walk, didn't join them inside.'

'Did you, by heavens! This could be enough to put an end to these O'Rourkes.'

The sergeant gets up and opens the door.

'Jenkins! Go upstairs and ask the Inspector to come down as quick as he can. This is going to be a night to remember. No second thoughts, I'll go and see the Inspector myself. You stay here and make sure this man does not leave. Better still lock him up so he *can't* leave.'

'Why are you locking me up!' Freddy demands. 'I've come here to report a killing and you treat me as if I am the murderer. I need to get home. My girl is looking after our son and she will be worried sick about me.'

'Nothing I can do about that. She'll see you in the morning all right and then everything will be fine. There is too much at stake here and I want you where I know we can find you. Just think about it – at least you will be warm and dry and out of the rain. We'll even give you a mug of tea for your troubles and maybe breakfast in the morning. Now me and the Inspector have got a raid to organise and to go and catch us some killers. The O'Rourkes at that! What a night! Oh what a night! ...'

Freddy is led downstairs to the cells and the door is locked behind him. The cell is no more than six foot long and a little less wide. The only things in the cell are a wooden bench without any mattress or bedding and a bucket. True to the sergeant's word, a mug of tea arrives fairly soon after and he is also passed the luxury of a candle in its holder and a blanket. The door is solid and has but a small grill about one-third the way up. There is no other light or ventilation in the cell.

*And this is how they treat the good guys!* Freddy says to himself.

Freddy eventually doses off when the stub of the candle finally burns itself down. He is awakened by a commotion of much shouting and swearing. It is hard for Freddy to hear everything that is said through his cell door and the place echoes as well, but the voices sound similar to those he has heard earlier. The O'Rourkes! Throughout the remainder of the night Freddy is kept awake by the continued shouting, oaths and threats from the latest 'guests' at Holborn police station.

After some considerable time, by which time Freddy

assumes it must be the morning, the keys turn in the lock to his cell. Freddy is beckoned out by a constable who has a finger to his mouth indicating that he should remain silent. Freddy is taken back upstairs and led into the room where he had been interviewed by the sergeant the night before. Waiting for him on the table is a plate of bread and cheese and a mug of tea.

'The sergeant will be with you in just a moment and then you will no doubt be free to go. Take your breakfast while you wait.'

The constable closes and locks the door behind him. A few minutes later the there is a sound of a key and the door opens and in walks the sergeant looking rather tired but obviously in high spirits.

'Look, lad, you have done well, you have done very well and no doubt you feel hard done by. If I had let you go, they would have had my guts for garters. Now there is one more thing you must do for us. It's been raining all night so any blood on the clubs you saw thrown away will have been washed off by now but I want you to show me where they threw those clubs.'

Freddy nods.

'Did you find that poor woman?'

'Yes we did and a right mess they made of her as well. Now there is just one more thing. Can you read?'

Freddy nods.

'Well, this here piece of paper I am giving you is what they call a subpoena. This means that you are required to come to court and give evidence on what you saw and heard last night. If you don't turn up, then the law will be after you and you will be spending sometime yourself in gaol. The O'Rourkes have a fearsome reputation and it is well deserved. It will be some weeks before they come up at the Old Bailey and we have other cases to build against them, not just this murder. We will keep your name from them and from their attorney as long as we can but I am telling you now, lad, that you should make plans to disappear after the trial. The O'Rourkes are not a forgiving lot and they will come after you even if the blighters that did the murder swing for it. Now go with the constable and let's see if we can find those clubs. So as not to draw attention to you, as soon as we have a date for the trial then one of my constables will be out of uniform when he brings round a letter with the details.'

Freddy is able to lead the constable to where he thinks the clubs or sticks can be found. There is a yard behind the fence in question that is used for rearing poultry. The weapons are easily found and are taken away. Freddy then rushes home as fast as he can.

Freddy at last comes through the door to the single dilapidated room that they have to call home.

'My love, I have been locked up at the police station all night and I could not get word to you. Last night I was witness to a murder and the police would not let me go. I am so sorry – you must have been worried stiff. Look, I must go now to work otherwise they will dock my pay and we need every penny we can lay our hands on. I'll come back this evening as soon as I can and I will try to explain all.'

Lizzie comes to him and they kiss briefly and passionately before Freddy pulls himself away.

'Tonight! I promise I will tell you everything tonight.'

Lizzie had been unable to say a word such was her relief and such was the short time that Freddy was there with her.

# Chapter 3

Throughout the day Freddy is distracted from his work. He worries about what the police sergeant has said about him needing to disappear and the possible dangers to himself and to his young family should he give witness against the O'Rourkes. He says nothing to Harry and George. He has to work things out for himself before he involves the rest of the family. In any event they are not mature or experienced enough to give him advice.

*If only Dad were still alive,* he says to himself. *He would have an answer, I'm sure.*

Freddy packs away his tools and makes his way home to Lizzie. As he enters Lizzie is standing by the small window at the end of the room and she smooths down her dress. It's her best dress and she has paid particular attention to her hair tonight.

'Oh Freddy, thank heavens you're home. I've been so worried. You've no idea of the horrible thoughts that have been going through my head.'

'You look lovely. I am so sorry to have worried you. I have lots to tell you so let's just sit down and I'll do my best to explain.

'When you said the other night that you think you might be expecting again it got me to thinking that I should try again to see your father and get him to agree to us marrying. That is why I did not come straight home from work. Well, a waste of time that was. By the time I made my way down across the river to where your parents live I was soaked through to the skin from the rain. Your father opened the door when I knocked and it was clear that he was drunk. I tried to have a conversation with him but he first threatened me with violence and then he slammed the door in my face. Nothing else that I could do then but to return home and this was what I did.'

Freddy goes on to tell her about the events of the night. 'Now this is the real scary bit,' he says at length. 'Not only will I have to give witness against the O'Rourkes but the sergeant said that I will have to disappear after the trial for my own safety.'

Lizzie gasps.

'What are we going to do, Lizzie? If only my dad was here, he would have an answer, I'm sure of it.'

Lizzie leans forward and takes both of his hands in hers.

'You are stupid but brave. Much better that you had done nothing and come straight home. How can we disappear? We have nowhere to go and you have your work. Look, can't you ask Mr Wilkins for advice? He may not care much for me what with me getting pregnant and all and us not being wed but he has your father's old job. He may have some ideas.'

'Wilkins is a fool. He may know his bookbinding but that's about all. No, Wilkins is not the answer.'

'Well, can't you go and see Mr Reynolds then? He's an educated man and your family have worked for his family for at least three generations.'

'Mr Reynolds, now that's a thought. I have just the once or twice had the briefest of exchanges with him, but I think Dad and he used to get on well enough. I'll try and talk to him in the morning. Is the baby fine and how about you? I've missed you.'

# Chapter 4

Freddy decides not to approach Jack Wilkins about his need to ask for Mr Reynolds' advice on a deeply private and personal matter. Wilkins would consider such an approach to be inappropriate and question why Mr Reynolds should be concerned about Freddy's problems.

Then after Jack Wilkins he has to get past Mr Reynolds' clerk, Mr Dougherty. Freddy prepares a note to hand to Mr Reynolds' clerk requesting such an interview. Knowing that Mr Dougherty is bound to read such a note first, Freddy does not explain why he is seeking Mr Reynolds' advice and he merely states that this is a most urgent and serious matter, and Freddy expresses the hope that, given the long association between his family and the firm, Mr Reynolds can see his way to sparing some of his valuable time.

During the mid-afternoon Mr Dougherty comes down to the workshop and approaches Freddy's bench with a look of disapproval on his face.

'Mr Reynolds will see you now, Clout. Come with me.'

Everyone's head turns to look and Freddy overhears someone behind him say

'I bet he's for the sack. I wonder what he's been up to. He got *another* girl up the duff, has he?'

Freddy follows Mr Dougherty into Mr Reynolds' office. The first time he has been into this inner sanctum. Freddy stands in front of the desk where Mr Reynolds is seated and is holding Freddy's note in his hand.

'Well?'

Freddy says nothing but gives a sidelong glance in Dougherty's direction.

'That's all, Dougherty, and close the door behind you.'

Dougherty exits and the door closes.

'Well?'

'Mr Reynolds, Sir, I do desperately need some advice and now that my father has gone I have no one to turn to and I know that my father held you in such high regard.'

'Did he now? Well, get on with it then – I am a very busy man. If it's more money you are after, you can turn on your heels and walk out of here right now.'

'No, Sir, it is nothing like that. I fear that my life and the lives of my family are in terrible danger.'

'Danger you say. How come?'

Freddy relates the course of the events of the night before. At the very first mention of the O'Rourkes Mr Reynolds shows a keen interest and lets Freddy continue uninterrupted. When Freddy stops talking Mr Reynolds is rubbing his chin.

'The O'Rourkes! Hah! So the police are going to nail them at last. There is many a fine man who will be glad of this news. Leeches – that's what they are. Leeches, villains and now going to be done for murder. That will be the end of their affairs, God willing. You have done well, Clout. You have done very well. Tell me, did the police mention any other matters in relation to the O'Rourkes?'

'The Sergeant did say something like they had other cases to build against them, not just the murder.'

'Did they now?!'

At this point Reynolds seems to go into a world of his own for a moment and mutters as if to himself. 'I must get news to the others.'

'Others, Sir?'

'Never mind that. Now what to do? What to do? You have had a child by the girl that used to work here, I believe. Are you married?'

'No, Sir, we are not married but we want to be. The trouble is that as Lizzie is under twenty-one – she requires her father's consent and he is not minded to give us his blessing. We will marry though just as soon as we can and we seem to have another baby on the way.'

'And your brothers are working for me downstairs?'

'Yes, Sir, they are my twin brothers, Henry and George, and they are living with my mother, who also used to work here some time ago, and I have another brother and a sister.'

'Far too many. Far too many. Can't do anything about them. They must change their names and just hope that's enough.'

'As for you, that is a different matter. The O'Rourkes have a hold on too many people. We need to get you and your young family away from here until the day of the trial. I wouldn't put it beyond the realms of possibility that they can find out how the police are building a case against them and do all in their power to ruin that case before things get to court. That would mean they would find out that you were a witness to the murder and they would have you … disposed of. I know your father could, so I take it that you can read yourself?'

Freddy nods.

'Good. My cousin Mr William Broadwater has a printing business in Uxbridge. He prints a newspaper for the district. I shall write him a note this very afternoon and ask that he takes you on and he finds somewhere for you to rent. You will stay there until the day of the trial and then you will disappear back there again. As far as all those people downstairs are concerned you have been dismissed. You'll have to explain things to your brothers as best you can.'

'You will do all this for me, Sir? I just don't know what to say or imagine how I can repay you.'

'This is not all about you, Clout, as admirable as your actions have been; I have my own reasons. It is about bringing to an end the O'Rourkes. You will testify against them or I will tell the police where to find you if you fail to turn up for the trial and if I do that the O'Rourkes are bound to find you. But it will not come to that, will it, Clout?'

Freddy shakes his head.

'As far as Dougherty is concerned you have been dismissed without pay and that's what the others will believe. Here are three sovereigns, part in compensation for not getting paid but also to help get you started in Uxbridge. You will need some money for the train fare. You are to go to Paddington and ask for a fare to Uxbridge; this will involve a change of trains at a place called West Drayton. My cousin's printworks are about a half a mile from the Vine Street station. I shall get a letter to him by late this evening and tell him to expect you tomorrow. In the meantime make your arrangements to quit London and think up a new name for your family to take. As for the trial date, I shall get word to my cousin and then him to you. I shall get to hear about this through my Lodge. They call you Freddy, I believe?'

'Yes, Sir, they do.'

'Well, Freddy, or whatever your name is or will soon be ...' Reynolds smiles. '... I don't expect to see or hear from you again but if you let me down I assure you, you will have great cause to regret it. You can go now and by go I mean leave the premises and then make your arrangements.'

'Thank you so much, Sir. I consider it my duty to give witness now at the trial and not in any way to let you down. Thank you, Sir.'

Freddy passes his brother George on the way out and says in a whisper: 'All is not what it seems, brother. Just keep quiet and ask no questions until you get home tonight.'

Freddy goes straight home to Lizzie and the baby. Within the hour they have packed all those belongings and clothing they can carry. As for their few sticks of furniture these, they know, will have to be abandoned. Tonight they will stay with Freddy's mother and brothers and sister and make their way to Paddington in the morning. Whenever Freddy goes to see his mother he passes a small bookshop that also undertakes small bookbinding commissions. Looking anew at the sign above the premises Freddy says to himself: *Clowes is as good a name as anything else.*

The family are all gathered in the two rooms in Great Wild Street. It is going to be rather crowded there tonight. Freddy has assured Lizzie that things will work out but he has resisted all calls for him to say what is going on until they are all there together so that he can explain things just the once.

Slowly and deliberately, just as if he was reading from one of Mr Dickens' accounts that he enjoys when he can afford the weekly publication, Freddy describes the events of the night before. Everyone is spellbound and there is no interruption.

Lizzie knows all this and eventually breaks in.

'Did you talk to Mr Reynolds? What did he have to say? Why haven't you told me? I'm scared, Freddy; what are we to do?'

'Mr Reynolds could not have been more obliging. He has written to his cousin, a Mr Broadwater, who runs a printing works and prints a paper out at Uxbridge, and he is to find us somewhere to live as well as a job. He says we should change our names and that he will get word to me when the trial is to take place. He has also given me three sovereigns. We leave for Paddington first thing in the morning and we will take the train to Uxbridge. I have never been on a train! Now you all need to take a new name as well. There is at least one O'Rourke still roaming free and he may try and get at us to stop me from giving witness against his family. As for a new name, how does the name Clowes sound to you?'

'Better than being reminded every day that you are called the same as a baby's diaper clout,' says Letty.

As far as Letty's children are concerned they have no idea that Letty and their father never married or that Will was married once but that his wife had vanished after the death of their three children. It is one of those family secrets that is never spoken about and is kept buried.

The family talk away until it is very late but eventually they do settle down for the night.

In the morning Freddy, Lizzie and the baby leave for Paddington with George carrying some of their things part of the way there before he heads off for his work.

Neither Freddy nor Lizzie has been so close to a steam locomotive before. They have seen and heard one in the distance of course but have never been this close. Clutching two third-class tickets, they board the train having asked a porter which way to go. It is not long out of Paddington that they come upon open fields and open spaces with so few people about. They have a considerable wait after they disembark at West Drayton for the smaller train that is to take them to Uxbridge. It is a grey day but at least it is dry and the wait is no burden as they enjoy the sight, the sound and the strange smell of the locomotives as they thunder past to Lord knows where. They board as soon as the little train with its two carriages arrives and some five minutes later the train pulls out on the short journey to the end of the branch line. At their destination, Freddy leaves Lizzie, the baby and all the things they are carrying and makes his way to ask for Mr William Broadwater at the printing works that he has already spotted along the road. It seems to Lizzie that it is not too long before Freddy returns.

'That is good, Lizzie. Mr Reynolds has kept his word and I am to start work tomorrow for Mr Broadwater. He has also found us some lodgings down in Bell Yard, which is just a little way in that direction.'

The place is so different from London. Why, in just several minutes it seems as though the buildings almost stop and you are looking out on open country with just a few buildings scattered here and there. They soon chance upon Bell Yard where the dwelling houses have outside sheds attached to them and there are a number of what are obviously lavatories around the yard.

'You know, Freddy, I think I am going to like it here.'

'I'm not so sure myself, Lizzie, but we have little choice in the matter. Well, for the foreseeable future anyway. Now let's see where No. 8 lies and get ourselves settled in and decide what we need for our creature comforts, as they say. I am told that there is a place down at the end of Windsor Street where we may pick up some used pieces of furniture.'

# Chapter 5

That very evening Hamilton Reynolds makes his way to his Lodge meeting. Tonight more than any other night he needs to seek out fellow Lodge member Judge Horace Taylor. As soon as he can he takes the judge by the arm.

'Horace, we must talk on a matter of the utmost urgency.'

The judge allows himself to be led out through the French windows leading onto the terrace.

'Horace, you will have heard that the O'Rourkes have been arrested for murder? Well, the witness works for me, or rather he did, as I have arranged for him to be tucked away safely with my cousin in Uxbridge just in case the O'Rourkes get to him before the trial.'

'Yes, it's good news, isn't it? I shall make sure that it is me that hears the case,' replies the judge.

'Good, good, but it seems that there is more. The police are looking into other issues and that will no doubt threaten many a gentleman who, shall we say, has partaken of a particular type of liaison. The O'Rourkes are animals and they have been trying to extort money where they think they have a hold over their, shall we say, clients. If this comes out into the open, Horace, it could cause a frightful lot of damage to the reputations of many a fine gentleman.'

'It won't come to that, Hamilton. I shall lean upon both the Superintendent in charge of Holborn and the Prosecutor for the Court and whatever papers the police may have found will never see the light of day. And for the trail itself I shall exercise what is known as judicial economy so that after I have sentenced them for murder any charges relating to extortion or blackmail will not need to be read, let alone heard. It will be the end of the O'Rourkes, Hamilton, rest assured!'

'That is fine to hear but as far as I know there is still one of them at large – the man I have sent to Uxbridge says this O'Rourke has a crooked walk. I am not so concerned about what he might do to my man if he found him after the trial but what would happen if he resurfaced at a later date and started to cause mischief?'

'We can only do what we can do, Hamilton, but you have done wonderfully well to spirit your man away until the trial. Can we trust him not to disappear?'

'I think so, Horace. He is in my debt and he knows it, but I have warned him of the severe consequences if he lets me down. We had best get back to the others but I think we can safely say we have control of the situation.'

'Rest assured they will swing for it. As for your man, let's not let the situation get complicated. Keep him away in Uxbridge until after everything is over. You should have him dressed as an old woman when he leaves the Old Bailey just in case there is someone watching.'

# Chapter 6

Some two weeks later Freddy is summoned to Mr Broadwater's office.

'I have heard from my cousin. The trial at the Old Bailey is the day after tomorrow, Wednesday. My cousin has asked me to give you the money for a return railway fare. This matter must be most important indeed for him to do this.

'You are to take the 7.25 morning train – there's a connecting service from West Drayton to take you to Paddington a few minutes after. This should give you time enough to walk down to the Old Bailey. It is most important that you keep your identity to yourself. You are not to give your name to anyone even if they look to be engaged at the Old Bailey itself. Here is a note to confirm that George Parsons – that's you – has an appointment to see Mr Brimelow at the Prosecutor's Office. It is Mr Brimelow that will be prosecuting the case. He will then tell you what to do. You will not let us down, will you?'

'No, Sir. I have given my word.'

'Good man!'

On the morning of the trial Freddy travels as he has been directed and then walks to the Old Bailey. Once there he asks for Mr Brimelow at the Prosecutor's Office and, when he is challenged as to the nature of his business, proffers the note confirming that he has an appointment. It is not until he is in front of Mr Brimelow that Freddy reveals his real identity.

'Excellent, excellent!' exclaims Brimelow.

'The trial or rather the trials are set for this afternoon. You are to remain in this room until then. It is through there you should go if you have to answer the call of nature and you will be given some refreshments. Now as for the trial itself, this is what will happen ...'

# Chapter 7

In the days leading up to the trial George and Henry become increasingly concerned as to how they could explain away their change of name from Clout to Clowes. If they stay in the employ of Mr Reynolds, then surely the ploy would not work. More likely they would be calling more attention upon themselves and increase the risks of being identified as belonging to the family of the man giving witness against the O'Rourkes No, they would have to leave Mr Reynolds' employ and find another bookbinder to take them on.

For his part, and upon deeper reflection, Mr Reynolds decides that he would also be glad not to have anyone on his books with the surname of Clout. He now wants to put as much distance as humanly possible between himself and the whole sordid O'Rourke affair and the dangers he has put himself in owing to his appetites. So it is that clandestine messages are passed between Mr Reynolds and the twins without the ever watchful clerk in the shape of Mr Dougherty having any idea that something is up and certainly without the knowledge of Jack Wilkins on the shop floor. So it is arranged that George alone would return one evening to Mr Reynolds' office some two hours after everyone should have left so that they can discuss the situation without fear of anyone finding out about their liaison.

It is agreed that George and Henry will leave at the end of the week thus terminating any association with the business of Mr Reynolds. For his part Mr Reynolds undertakes to speak to someone with whom he is personally acquainted with so that the twins can be engaged from the beginning of the following week at a premises nearly three-quarters of a mile distant. Here they would be known as George and Henry Clowes from the very first hour of the very first day in their new jobs. It is through his 'friendship' with a fellow Lodge member who also has an interest in the fate of the O'Rourkes that Reynolds is able to make all this happen.

# Chapter 8

Lunch has been taken and the court has reconvened for the afternoon session. Standing in the dock are James and Mary O'Rourke who run and maintain the establishment known as The Flute. The courtroom is filled and the jury are assembled and all await the arrival of Judge Horace Taylor who is to hear and to try the case. This is the first of two cases involving members of the O'Rourke family to be heard. Judge Taylor enters, the court rises and settles down after he has seated himself and the niceties have been observed. At the indication of the judge, the clerk stands to read out the charges.

'James and Mary O'Rourke, being husband and wife and involved in the management and running of the establishment known as The Flute, located in the parish of St Giles, are charged with the following offences: the running of a disorderly house and a brothel being at the afore-mentioned premises known as The Flute; under threats and coercion unlawfully taking away Ann Green, an unmarried girl, aged fifteen years, from the possession of her father, and against his will, he having the lawful charge of her; falsely imprisoning the said Ann Green for the purpose of prostituting her; unlawfully taking away Jane Kemp, an un-married girl, aged sixteen years, from the possession of her mother, and against her will, she having the lawful charge of her; falsely imprisoning the said Jane Kemp for the purpose of prostituting her; living off of the immoral earnings of at least four women of full age.'

There are mutterings of disapproval from members of the public before Judge Taylor speaks.

'Mr Brimelow, you are prosecuting in this instance? Are you ready to call your first witness?'

'I am indeed prosecuting, Your Honour. I should like to call Sergeant Haines of the Metropolitan Police Constabulary.'

The sergeant comes to the front of the court.

'You are Sergeant Haines?'

'I am, Sir.'

'Will you explain to the court your role and that of the police in relation to the charges against the two persons standing in the dock.'

'I am Sergeant Haines, one of the sergeants serving at the Metropolitan Police Constabulary based at Holborn. Following information received the day before in relation to another matter soon to be heard in this court, I was authorised and empowered to take with me eleven of my constables, this being the full complement of the Watch, to The Flute in St Giles to find evidence that the establishment was being used as a brothel.

'We arrived at The Flute at exactly eleven o'clock in the

evening of 19 April 1859. With three of my constables at the rear of the building should anyone attempt to vacate the premises, I led the rest of my men into the front of the premises. Upon entering, I observed a number of men taking drink and some women in revealing costumes. One of these women was leading a man up the stairs. I left some of my men at the front door and with four others I went to take the stairs to investigate the premises further. At the top of the stairs was seated the accused Mary O'Rourke. My men then went into each of the rooms leading off from the landing – each of these rooms was set out as a parlour or bedroom. In two of these rooms we found men with prostitutes in various stages of undress. At the end of the landing, two of the rooms were locked. I demanded the keys from the accused woman but she refused.

'My men then broke down the doors where we found two young girls later identified as Ann Green aged fifteen and Jane Kemp aged sixteen. Their hands had been tied and secured behind their backs.'

'And where was the accused, James O'Rourke, at this time?' asked Brimelow.

'He was in a parlour on the ground floor next to what passes for the kitchen to the rear of the area where drinks are served.'

'Was he with anyone?'

'No, Sir. He was alone and had clearly been taking several bottles of beer – from what I saw beside him on the table and on the floor. I would say he was quite drunk, Sir.'

'What of the two young girls? Though let us call them children for that is what they are!' exclaimed Brimelow. His words are received with noises of approval from the public. 'What have the police learnt of their situation?'

'It is most upsetting, Sir. I have daughters of a similar age and in all my time in the police I have not come across such a sickening and sad tale.

'Taking the youngest, Jane Green, first, Sir. It took me quite sometime after untying her to gain her confidence and to reassure her that she would not have to face the accused or their sons. The wretched girl had been locked away for what she thinks was about three weeks. She was first brutally raped by what she believes to be one of the sons of the accused. This is a man with a limp. By her description I believe the assault on this poor wretched girl was done by the son, Thomas O'Rourke. We have been unable to find him.

'Since that time the girl has been forced to have sexual relations with a number of men. Some, she has told me, judging by their clothes and the manner of their speech, were gentlemen, although that is a matter of opinion in my eyes.

'There is a history between the girl's father and the accused. Mr Green found his small business was struggling but he was hopeful of pulling things around but needed to borrow some money to overcome temporary difficulties. He was unfortunate in that it was to the O'Rourkes that he owed the money. The business failed and it was then that the accused took away the girl Jane Green and did those things to her. As for the father, he was threatened with extreme violence and told that further harm would come to his family if he went to the police.'

Judge Taylor intervenes.

'Sergeant, are the circumstances concerning the other young girl of a similar nature?'

'They are, Your Honour, although the manner of the taking away of the child from the mother was different.'

'Mr Brimelow, I think the court has heard enough of the sordid details affecting these two unfortunate girls. In the interests of public decency I think there is no need to hear any more. I have read the police report and I am quite satisfied on that account. Is the father of the first girl to be called as a witness?'

'No, Sir, he is not. It seems that a few weeks ago the whole family, including the girl, packed up and left and I have no knowledge of where they have gone.'

'Then I hope that father and daughter are now reunited and that they find peace. Does the prosecution have any further witnesses?'

'No, Your Honour. There is just the sergeant's testimony and the police report that you have seen.'

'And a fine testimony it is. You should be commended for your diligence and attention to detail, Sergeant. You may stand down. Mr Phelps, do you have anything to say on the defendant's behalf?'

'No, Your Honour. I have nothing to say.'

'Gentlemen of the jury, you have heard the clear evidence of an experienced police sergeant and no defence has been offered. What is now required is your verdict based upon the admirable evidence from the policeman that you have heard.'

The jurymen are seated along two six by six rows one behind each other to the left of Judge Taylor and immediately opposite the accused. Without rising from their chairs they start to confer with each other. It takes just a few seconds. The foreman at the end of the first row and closest to the judge raises his hand.

Upon a nod from Judge Taylor, he declares:

'Guilty, Your Honour, on all accounts.'

Judge Taylor addresses the court.

'I would normally give a sentence of six or twelve months for those running a brothel but this wicked case goes beyond that. You have ruined and abused the lives of two young girls and kept them captives for your own immoral purposes and gain. It is a great pity that the sentence of transportation has started to die out. This great city would continue to be best served if the worst of society be moved to the other side of the world. Mary O'Rourke, your sentence will be ten years' transportation.'

James O'Rourke shouts out: 'That is a death sentence! No woman, particularly a woman of her age, can expect to come through such an ordeal.'

Judge Taylor continues.

'Silence! I will have you removed and the court will continue in your absence! James O'Rourke, your sentence will be the same except that the man should be taken as being the most responsible in any crime. For you it is fifteen years' transportation, although it is unlikely that this sentence will ever be served given the more serious case to be brought against you very shortly.

'There is also the question of the rape of Jane Green by the person believed by the police to be Thomas O'Rourke. This case and matter remains open and should not be considered closed. Take the prisoner Mary O'Rourke away and we shall commence the trial concerning the murder of Mary Peters involving James O'Rourke and Charles O'Rourke immediately.'

The first trial has taken less than ten minutes from beginning to end. Judge Taylor prides himself in the efficiency of his court.

James O'Rourke remains in the dock and his son Charles – 'Charlie' – is led up from the cells below to join him. Again with a nod from Judge Taylor the Clerk reads out the charge.

'James O'Rourke and Charles O'Rourke, you are charged that on the evening of 18 April 1859 in the presence of a third person believed to be one Thomas O'Rourke you did maliciously murder one Mary Peters who had been working at The Flute in the parish of St Giles as a prostitute.'

'Mr Brimelow, you are prosecuting in this case as well?' asks Judge Taylor.

'I am indeed, Your Honour.'

'And you, Mr Phelps, I take it that you may speak for the defendants?'

'I do, Your Honour.'

'Very well, Mr Brimelow, would you call your first witness.'

'Witness for the Court is Frederick Clout.'

Freddy takes a deep breath and makes his way to the front of the court. He has been standing, he hopes unnoticed, towards the back of the court during the first trial against the O'Rourke family so, as Mr Brimelow has suggested, he could see the sergeant give his evidence and know what was expected of him as a witness. Over the past week or so Freddy had been wondering what he should say in the court so as to give away as little information as possible about himself, his family and where they could be found.

'I would like you, Mr Clout, to tell the court how you found yourself to be in St Giles on the evening of the murder, what you saw and what you heard and the course of events up until the time that you found yourself at the police station in Holborn,' Brimelow demands.

Freddy tells his story as truthfully as he could, up until the departure of the three assailants.

'What did you do then?' Brimelow asks. 'Did you go to the woman?'

'No, Sir. I thought that if she was done for there would be nothing that I could do, so I decided to follow the men instead. It was not difficult as there was hardly anyone about. After a few minutes I saw them throw the clubs away over a fence and I continued to follow them until they came to The Flute. It was then that I decided to go to the police and tell them what had occurred and what I had seen and heard.'

'That is very commendable and it is a fine thing that you have done so that the court can today hear of the horrors that went on that dreadful night and the wilful and brutal murder of Mary Peters committed by these two men.' Brimelow dramatically points an accusing finger at James and Charles O'Rourke.

For the first time Phelps stands up.

'You admit it was a foul night with heavy rain?'

'Yes, Sir, it was.'

'And there are many twists and turns in the streets and lanes, are there not?'

'Yes, Sir, there are but it was them that I followed all the way from the scene of the murder to The Flute.'

'They must have been out of your sight on occasions – you could have lost sight of one group of men and started to follow another party altogether?'

'No, Sir, I know it was them because it was the same man that was with them that had a crooked walk.'

Judge Taylor intervenes.

'That seems a clear enough explanation to me, Mr Phelps. Do you wish to call further witnesses, Mr Brimelow?'

'I would like to call Sergeant Haines of the Metropolitan police station at Holborn.'

Haines re-joins the front of the court.

'Sergeant, we have heard the previous witness state what he saw and heard of the murder itself. We have heard that the witness saw the men discard their murder weapons and how he followed the same men to The Flute. What can you tell the court?'

'Well, Sir, when that witness started to give his account at the police station of what he had seen I did send two of my constables to look for the murdered woman. They did in fact find her near to where we expected to find the body except that she had been moved out of the weather into the doorway of a shop nearby. Someone had not wanted to leave the poor wretch where she lay in the rain. She was then taken to the mortuary. It was the day later, after we had raided The Flute, that one of the prostitutes we had arrested identified the dead woman as Mary Peters, even though her face and head were all battered and cut up, and it was confirmed that she too had been working at The Flute whorehouse.'

'And what of the murder weapons?' Brimelow asks.

'The witness that has just testified was able the following morning to lead one of my constables to where they had been thrown away. We had kept him in one of our cells overnight as we did not want him to disappear on us. As far as the police are concerned, all and every account given by the witness and what he had told us is accurate and true.'

'So,' Brimelow starts, 'we have a clear testimony from a witness who saw and heard this dreadful and callous murder being committed. We have heard how the police later confirmed the identity of the murdered woman as Mary Peters, a prostitute from The Flute, and we have heard that the police have recovered the murder weapons from where the witness said he saw them discarded. There should be little doubt in any person's mind as to what the outcome here should be. Those murderers deserve to hang for what they have done!' Brimelow once again dramatically points an accusing finger at the O'Rourkes.

'Mr Phelps, have you anything else you wish to say?' asks Judge Taylor.

'No, Your Honour.'

'Very well. Gentlemen of the jury, I think you know your duty.'

After the briefest of conferring and nodding between the men, and as in the previous case against the O'Rourke family, the foreman confirms a verdict of guilty – to which there is some considerable cheering around the courtroom.

The court usher places the regulation black cloth on the head of Judge Taylor.

'James O'Rourke, you have been found guilty of a callous and wicked murder. You will be taken from here to a place of execution where you will be hung by the neck until you are dead. Charles O'Rourke, you, too, have been found guilty of this callous and wicked murder. You will also be taken from here to a place of execution where you will be hung by the neck until you are dead.

'As in the previous trial, the name of Thomas O'Rourke has featured, although he remains at large. Let the warrant for his arrest now also include murder as well as rape and taking part in false imprisonment, for he is as guilty as if he too had taken a weapon to this woman. Fallen as she was, she did not deserve to die in such an appalling manner.'

At this point James O'Rourke points his finger directly at Freddy.

'You have crossed the O'Rourkes. They may stretch my neck but we will be avenged. No matter how long it takes, the O'Rourkes will seek you out and your family and we will destroy you as you have destroyed us.'

Freddy is knocked back by the fierceness and the venom of this threat. He is scared that it is a promise that will come true. As instructed before the start of the two trials, Freddy returns to Brimelow's office. Brimelow has other cases to prosecute but his clerk, Mr Symes, is there waiting for him. Freddy appears with all colour drained from his face.

'We need to get you away from here as soon as we can. Mr Brimelow has instructed me to ask you to put these women's clothes on. It may seem undignified but in case anyone is watching for you leaving they hopefully will not be giving an old woman a second look. Here is a dress, a shawl and a bonnet. Walk away slowly with your back bent as if with old age. Keep these things on until you get to wherever it is you are going and do not be tempted to take these things off until you are inside at your destination. Even I do not know where you are going and that is how it should be. The less people know of your whereabouts the safer you will be. Good luck to you. You have done a great service and justice has now been served.'

Freddy does not object and meekly dons the clothing and slips out into the street before making his way back to Paddington. He continues to make the pretext of being an old woman so does not stride along in his normal manly manner. He has quite a wait for the change of trains at West Drayton and by the time he gets back to Uxbridge it has started to rain and the light is beginning to fade. Freddy smiles to himself and decides he will play a trick on Lizzie.

All things said and done, things have worked out quite well, although Freddy still has doubts about whether he will ever feel settled in such a backwater as Uxbridge and he misses seeing his mother, brothers and sister. He has now been on the train either to Uxbridge or to London three times. Not many people on his wages or from his background can say they have done that and Freddy smiles to himself again.

Lizzie, he thinks, won't want this old dress they have given him but they can at least get something for it at the market and in return buy some clothes for the baby.

*Nearly there now*, Freddy says to himself. He has in his hand a bunch of wild flowers that he had picked from the nearby field at West Drayton station. They are intended as a surprise for Lizzie but first of all he will play the role of an old gypsy woman trying to sell the said flowers. Lizzie is not taken in when she answers the knock at the door. Freddy cannot keep a straight face and soon starts to snigger.

# Chapter 9

With the trial now over, Freddy reverts to being just another worker and he is fairly content. There is no reason for him and the paper's owner, Mr Broadwater, to have any communication and he never hears again from Mr Reynolds. The newspaper, now known as the *Buckinghamshire Advertiser, Uxbridge Journal and Middlesex Gazette,* is apparently doing well and the printing works have just moved into more spacious premises in King's Arms Yard. At the time of the printing works being relocated in King's Arms Yard, Lizzie is just a few weeks away from giving birth to the new addition to the family. It has been a hot August day and, although they have been sitting outside most of the evening, the air is still close and it has remained uncomfortably warm. Freddy is fatigued from working in the heat of the printing works and is in need of a good night's rest and sleep. They come inside and climb the wooden staircase to their first-floor room. If the air outside was still, the atmosphere in their room can be stirred with a stick. They lay on top of the bed in little more than their underclothes, waiting and hoping that the temperature will soon start to drop and they can get to sleep. Once again, they go over a familiar conversation.

'So we are agreed then, Lizzie? If it's a girl we will call her Elizabeth Rose after you and if it is a boy we shall call him Albert after the Prince Consort?'

'Yes, dear, that's what we said we would do. Now why don't you try and get some sleep?'

'And we will not have the baby baptised yet then? I mean with us still not wed and not going to church, we just don't know what questions the vicar might ask of us and we are still trying to keep my real identity a secret. We have to have the birth registered of course but that is a different matter. Who's to know that we are not married if we tell them we are?'

'Yes, dear, that's what we said we would do. We *are* going to get married though, aren't we, Freddy? There is nothing my drunken father can do about it after I'm twenty-one. I am better out of it and away from him. I hope I never see him again in my life. It is my poor mother that still has the worst of him. He beats and abuses her and won't ever take no for an answer, if you know what I mean. I hate him to his boots. I can't wait to stop being a Sparrow and to take your new name, Clowes. It sounds so grand, Freddy.'

'Then Mr and Mrs Clowes it shall be, my dear, and to hell and back with your father. As soon as we can, we will be wed.'

Baby Elizabeth Rose arrives on market day on the eleventh of September and both mother and baby are in good health and are doing well according to the midwife. Neither Lizzie nor Freddy have any regrets about what they have said and felt about Ephraim Sparrow when news of his death arrives in the form of a short note from Freddy's brother, George. Lizzie's mother had brought the news to Great Wild Street. She was far removed from being the distraught widow.

# Chapter 10

'What's all this commotion going on here!' barks Sergeant Haines. 'This is a police station not a circus.'

'We have arrested these three men for fighting in the street, Sergeant,' replied one of the constables.

'We knew the others involved in the fight but not these three. With there just being the four of us, we concentrated on these strangers. They did not appreciate our interest at first so we had to call upon our dear friend the pacifier,' says another constable with the broadest of smiles as he pats his long stick. The other constables burst into laughter before the sergeant joins in himself. They are all big men these constables. Tough but far from clever. They were employed for their brawn and not for their brains.

'Well, your pacifiers certainly seem to have left their mark, given the blood and all. Where did you find them and what were they fighting about?'

'We came across them just down the side of St Giles' Church, Sergeant. We did not see the fight start but we heard a commotion and Bill here started to blow on his whistle and as soon as four of us had arrived we decided to get stuck in ourselves. It's a bit odd really – we know the Carters like their drink but it's unlike them to get into a fight in the street. We know where to find them anyway so as I suggested we concentrate on bringing this lot in. Must say, though, even with the aid of me pacifier it was the devil's own job to cuff 'em.'

'Well, it's getting late now and I'll soon be going off duty. Mrs H has promised me something special for supper tonight so just bang 'em up for the night but I'll have their names first,' said the Sergeant.

'Sod you, copper!!' one of the battered and bloody arrested men shouted.

This provokes the biggest of the constables to resort to use of his 'pacifier' with a hearty end first push into the man's gut that causes the man to double up in pain.

'That's the way of it, is it! Bring that one over here to me.'

As the constable goes to grab his arm, the prisoner barges him away and refusing to let them see that he is hurt walks upright towards the sergeant's desk. He walks with a very pronounced limp. The sergeant frowns.

'Show me his face!'

The constable pulls the man's hair back so that he now looks directly at the sergeant behind his raised desk.

'O'Rourke! After all this time! Thomas O'Rourke, we have you at last. Not the magistrate for you. You'll be going to the Old Bailey. Now let me see the others' faces. I don't know you two but if you are fighting on the side of O'Rourke then I bet my last shilling you'll be related in some way or another. Oh what a night! What a night! There are times when a man can truly take pride in his job. Well done, lads, well done! Now take this scum downstairs and lock them up and make sure they're not in the same cell and can't ever talk to one another. O'Rourke, every time you close your eyes I hope you feel the rope around your neck. The rope that is going to see you hang. As for you other two, we will sort you out in the morning. If you know what is good for you then you'll sing like a bird.'

'Go to hell, copper. We are family and we ain't ever going to tell you anything.'

'So, more O'Rourke scum to feel Her Majesty's justice. My night gets better and better.'

# Chapter 11

Judge Horace Taylor pulls Hamilton Reynolds to one side just as everyone is about to leave the Lodge meeting.

'Hamilton, I thought that you would like to know that the law is about to bring outstanding matters involving the O'Rourkes to a satisfactory conclusion.'

'The O'Rourkes, Horace? I thought I had heard the end of all of that. Why do you raise this after all this time?'

'Thomas O'Rourke has been found and is in gaol waiting for me to try him as an accessory to murder next week at the Old Bailey. He will hang of course, just like his father and his brother. Thomas O'Rourke got himself and two of his cousins into a fight in the street and it was fortunate that some rather tough and uncompromising constables were able to bring them to Holborn Police Station. It was there that the sergeant on duty that night was able to identify one of them as Thomas O'Rourke.

'I have never asked why, Hamilton, you have a personal interest in the affairs of the O'Rourkes and as your Lodge brother I do not need to know nor do I *want* to know. Now what shall we do about the two cousins? Much as I would like to, I do not have enough to send them to the gallows but it is clear to me that they are of the same type as Thomas O'Rourke and the two that I have already sent to the hangman.'

'Well, it would be reassuring to know that they are well out of the way and are unlikely to cause any mischief but I am not certain how to ensure that happens.'

'In my time as first a lawyer and then a judge I have seen some strange goings-on, Horace. Have you ever seen a trial at the Old Bailey?'

Reynolds shakes his head.

'Well, from time to time it has been known for witnesses to be bought. This is of course not quite proper but when a case involves prosecuting the worst of all possible types it could be said that the practice has its advantages. Some shall we say "astute" prosecutors have been known to find a man of straw to speak against a defendant. Such men of straw can be seen sometimes out in the street outside the court with a piece of straw sticking out from the front of their shoe or boot and for a little monetary consideration such men of straw will say whatever is asked of them. So, if, for example, the O'Rourke cousins were not just involved in a simple affray in the street but had been seen to set about persons unknown with a view to robbing them then the court would have to take a much more serious view of the matter.'

'Would they indeed, Horace? That is a very interesting tale. The intricacies of the law never cease to amaze me. Maybe it is time I saw justice in action.'

# Chapter 12

Someone once said to Freddy to expect things to happen or arrive in threes. On this one occasion, and perhaps for the only time in his life, that advice rings true. Just a few weeks after the birth of his daughter, and news of the death of Lizzie's father, Freddy receives another note from his twin brother, George. Thomas O'Rourke has been found and arrested, the note said. Having escaped, apparently to Ireland, after the arrest and before the trial of his father and brother, he had returned to London, though whether this was with the intention of seeking out Freddy and keeping his father's promise that the O'Rourkes would be avenged, or simply because he was running out of money, wasn't clear. George promised to send another note to Freddy as soon as the trial was over.

Some three weeks later the expected note from George arrives. Freddy learns, much to his relief, that Thomas O'Rourke has been sentenced to death by hanging and the two cousins are to be transported for life. It was Judge Taylor who had charge of the trial, the same judge as before.

Freddy remains restless living out in Uxbridge. The air is sweeter but Freddy is a town man. Here everyone seems to know everyone and he is sick and tired of the vicar pestering him and Lizzie to attend church. He is now a printer. There is plenty of work for printers back in London and now with Lizzie's father dead and gone they can go back to London and get married, and Freddy can safely visit his family again now that the O'Rourkes are no longer a threat.

Lizzie knows that Freddy is unsettled and is content to agree with their removal. After all, being Mr and Mrs Clowes is what she wants the most. Unlike when they had to leave London for Uxbridge in such a rush and leave some of their meagre possessions behind, this time they can take everything with them back to London. Freddy has been to the clerk's office down on the canal and has booked room for himself and the family and all their possessions to be taken by barge to London. This isn't the normal business of the bargemen but since the coming of the railways they take whatever business they can find. Freddy still has to pay for a cart to take them down to the barge but it's still cheaper to travel by barge than by train. Brother George has been able to find them somewhere to live back in Holborn.

Just two days after they arrive back in London the sad news is announced that Prince Albert the Prince Consort has died of typhoid fever at the age of forty-two. Freddy feels the same sadness at this news as do many poor people but it was not something to dwell upon. The struggle of everyday life ensures that there are far more pressing matters for the ordinary man and woman to concern themselves with.

# Chapter 13

Freddy finds it fairly easy to get a job as a printer in London and the job is better paid than some and certainly better paid when compared with what he used to bring home as a bookbinder.

Life, though, does become increasingly hard as the family rapidly increases in size. First there are the twins Emily and Albert, although poor little Emily succumbs to the cough at the age of just five years old. Lizzie starts to lose her looks and takes less care of her appearance and eventually there are twelve children in all, not counting the little girl that was stillborn when she arrived early. All this before Lizzie reaches her fortieth birthday. By the time Ben arrives, Freddy Junior and Elizabeth are already out to work bringing home what earnings they can. Young Freddy starts as an errand boy/messenger at the same place where his father works and young Elizabeth becomes a feather curler at a nearby milliner's. As things are to turn out first Albert (Bert), Walter (Wally) and then Arthur start work as errand boy/ messenger before becoming compositor or printer apprentices. A dynasty of printers has been started.

Lizzie is becoming increasingly tired and finds it more difficult to get going in the mornings. Beatrice is a great help with preparing breakfasts in the morning before she goes to work and Harriet who is now twelve does most of the work around the house. Freddy just thinks Lizzie is tired and that all she needs is rest and then she will be right as rain again. If he has noticed a change and a deterioration in her state of health, then he is either keeping things to himself or he is in denial.

It is that time of the year for colds and sniffles and the Clowes household is no different from others. First it is some of the children who fall ill – hardly surprising given that the youngest boys are head-to-toe and four in a bed and the three girls also share the same bed. Lizzie also catches a cold and whereas the children start to improve and recover after several days Lizzie does not. She develops first a hacking cough and then loses her appetite almost completely. Lizzie takes to her bed and only gets up when she needs to visit the lavy. After nearly three weeks of this Freddy asks the doctor to call. This is going to cost money – money that Freddy can ill afford.

'Well, Doctor? Why can she not get better? It just started as a cold like what the kids have had.'

'First things first. Have you the three shillings before I look at her?'

Freddy counts each shilling out slowly and purposefully, as he places them in the palm of the doctor's outstretched hand.

'She is worn out. You must keep her warm and in bed and try to get her to at least take broth as often as you can to keep her strength up. I will give you some powders for her to take once in the morning and then once in the evening.'

After handing Freddy a flask containing some white powder the doctor dons his hat and leaves without another word.

'Bloody old quack! He has told me nothing I hadn't already worked out for myself. Three bob for these powders! They had better work.'

None of the children say anything. They are too worried about their mother to think of anything to say. The powders have no effect whatsoever and Lizzie continues to suffer from her hacking cough and can barely take a spoonful of broth.

Her whole chest and sides and stomach are aching from her coughing so much and her skin has taken on a sallow look and her eyes seem to have shrunken back into their sockets. Lizzie is now too weak to make even the short trip to the lavy. The one saving grace is that she is now sleeping for longer and longer periods.

'Pa, should we not ask for the doctor to call again?' asks young Elizabeth.

'And what good will that do? Just more money for some useless powders? No, all that we can do is hope that somehow she will pull round and start to get better.'

Deep down Freddy knows that that is not going to happen. It is not long after that Lizzie leaves this world.

# Chapter 14

Soon after the loss of Lizzie Freddy starts to frequent the alehouses to the extent that sometimes the children go to bed with less than a full stomach as there is not enough money to buy all the food needed. This is something that he would not have dreamt of doing when he and Lizzie first got together. Now things were different. There is no Lizzie and the beer does sometimes dull that empty aching feeling he feels at the loss of his wife.

Things, though, do improve slightly as more and more of the boys go out to work, but Freddy continues to stop off at the alehouse on his way home from work – almost every day. He prides himself that he is still able to hold down his job. As the sons and then Elizabeth make their own way in life and settle down and marry, Freddy's life undergoes a further change. He finds it more and more difficult to find enough money to satisfy his desire for beer. His habits and his behaviours put increasing strains on his relationship with his children and it is Beatrice that finds things most difficult of all.

Beatrice has done well at school and has shown a remarkable aptitude for music. Her teachers, and Miss Watts in particular, recognise in Beatrice an incredible musical talent. Freddy sees no point in encouraging the girl to take up music. She is just an ordinary girl from an ordinary working family background and should not be wasting her time and filling her head with such things as music. That's not what schools are about, Freddy convinces himself. Why are they spoiling the child? With Lizzie gone, Freddy considers that Beatrice's place and her duty is to look after her widowed father and the house.

The matronly and plump Miss Watts has taken a shine to Beatrice. Miss Watts has now made it her vocation to encourage the most musical child she has ever met. Miss Watts is a spinster and is fortunate in that her recently deceased father was able to leave her with some degree of security and a roof over her head that she could now call her own. Nevertheless, Miss Watts lives on her own and she finds her life rather empty. Beatrice can change all this. She determines to bring Beatrice and music closer and closer together and at the same time Beatrice can provide the companionship that Miss Watts so much needs. This all starts with Miss Watts inviting Beatrice to her house so that she can take up violin lessons and Miss Watts lets Beatrice use her late father's violin.

Miss Watt's late father had been a concert violinist and had toured the country and sometimes overseas. Miss Watts had lost her mother when she was only nine years old and thereafter travelled wherever her father went – she was bought up with music and loved it passionately. However, she has some time ago accepted that she does not have the talent and flair to emulate her father. She would never be more than competent and besides as a young woman it was so much more difficult to make your mark than it was for a man. When her father's professional career was drawing to a close Miss Watts applied for her current teaching position. By then she was well into her forties and she had for many years been resigned to spinsterhood. With her plump figure and moon-round face, sober dress with a high neckline and her hair done up in a bun at the back, Miss Watts appears to be a very respectable but very plain lady. Her job as a teacher is to equip her charges with a basic understanding of reading, writing and arithmetic. The head teacher and the school board, aware of Miss Watts' background and musical inclinations, take a relatively liberal approach to Miss Watts' attempts to encourage her pupils' musicality, provided that this does not disrupt the running of the school or the girls' more basic education.

At first, whilst not entirely happy or understanding why Beatrice should take an interest in music, Freddy went along with the arrangements Beatrice had with Miss Watts to advance her musical talents outside of school hours. Now, however, things are changing. Freddy can no longer carry on working as his eyesight has begun to deteriorate and his hands have started to play him up. Beatrice would now have to go out and find work and bring some money into the household.

'I'm telling you now, Bea girl, you have to find work as well as spend time looking after me and the house and the rest of the boys whilst they are still with us. This music business of yours is going to have to stop.'

'But, Pa, music is the only thing I really care about and I love learning to play with Miss Watts so very much. Miss Watts says that I have an exceptional talent. Please don't make me stop, Pa. Please!'

'My mind is made up. Your place is here looking after me and that means finding a job. Now that's the end of it. I will hear no more of it. I am taking you out of school as soon as I can find you a job. Think yourself lucky that I have allowed you to stay in school for so long. Most girls start work when they are eleven or twelve and I have allowed you to stay on some three months now after your twelfth birthday. Now off to bed with you.'

Bea cries herself to sleep and it takes her a long time before she does fall asleep. There is no way out of her predicament. Tomorrow or the next day could be the last time she would be able to hold a violin, let alone play one. It is a red-eyed and tired Beatrice who goes in search of Miss Watts the following morning before the rest of the class turn up for their lesson.

'Why, Beatrice child, you have been crying! Now what is it?'

Bea blurts it all out, her sorry tale interspersed with bouts of sobbing. Bea cannot see through her own blurred vision, and she is looking more at the floor than anywhere else. She does not see the look of great disappointment that comes over Miss Watts' face. Miss Watts even allows herself to place a comforting hand on Bea's shoulder but as much for herself as for the child's sake.

'The class will be here any minute. Now try and pull yourself together. Now will you do that? And stop wiping yourself on your dress. Here, borrow my handkerchief and go and tidy yourself up before I start the lesson. I need a little time to think things through so perhaps after school tomorrow you can come back to my house and we can talk about things.'

There is precious little time for Miss Watts to marshal her thoughts during the day but she knows that she must find a solution to the problem if she is to find a way for Bea to keep her company and to provide her with an objective in life. That objective being to turn Bea into the type of musician that she was unable to become. It is only when Miss Watts comes back to her own quiet and empty house that she is able to fully concentrate on the problem. As the evening wears on, Miss Watts starts to form a plan and what she hopes will be a strategy for handling Bea's father. More and more it occurs to Miss Watts just how attached she has become to Bea. She decides that she must move quickly and decisively and the sooner she goes to see Mr Clowes the better. In fact, having slept on the matter Miss Watts decides she must call on Mr Clowes that very evening. She now has a proposal to make to Mr Clowes. She just hopes that Bea will accept what she has in mind.

'Bea, how would you like to come and live with me? What you can do is help keep the house for me. I have Mrs Perkins who comes in every other day and cleans and washes up and does the laundry for me but she does not live in. I do not entertain and I usually provide for myself in the evenings so there is just me in the house in the evenings and during the night. Now if you like you can come and stay with me and perhaps I can convince your father that this could work out well if I was to pay you for being both my help around the house and company for me in the evenings. That way you can continue with your music lessons and maybe for two days a week you can then go back to your father and help him in whatever way he thinks he needs. There now. What do you think of that?'

'Oh Miss, Miss! You would do that for me?'

Miss Watts pulls herself up straight and assumes a tone that she hopes hides any sign of emotion.

'Well, I hate to see all my time and effort wasted in teaching you music and the violin. What time does your father arrive home in the evenings? Perhaps I can call on him tonight?'

'Tonight, Miss? Well, I don't know. We sometimes do not know when he will arrive home.'

Then after a brief pause for thought, 'Sunday morning, Miss! Could you perhaps make it this coming Sunday morning? Why it is Friday today already and I can give you the address if you like or I can come and fetch you. It will be no trouble.'

Bea is wearing the broadest of grins and it is the first time she has not been sad in days. Miss Watts decides that the matter in hand is that important that she will forgo her own attendance at Sunday morning service. She and Bea agree that Miss Watts will make her own way but that Bea will wait for her at the corner of the street.

Bea does not mention any of this to her brothers and her baby sister as she knows that it would suit them better if she were to remain at home running the house. Bea thinks that is maybe why her older sister Harriet agreed to getting married before she was nineteen years old. It was her own escape from becoming an unpaid family servant. She thinks sadly of her younger sister, Jane.

It is only at the very last minute when her father is having a rather late breakfast that Bea tells him that someone is coming to call and would like to speak to him.

'And who wants to speak to me on a Sunday morning, Bea? I have barely finished my breakfast.'

'Sorry, Pa, I must go as I am meeting her at the corner. Back in a few minutes.'

Bea is out of the door and gone in a flash before her father can respond. Cursing and muttering under his breath, Freddy looks for his collar studs and a clean collar so he at least looks a little more presentable to receive this unwelcome and unwanted caller.

'Pa, this is Miss Watts. She is my teacher at school. She would like to speak to you if that is possible, please'

Not forgetting his manners, Freddy rises from the chair at the table where not so long ago he had been taking his breakfast. He extends a hand.

'Miss Watts, good day to you. I was not expecting your visit but please will you be seated and then perhaps you would like to tell me why you are here?'

Miss Watts takes one of the wooden chairs around the table as pointed out by Freddy.

'Would you like some tea, Miss Watts?'

'No thank you, Beatrice. I do not want to impose upon your father and his time any longer than is necessary as I am sure he is a busy man and has important things to do.' Miss Watts cleared her throat.

'Mr Clowes, if I may be so bold and come straight to the point as to why I am here. Perhaps you will allow me to offer a proposal that may suit the pair of us when it comes to young Beatrice?'

Freddy nods.

'Well, Mr Clowes, since the passing away of my dear father some years back I have been living on my own and although I have a daily help she does not live in. Beatrice has told me that it is now your desire that she finish with school and start to make a living and that she continue to help with the running of your household.

'I do not know how much Beatrice has told you of her musical abilities, Mr Clowes, but please allow me to say this. Beatrice is a most exceptional young talent and I truly believe that she has the capacity to play the violin to a very high level. My dear late father was a concert violinist and it is in fact on his violin that Beatrice has been learning to play. Mr Clowes, I see in Beatrice a bright future if it were possible for her to continue with her tuition and practice. I wish that I had had her talent when I was her age. Oh I can play, Mr Clowes, and I credit myself in being a fine teacher of the violin but I lack that special talent and spark that marks out someone who is a merely a competent player from someone who can perform at the highest levels.'

'Where is all this leading, Miss Watts?'

'Mr Clowes, just one more minute of your time, please. As I have said, I spend much time in my own company but I also need someone to help me run the house and to be there in the evenings especially. Now how can I best put things? For any possible inconvenience it may cause you, Mr Clowes, I would be happy and willing to provide Beatrice with food and accommodation and a small amount of money for those things that a young girl and a young woman may need but also to offer you some form of compensation for taking Beatrice away from you. If you so desire, perhaps Beatrice could come and visit you, say, twice a week, to keep you company and perhaps to help with anything that needed doing here? Then, if you have no objection, Mr Clowes, I could in the evenings continue with Beatrice's music and other tuition. I am sure that I can make of her a daughter that you could be even more proud of than I am sure you already are.'

Freddy is silent for a good few minutes. His forehead is furrowed and it is clear that he is in deep thought.

'Bea, leave us and close the door behind you. Miss Watts and myself have some personal matters to speak on.'

A few moments later he continued:

'I recall you mentioned a matter of some compensation, Miss Watts? Perhaps you would care to elaborate on what you have in mind.'

# Chapter 15

The arrangement between Beatrice and Miss Watts works out extremely well and suits them both. Miss Watts enjoys seeing Beatrice grow from a young girl into a young woman and developing into such a great talent with the violin. When she plays she uses the same violin that once belonged to Miss Watts' father. At such times she exudes self-confidence.

Where Beatrice – for that is what she is always called now, never ever the more familiar, shorter version of her name – is less confident is moving in social circles and in conversation with others than Miss Watts. This is particularly so with those young men whom she is either introduced to or comes into contact with through her musical engagements. Beatrice admits to herself that she is rather plain-looking and does not have that type of figure that men seem to admire, it being rather too narrow and lacking in shape.

Thanks largely to the efforts of Miss Watts and her contacts and introductions, one day Beatrice is offered the opportunity to audition for a role in an orchestra. Beatrice passes both the audition and the subsequent interview with the director and the conductor. This is the pivotal point in Beatrice's career and the turning point in her life as everything thereafter springs from this moment. Her orchestra plays in London and also tours the country and when she can Miss Watts accompanies her. Then one day, during rehearsals in Birmingham, the director makes an announcement of a forthcoming tour to the United States of America. A young woman of her age, Beatrice is going to America. Miss Watts is so proud of her and this is something that she decides that they both will not miss for all the world. Her prodigy and her sweet young companion has repaid all her faith in her.

On 18 April 1903 Beatrice, the orchestra and Miss Watts sail with the other passengers and crew from Southampton bound for New York on the SS *Philadelphia*. The orchestra's subsequent tour is a success and in many instances the concerts are sold out. The amount of travelling though becomes increasingly tiring and the now somewhat elderly Miss Watts obviously is the most travel-weary and tired of them all.

Towards the end of the orchestra's tour Miss Watts falls ill in Houston. At first it is thought that it is merely a matter of exhaustion and that a degree of rest will put things right. Beatrice insists on quitting the tour and looking after her 'dear Miss Watts'. Never, after all these years, has Beatrice called her mentor anything other than 'Miss Watts'. It was and always will be Miss Watts. As close as they have come, and they had become the very best of friends, their differing backgrounds and class origins and difference in age make it inappropriate for Beatrice to use Miss Watts' Christian name.

As the days pass, it becomes more evident that it is more than a matter of exhaustion that has led to Miss Watts' condition. The days then turn into weeks with no sign of Miss Watts' improving. It is during this time that Beatrice becomes acquainted with a young American doctor who attends Miss Watts more and more frequently until he visits almost on a daily basis as her condition starts to deteriorate further.

At first the conversations between the doctor and Beatrice are very formal and are concerned solely with the issue of Miss Watts' health. As time goes by the nature of their conversations begin to develop and become less formal and more prolonged.

He is clearly a man who looks beyond Beatrice's perceived plain looks and her somewhat reserved and socially clumsy air. He is interested in making more than just the expected polite conversation during his calls upon Miss Watts. He sees the real woman hidden away inside. The woman that Beatrice herself begins to discover for the very first time as she becomes more and more comfortable in the doctor's company and then begins to look forward to his calls. Doctor Watkins has a nature completely the opposite to Beatrice's. He is confident and easy-going and has the ability to put Beatrice at her ease. No other man has ever had such an effect upon her. After some attempts at self-denial Beatrice starts to find that she is very much attracted to this tall, slim and relaxed young doctor. Why hasn't he found someone before? Beatrice asks herself. He is tall and he is handsome and he is intelligent and kind and he is a doctor as well as all that. Why has he not settled for anyone else? He can't surely be interested in plain old me.

After a relatively long illness, during which Miss Watts is largely confined to her bed, Miss Watts slips away but in her final days she is happy because she can see a growing bond between her Beatrice and Chad Watkins. Towards the end, on one evening when Beatrice is reading to her, Miss Watts raises a hand for Beatrice to stop.

'Beatrice my dear, I think that young doctor of yours is quite taken with you.'

'*My* young doctor? What nonsense! He is not *my* young man at all. I'm sure that he has plenty of admirers.'

Miss Watts smiles.

'I have seen the way that he looks at you and the way that his eyes follow you across the room. Do not end up as an old spinster like me, my dear. Don't push him away, just open yourself up for once. You are fond of him, are you not?'

'Yes, I think I like him very much.'

'Good, then that is settled. Now I think I will go to sleep; I am feeling rather tired.'

Unknown to Beatrice, Miss Watts also gives Doctor Watkins words of encouragement when he attends her the following day.

'Doctor Watkins, I can feel my life energy slipping away and I welcome the opportunity to go soon to my creator as I am so terribly tired.'

She waves away Doctor Watkins' attempt to contradict her.

'Now, Doctor, I need to talk to you most earnestly. I need to talk to you about Beatrice.'

'About Beatrice, Miss Watts?'

'Yes, Doctor, about Beatrice. I have seen how you have become attracted to her. I have seen the way that you look at her and how you follow her with your eyes when you think she is not looking. I may be an old spinster but I can still see when two people are attracted to each other and you two are attracted to each other, I know it. Now, Doctor, when I am gone I shall be leaving a small sum to Beatrice. Not a great deal but enough for her to be secure for the time being. There is nothing for her back in England, Doctor, and I am sure that if you were to put the question to her she would be more than happy to settle here with you. I have known Beatrice now for some fifteen years. I have seen her grow from being a child from very ordinary circumstances into the good, the gifted and, now I believe, the loving young woman she is now. Oh she may try not to show her feelings or to admit that there has been a change about her of late but there has, Doctor, and it is all down to you. Now you do have feelings for Beatrice, do you not?'

'My, Miss Watts, you are full of surprises,' he laughs. 'I do not deny it.'

'Then go to her, Doctor. Go to her before you leave this house. Make an old woman happy. I have grown to love that girl as I am sure you will if you do not know it already yourself.'

Doctor Watkins does not have to seek Beatrice out. She is seated, as she always is these days after he comes down from Miss Watts' bedroom, on the couch in the saloon to the right of the staircase. They talk for more than an hour, thereby making the doctor seriously late for his next appointment. He looks at his watch once more.

'Miss Clowes, Beatrice, I must go now to call upon another patient. Beatrice, I have so much enjoyed this past hour. The time has passed far too quickly for my liking. May I call back this evening, say around seven o'clock? I feel that I still have so much to say to you.'

'You wish to call upon me this evening, Doctor? Is it Miss Watts that you need to see again? You have not made evening calls upon her before. Should I be concerned?'

'No, I don't need to see Miss Watts again today but I will call upon her tomorrow morning as usual. It is *you* I wish to see, Beatrice, and it is Chad not Doctor, if you please. I think there are other personal issues that we need to explore. So this evening it is then – I look forward to our meeting very much.'

Beatrice, still showing the shy aspect of her nature, just looks at the floor as Chad Watkins rises to go and lets himself out. Beatrice is confused but elated both at the same time. All through the day she continues to ask herself the same questions: 'Can he possibly be interested in me?' 'I don't think I could bear it if he didn't but does he have feelings for me?'

Beatrice is never to leave America's shores. That very evening, perhaps because he knows that Miss Watts is going to die soon, Chad Watkins proposes marriage. Beatrice can only give one possible response. Miss Watts goes to her creator knowing that Chad Watkins and Beatrice have become betrothed and they do so with her blessing. Beatrice continues with her music career, mainly as a teacher, for a short time but then she puts this all to one side for her new life as a wife and then a mother.

Once or twice a month Beatrice goes to the cemetery and lays flowers on the grave of Miss Watts. At first she does this on her own and later with her daughter, Dorothy Beatrice, and her son, Thomas Chadwick Dickens. Chad being such a great admirer of the books of Charles Dickens suggests naming their son after his favourite author. As for their children, they are to be told of Beatrice's incredible journey from being the daughter of a printer back in London to being a doctor's wife in Texas. In America class background is not a thing to be ashamed of. Nevertheless, Chad is a doctor and in a highly regarded profession and he attends people from important families. America does have its own society of the nouveaux riches. Different, of course, from the old class distinctions back in England but in some respects there are similarities.

Beatrice teaches her own children to play the violin. Whether they take this up for just their own pleasure or take music more seriously, that will be down to them to decide.

They may decide to become doctors or do something else and that is possible in America. It will be up to them to decide, although the very young Dorothy is already being described as a delightfully pretty child and by one person as being what they call a 'picture painting'. If she grows up to be as bright as she is obviously going to be pretty, Dorothy is bound to marry into one of the important and rich American families. That is for the future. In the meantime the house is and will be full of music.

# Chapter 16

From the time that the young Bea leaves home to take up with Miss Watts Freddy leads an increasingly intemperate life. Almost every penny he can get his hands on goes on beer. Freddy becomes increasingly bad-tempered and it is the last of the children still at home that experience and feel the worst effects of their father's deterioration in character and then in health.

Arthur is unhappy at home. Arthur is unhappy with his lot as first an errand boy and then as a compositor's apprentice. Better off than most, so his father tells him, and that may be the case and it might suit his brother Wally but this is not the life for Arthur. He wants adventure and he knows where to find it. He will join the British Army and fight for Queen and Country against the Boers. Now that will be an adventure and there is nothing that his father or anyone else can do about it. He is old enough to enlist and then he will tell the family afterwards.

The British Army – the greatest army the world has ever known, or so Arthur thinks and few disagree with him – has been defeated three times within a week at some places called Ladysmith and Kimberly. Arthur has read all about this in the newspaper printed where he works. Britain is now to take out reinforcements to the Cape Colony and to put things right. Arthur is going with them wearing that wonderful red tunic. He may be just a raw recruit and a private but the army and the Empire needs men like him, he thinks to himself. Arthur is going to do his duty and get away from the life he is dissatisfied with.

Arthur seeks leave of absence from his overseer and upon explaining that he needs the time to enlist to fight against the Boers the leave of absence is most willingly granted. The newspaper owner is a most patriotic man and his newspaper has been calling out for the need to correct the aberrations in history recently created by the Boers.

Arthur decides he will take a leaf out of his father's book and call in for a few beers until such time as he knows everyone will be at home and he can break the news to everyone at once. He does not go to the same place where his father normally drinks.

After several beers Arthur is filled with bravado and decides that he is going to make a grand entrance. He has a rough idea of when his father will have had his fill of beer, or more likely run out of money. He leaves it until a good half an hour after that.

The door sweeps open before him.

'I've joined the army and I'm off to fight the Boers!' he proclaims.

Ben, Wally and then Jane look at each other. Their father has started to eat and nothing now was going to interrupt him.

'Didn't you hear me?! I'm off to fight the bloody Boers and they are shipping me out to the Cape Colony in six days' time. I'm to go to work tomorrow morning and quit and ask for what money is owing to me and then I'm off to a transit camp near Southampton and then we sail out to the Cape after that. Now what do you have to say?'

'Not much that we can say is there, brother,' says Ben.

'You've enlisted and that's the end of it and you are leaving me and Wally and Jane to deal with things on our own.' Ben jerks a thumb in the direction of his father.

Arthur sets sail as scheduled just a few days later. Crossing the Bay of Biscay is the most unpleasant experience as the ship bucks up and down and from side to side and sometimes both at the same time. Arthur is amongst many others who succumb to seasickness. For days later after he has landed when he lies down to go to sleep he can still feel the motion of the boat as if he is still out there at sea.

There is a degree of urgency upon arrival of the fresh troops in the Cape Colonies. The priority is to relieve Mafeking – both for the sake of those trapped within the garrison and for public consumption back at home. Arthur is not to go with the forces under the command of Lord Roberts that eventually relieve the garrison. Neither is Arthur to see the action he desires in the taking of the Boer strongholds of Bloemfontein and Pretoria.

Arthur is not to know it but when the news reaches home about the relief of Mafeking there is much celebration in the streets and elsewhere. It is perhaps the one time that Freddy in his later years shows pride in one of his children. Almost everyone down at his local is told more than once that his son was out there doing his duty for the Queen Empress, for Britain and for the Empire and that no doubt his son Arthur was right in the thick of it all.

In the end it is that wonderful red tunic that is Arthur's undoing. After losing their major strongholds to the British the Boers revert to a form of guerrilla warfare. The Boers in their khaki clothing can so easily blend into the surrounding countryside whereas the British in their red tunics are easy targets for sniping Boer sharpshooters. It is such a Boer bullet that despatches Arthur and in all his relatively short time out there Arthur never sees a Boer at whom he could shoot in anger.

None of the people back home that throng into the streets to celebrate the end of the war just under two years after Arthur's death likely know or hear or care about the shame of the British concentration camps or about the British confiscation of food and property or about the scorched-earth tactics aimed at hitting the Boers the hardest. Perhaps like the Arthur despatched by a sniper's bullet people's romantic ideals about the Empire and the civilising influence of the British remain untarnished.

Arthur is just one amongst the 22,000 British troops to lose their lives during the three years of fighting between 1899 and 1902. In British eyes he and his fellow dead are to be honoured as heroes. As the public celebrate the end of the war, many waving the flags they have bought the year before to celebrate the coronation of King Edward VII, little or no thought or regard is given by any right-thinking British man to the 25,000, mainly civilian, Boers who have lost their lives in this the second of the Boer 'Freedom Wars' against the British Empire.

# Chapter 17

Freddy's time is coming to a close. Ben and Jane are the only ones now still at home with their father and this means that it is down to Jane to tend to Freddy and to be on the receiving end of Freddy's worsening nature when he can say the most horrid and hurtful things. Sometimes he even hits out with his hands.

Ben comes home from work promptly. He is very particular in his habits as he knows just how much a strain his sister is under.

'Ben, I just cannot cope any more and father's pain seems to be getting worse. I am sure he did not mean it but he

127

nearly broke my arm this morning and the things he was shouting! Some of the words I don't think I have ever heard before but they sounded vile.'

'There is only one place for him to go if he weren't here at home. You know that, don't you, Jane?'

'The workhouse! The workhouse hospital. Well, at least they can care for him better there because I don't think I can take any more. I have more than done my duty to him these past few years.'

'Then we agree, Jane? It's all right for the rest of the family – they have their own lives to lead and they are not here every day like you and me are, especially you, Jane. I shall start to make the arrangements tomorrow and hopefully there will be room for him in that hospital.'

So Freddy ends his days in the hospital down in Shoreditch belonging to the Holborn Union Workhouse and he succumbs at the grand old age of seventy-two.

'Jane! I have his death certificate here and it says that father died from gout. I have never heard of anyone dying from gout before. I've heard that drink can bring on the gout but it can't be as simple as that. They just couldn't be bothered to find out the real cause, that's for sure.'

# Part IV

# Certain Things We Just Do Not Talk About

# Chapter 1

While Freddy and Lizzie first went into hiding out at Uxbridge and later when they return to London and start to grow what will eventually be their big family, the twins George and Henry and Freddy's sister Letitia have been leading their own lives. Their mother Letty continues to enjoy the best of health yet even now, some ten years after he has gone, Letty still misses Will so very much. Not for her though the widow's weeds and she certainly has not become a recluse like Her Majesty The Queen has done for so many years.

Letty is determined that she must show that she is strong despite the feeling of a loss that she must bear in private. Letty has no intention of becoming morbid or depressed or dragging any of her children down with her. Will would not have wanted that. Not today especially for George is bringing round his young lady for tea for the very first time. Ann is her name, although evidently her proper name is Susannah Ann, and she is a book-folder – in other words she sizes and cuts the paper before folding it into signatures for others to work upon. She and George know each other from work. This makes Letty smile as she remembers those early days when she and Will had met and fell in love.

They are all there sitting around the table that is used for food preparation, for serving and eating food, or just for putting things for the time being. Letty, Henry and Letitia were waiting and all that is needed now to complete the company is George and his young lady. The best tablecloth has been brought out of its drawer. Letty and young Letitia have made sure that the main room is clean and neat and tidy. The curtain that separates the main room from the kitchen area had been washed the day before and is now drawn across. Letty is determined that, if George is to marry this girl, then she should be shown how a house should be kept tidy and clean no matter what one's circumstances.

George enters the room closely followed by Ann. Before George speaks, Letty takes in her appearance noting that she seems so young. Why, she couldn't be more than sixteen or seventeen! She is some two or three inches shorter than George, and he is far from being a tall man just someone of average height. Her light-brown hair is tied back. She is neither pretty nor plain and has a rather square jaw, but what catches Letty's attention the most is her eyes. Even from a few feet away her dark-brown eyes seem so large and her gaze is almost penetrating. She has a rather full bosom and Letty smiles inside herself: *Just like your father George, aren't you?* She further thinks: *I hope you haven't been messing about with her.*

'Mother, Henry, Letitia, this is Ann.'

'Ann, meet my family.'

'Hello.'

'Nice to meet you,' says Henry, rising to his feet and extending his hand but he then finds himself having to avert her gaze and then finds it equally difficult not to appear to be looking where he should not be looking.

'Come and sit by me,' says Letty. 'Letitia, would you get the tea on the go, please.'

Ann sits herself down while George appears to hover as if he is awkward in his own house before he finally pulls out the chair and sits himself down. Letty starts a conversation but finds that the conversation is rather one way with her asking questions and Ann answering but not expressing herself or giving much of an insight into her nature in return. Letty later puts this down to the fact that the girl is meeting what are after all strangers for the first time and that she is young and perhaps nervous.

What Letty does find out is that both Ann and her mother were born close by and that Ann's father Bill is a bookbinder who came to London from Portsea. As for the rest of her family, Ann at the age of seventeen is the eldest out of the four girls and older also than her surviving brother. That makes her between five and six years younger than George. Whereas Letty and her children are irregular church attenders, it seems that the Germains attend church only for family baptisms, weddings and funerals and there have not been many of those of late, only the baptism of younger sister Jane some two years ago. From what Letty can gather it seems that Ann's father some years ago turned against the church and religion for some reason and that is why the family just 'keep it to the basics', as Ann said. After this almost question-and-answer conversation it is George and then Henry that dominate the conversation with Ann contributing nothing other than acceptance or polite refusal when offered something from a plate or another cup of tea. *At least the girl has good manners*, Letty says to herself, but there is something about her that I just can't put my finger on.

# Chapter 2

Letty has been waiting for the opportunity to speak to George alone. With George and Henry working together and leaving and arriving back at home at the same time, there is little opportunity to have such a conversation without fear of interruption. Henry has, though, unusually gone out this Sunday afternoon on his own. Letty sends Letitia out on an errand. At last she and George are now on their own.

'Son, are you sure you want to marry this girl? She does seem rather young to me and she has this thing about her that I can't put my finger on. How is she with you?'

'She's fine, Ma. I liked her from the first I saw of her and things have just grown from there. I've met her family and they seem fine and her father is willing to consent to us getting married. I am old enough to marry in my own right, you know, and Henry has already agreed to be one of the witnesses. You're not going to be difficult about this, are you, Ma? How old were you when you and Dad got married?'

This is a question that Letty does not want to answer as none of the children are aware that their parents never married.

'No, son. I'm not going to be difficult, as you put it. I just want to make sure that you are sure that is all.'

There is the sound of footsteps outside the door and the handle turns and the door opens. It is Letitia returning from running her rather unnecessary errand.

# Chapter 3

It is just two weeks before they are due to get married and George and Ann have gone to look at the two rooms that George hopes to be able to rent. They will have to make a decision quickly as George has to put some money down if they are to secure this place as somewhere to live.

'You know, Ann, I hope that you are agreeable to us starting our married life here. The place has an interesting story to tell. Well, this street does anyway,' says George.

'Is this going to be another one of your long stories? You are always telling me about things you have picked up from books or what someone else has told you.'

George pretends not to have heard.

'You see The Old Red Lion over there,' he continues, pointing out of the window. 'Well, here is the story. I am going back almost exactly two hundred years ago, and to a time some eleven years after King Charles had had his head chopped off. The Red Lion had always been a boisterous and rough-and-tumble place so what I have to tell you, shall we say, just adds to its character.

'Well, The Red Lion was to be visited by Oliver Cromwell.

134

Well actually by his body. He had been in the ground for over three years and it was decided to dig him up along with his son-in-law – a man called John Ireton by the way – and another man called John Bradshaw who was the President of the Commission that had tried the King and ordered him to be done away with by public execution in Whitehall. Anyway, having dug the three of them up, it was decided to keep the bodies in The Red Lion overnight before taking them to Tyburn the following morning.'

'Why on earth would they take the remains to Tyburn? That's where they used to hang people,' says Ann.

'Exactly! That is what is so strange about the whole thing. You see the mood was that there must be a public hanging of those responsible for having the King executed and the only way they could do this was to dig their bodies up and then string them up at Tyburn for all to see. Then, after they were well and truly hung, they were cut down and had their heads chopped off. They then stuck the heads on stakes so that they could be displayed for all to see in front of Westminster Hall.'

'That's the most disgusting and revolting thing I have ever heard. Why did you want to tell me that, George?' complained Ann, pulling a face.

'But that's not all of it,' George smirked, determined to carry on.

'No more! I don't want to hear any more!'

'Well, Susannah Ann, they said that Bradshaw's body had not been properly embalmed and if they had left him hanging much longer his head would have fallen off and they would not have needed to take an axe to it.'

'You utter beast, George Clowes. I don't know what I see in you, let alone why I should still want to marry you! Your story is horrible and *you* are horrible and … and … you know how I hate that name Susannah!'

'Horrible, am I?'

George pulls Ann towards him and she feigns some

resistance but not for long though. Cold as it is and even with no furniture in the room the young couple cannot wait for each other any longer. It is the first time they have been alone and in private for more than just a few minutes. Then after a few minutes Ann pushes George away and says in a whisper,

'No George! Someone's watching us.'

George lifts himself up by his arms and quickly looks round the room that remains empty but for the two of them. The door remains firmly closed. The room is on the first floor so there is no chance of anyone spying on them through the window either.

'You silly goose! There is no one there.'

'There is, George, I know there is. I can feel it. Now get off me. You'll just have to wait until we are married.'

Somewhat perplexed and even more disappointed, George does as he is asked. In silence he extends a hand to Ann to help her to rise from the floor and she starts to do up the buttons at the top of her dress, that being as far as George has been able to get intimate with her.

George opens the door and they start to leave. Looking in both directions down the narrow hallway, first to the door at the end leading to another set of rooms and then the other way to the stairs leading up to the next floor and down to the street, there is no sign of anyone.

'I told you, Ann. There was no one here.'

'There was, George, and now I want to go home, please.'

George puts the experience down to Ann's nervousness and it being her first time – or would have been – but then it would have been George's first time as well.

'Shall we take the rooms then, and then I can go and get some furniture and a small stove?' George asks.

Ann merely nods and they continue the walk to Ann's lodgings in a rather uncomfortable silence.

Two weeks later and on a bitterly cold Christmas Day some

six months after Susannah Ann's eighteenth birthday they are married. It was a busy day both for the curate and for the vicar but agreement was reached for the curate to conduct the ceremony in between the services held on that holy day. This is one of those occasions when Ann's father is prepared to 'keep to the basics' and attend the church ceremony for the wedding of his daughter. Nevertheless, even though as the father of the bride he has a role to play in the short ceremony, he is in the main silent throughout including when prayers are said and he has insisted that no hymns are to be sung. With such a small wedding party the hymn singing would have been rather feeble and ragged anyway. 'Short enough' is all William Germain would say about the ceremony afterwards.

It being Christmas Day, they go from the church to the Clowes household that will from today no longer be George's home. The main room is crowded and there is little room for the younger brothers and sisters of Ann to amuse themselves indoors but at least it is warm. The cooking stove is too small to accommodate the cooking of a goose for this many people. Goose, apple sauce and mashed potato; that is what George has had on Christmas Day for the past few years. It's a treat that they always look forward to. On this occasion, though, they would all have to make do with rabbit stew warmed up again until it is nice and hot. Letitia is sent off to the baker's shop to collect the ordered Christmas pudding. Many families purchase cooked puddings from the baker on Christmas Day and some families with little or no cooking facilities take their entire diner to the baker to be cooked for them.

Letitia took a long time to re-join the party but then she has stopped along the way to light the fire she has previously laid in the grate so that her brother and his bride do not come home to a freezing-cold room.

For the men there are a few bottles of beer to be had and

William Germain starts to complain about how fussy and sentimental Christmas has become ever since Dickens wrote that book about Scrooge.

'I hope we get no carol singers calling here,' he says. 'There certainly is no joy this Christmas in the Royal Household following the death of Prince Albert, and in the United States of America brother countryman is fighting brother countryman.'

'Mr Germain – William – can we at least have some joy in this household today. It is Christmas Day as well as the wedding day of my son and your daughter after all. We should be grateful and thankful for what we have got.'

# Chapter 4

Life begins to settle down for George and Ann as they adapt to living together as husband and wife. There are times though when Ann seems unduly apprehensive and George will see her on occasions looking around the room. On other occasions when they are about to become intimate Ann pushes George away and says something like 'Did you hear that?' or 'I think someone is here.' George reassures her that everything is fine but by then the spontaneity and the magic of the moment has been destroyed and Ann assumes a more passive role, although that is not to say that this is always the case.

One night, when the two of them are finding it difficult to get to sleep as it is so warm and close in their rooms, they are lying on the bed in almost complete darkness. Neither of them has spoken for quite some time. Then Ann says something in almost a whisper.

'George, you do believe in the spirits and ghosts, don't you?'

'Oh for heaven's sake, Ann, it is hard enough to get to sleep without you asking me this sort of rubbish.'

'No I mean it, George. I think this place is haunted. Please, please, George can we not find somewhere else to live! I'll be much happier if we can. Do this for me, please, if you still love me.'

The following Sunday George goes to see his mother.

'Is Ann not with you?' Letty asks.

'No, Ma. She insists on staying behind to clean the rooms. Every day she cleans and sometimes she does it twice a day. I love a nice clean place but there is a limit.'

'Is everything all right between you two?'

'She wants to find somewhere else to live, Ma. She seems to think the place is haunted. She says if I love her then I'll do that for her.'

'Haunted? What rot! Sounds to me, as we used to say back home in Frimley, that's she's got bats in the belfry.'

'What's that mean then? I've never heard you use those words before.'

'It means, son, that I think she may be a bit funny in the head. The first time I set eyes on her I thought to myself, "What is it about you, girl?" but then I could not put my finger on it. Still you are married now and it is up to you to decide whether or not to find somewhere else to live and to see if that will please her and make her happier.'

George finally relents, not least as Ann insists on turning her back to him and going to sleep until her wishes are met. Some weeks after Ann's first plea for them to move, George secures rooms a few doors down and on the opposite side of the street.

After the move Ann appears to be more settled, yet at times her behaviour is erratic and beyond George's comprehension. She will call out and shout sometimes in her sleep but then have no recollection of having done so when George wakes her.

# Chapter 5

Two years into their marriage Ann gives birth to a baby boy. The child appears strong and healthy and yet shortly after baby Charles' first birthday he perishes. The doctor is called and confirms the death as having resulted from natural causes and declares that he unfortunately sees such things happen on far too many occasions.

George is struck with grief and a feeling of remorse as if he might be to blame for the loss of his first-born. George is also worried as to how this may affect Ann's state of mind. Yet to his great surprise Ann shows great resilience and seems to come through this difficult time better than he does.

The following year sees the birth of Arthur Frederick and the year after that of William Harry. Ann seems settled and motherhood seems to suit her. George puts out of his mind his concerns and worries about Ann's state of mind and her belief in spirits and in ghosts. He is happy that they are a family as he continues day after day to carry out his work as a bookbinder.

# Chapter 6

*Some years later…*

George is more than worried. He is deeply concerned. Of late Ann has been acting in a manner that is beyond his comprehension. He has tried to talk to his twin brother Henry but he is too wrapped up in his own affairs and his forthcoming marriage to Jane. He can't talk to anyone outside of the family as this is such a personal matter. He can only turn to his mother Letty. He does not want to burden her with his problems but he needs someone to confide in. During his regular Sunday afternoon visit he tells her that he

140

needs to talk to her and asks if they could do this away from the house to ensure that they will not be overheard or interrupted.

Letty's intuitive response is to nod and say, 'It's about Ann, is it, son? Well, why don't we go for a walk. I fancy a stroll down to Regent's Park anyway. Did I ever tell you about the time that your dear father bought me a bird in a cage?'

George pretends he has not heard this story a hundred times before – he knows that his mother still misses his dad so much. George's sister Letitia comes back in from the yard out the back and sees her mother putting on her bonnet.

'Where are you two going, Ma? Can I come along as well?'

'Not this time, pet. George and I have something to talk about.'

On their way to the park Letty recounts for the umpteenth time the story of the bird in a cage given to her by her 'husband', as she always describes their father to her children, and how she could not stand to see the creature kept in such a condition and how they let the thing fly free. The park remains enclosed, as it did all those years ago, and the public continue to have no access. Nevertheless for Letty even its margins are a pleasant place to have a stroll.

'Tell me all then, son.'

'She is acting so strange, Ma. It is almost frightening and Arthur in particular seems to be upset. Ann is sometimes talking to herself and sometimes it's as if she is having a conversation with another person there in the room. At times she is shouting as if she is having an argument and she can be so very angry. As I said, Arthur in particular is affected and I think that he is scared now of his own mother. Then there are other times when she is quiet and it is difficult to get a word out of her and she seems so low in spirit. I fear that she is losing her mind. I am at my wits' end, Ma, and I don't know what to do. The kids need their mother and I can't cope without her being there to keep house and to look after

141

the kids. I now question my own feelings for her but what can I do?'

Letty says nothing for a few moments.

'Arthur is very bright and, as you say, a sensitive lad. As long as she does no harm towards the children you will just have to make do. I think you will have to talk to Arthur. Tell him that his mother is not very well and that she needs the love and understanding of you all. Say to him that as the eldest child, and now that he is growing to be a young man ...'

George goes to interrupt but Letty holds up her hand.

'... Yes I know he has just turned eight. Say to him that you are looking to him as the next man in the house to be very grown up about this and to look out for his brother and sisters. That's all you can do for now, George. It will not be long before you will have to talk to young William in much the same manner. As for the girls, well they are so young, so we do not have to concern ourselves with that for the time being. Well, I hope so anyway.'

George decides to take his mother's advice. He is not going to get advice from any other quarter. Next week George will tell Arthur that it is time that they paid a visit to the bathhouse before he goes off to Sunday school. That will be the time to take him into his confidence. They may not be due a visit to the baths for a week or so yet but George will make up some excuse or story. Maybe he will say he's going to show him where he works and what he does as a bookbinder and he wants Arthur to make a good impression. After all, he is more than likely to follow in his father's and his grandfather's footsteps and to become a bookbinder, too. 'Yes, that's it. That's how I'll do it,' George decides after dwelling on the matter for a while.

So that is what happens. On the way back from the bathhouse they pick up William so that he can go to Sunday school with Arthur as is usual. For a lad of his age, Arthur is taking a great deal of interest in his religious instruction and what his teacher is telling him. George just hopes that Arthur, and William of course, are being told and taught the right things. George has heard that some of these what are now called 'Bible thumpers' are well capable of turning a person's head, particularly someone as sensitive and perhaps impressionable as Arthur.

Ann starts to be shunned by the neighbours and she has the reputation of being 'a madwoman'. There are few, if any, callers and even the family choose to keep away if they can. It tends to be George that goes to visit them, sometimes taking one of his sons or daughters with him but never with Ann. George does though sometimes get his wife out of the house on Sunday afternoons or late on a summer evening after he comes home from work and he is not too tired. Mainly this involves a walk up to Regent's Park or to Primrose Hill. Life is not easy for anyone in the Clowes household, least of all for Ann.

As for Arthur, he starts work with his father and begins to learn about how to become a bookbinder. Arthur is now taking religion even more seriously. He attends church up to three times a day on Sundays and sometimes in the evening after work – that is, if he is not attending Bible classes. Yet in spite of all of this Arthur is developing a friendship with Caroline who works with him at the bookbinder's.

# Chapter 7

Ann, for no apparent reason and without warning, takes a swing at George with a lump of wood when they are outside in the backyard one Sunday morning. George evades the swinging lump of wood but in doing so loses his balance and falls amongst a pile of broken wooden crates. The wood from these crates is intended to be used to get either the fire or the small stove going. George's trouser legs are torn on some nails.

'Hell's bells! exclaims George. 'What has got into you this time, you madwoman?'

'I'm not mad. I'm not mad. You don't know what it's like. They won't leave me alone.'

Ann then turns on her heels and goes back into the house and a few moments later George hears the sound of the front door leading into the street crashing shut.

George picks himself up and extricates himself from the wooden pile. He then inspects himself. Well the trousers can be repaired with a bit of darning when Ann is in a more reasonable frame of mind. George then rolls up the trouser legs and finds that he has some deep gashes and one or two scratches on both legs. Cursing away to himself, George starts to wash away the blood from his wounds using the rainwater in the pail kept by the staircase entrance to the yard. He does this several times and in between times uses the rags he has pulled out of his trouser pocket to try and stem the flow of blood.

It is starting to get dark and it has been several hours since the incident when Ann eventually returns home. On the surface at least she seems to have calmed down. William has attended church that morning and has stayed out for most of the day. The two girls have gone to see their Grandma Letty so the remainder of the family are unaware of that morning's event out in the backyard. When they come home and ask of the whereabouts of their mother George just explains that she has gone for one of her strolls.

As the days pass there is little sign of the wounds on George's legs beginning to heal. Indeed, to the contrary, the marks have become inflamed and very red. George has had to put bandages over the wounds to stop his trouser legs chafing the wounds. He awakes one morning feeling very groggy and nearly loses his balance as he goes to get out of bed.

'Oh Lord,' he whispers to himself as Ann lies there still asleep. 'Don't say I've come down with something on top of these bad legs.'

William is already up as it is his turn to relight the stove. The stove not only heats up the water in the kettle but it also takes some of the chill out of the air first thing in the morning. George gingerly makes his way over to the chair placed next to the stove.

'Make us a cuppa, Billy Boy, there's a good lad.'

A little while later the water is hot enough for the pot and everyone else has started to get up and get dressed for the day ahead. George grasps the mug with both hands and slowly drinks his morning cuppa. Some ten minutes later George turns his head and he can't stop himself bringing everything back up into the coal scuttle right next to his chair and the stove.

'William,' says Ann, 'give me a hand to get your father back into bed. He can't go to work like this. You'll just have to explain that he is sick at the moment.'

George spends the day in bed and later develops a fever. He is unable to keep any liquid down let alone take food. The following day Ann has the gumption to realise something is very amiss and that they will have to spend the money and call out a doctor. The doctor arrives the following evening by which time George has become delirious and slips in and out of consciousness. Listening to their father's delirium, the youngest of the girls starts to think that their dad is going all funny just like Ma.

'He has a fever,' says the doctor, a rather elderly man whose jacket and trousers have a shiny appearance.

'Well, even I can see that!' replies Ann.

'Don't sass me, woman! Now if you pay me my three shillings then I will examine him further.'

Ann slowly counts out two shillings and then two tanners into the doctor's open hand.

'That's better. Now how long has he been like this?'

'He has had the fever for these past two or three days and he can take nothing to drink or to eat. And then there are his legs that just won't get any better.'

'His legs, what about his legs?' as the doctor pulls back the counterpane and the blanket and sees the now badly discoloured bandages around the lower part of both of George's legs.

'When were these bandages last changed and what is there underneath?'

Ann does not respond and the doctor reaches into his bag and taking out a pair of scissors starts to cut away the bandages. The smell of the putrification is most unpleasant.

'Good heavens! When did these injuries come about? No matter, no matter. Let me clean this up first and so I can see what is going on.'

The doctor again reaches into his bag and pulls out a bottle filled with a clear liquid and 'Spirit' printed on the label. Taking a clean swab he starts to clear away the decaying tissue from the unhealed wounds.

'I have seen this type of thing before,' says the doctor. 'He needs to be in a hospital otherwise he'll be taken out of here in a box within days. He'll have to go now and we'll hope that the parish will pay for his costs. Is he, or rather I should say has he, been working?'

'Yes, Doctor,' replies William. 'My father has never been out of work and he, myself and my older married brother Arthur are all bookbinders. This family has never had to call upon the parish here or elsewhere for relief.'

'Well, that could make things easier. I will write you a note that you should take with you when you deliver your father to King's College Hospital.'

'How will we get him there?' asks Ann.

'Leave it to me, Ma. I'll get him there even if we have to borrow a cart to do so.'

Within the hour George is in hospital. Within the week he is dead – it is said from 'carbuncles'.

'What are these carbuncles?' asks Arthur on being handed the death certificate. 'I thought a carbuncle was some sort on stone as in jewellery.'

'I asked about what it meant,' said William. 'They told me that to medical people a carbuncle is how they describe an inflamed boil. I was then told that younger doctors now coming out of medical school call them ulcers for some reason.'

'Now that is a term I am acquainted with,' says Arthur.

The family rally round for the funeral, which takes place at a small chapel at the cemetery beyond the Finchley and Hendon railway station. Perversely, it is called St Pancras Cemetery but this is only because the local authority has purchased land there some years back to be used as a burial ground as the churchyards within the parish were full and there was no room for further burials. Despite the costs of the train tickets the entire family attends and even their recently widowed Uncle Freddy turns up. Ann sits through the day grim-faced, barely saying a word to anyone and often appearing to the guests and mourners that her mind is in another place.

There is so much space available that Arthur is able to arrange for the place where George is buried to be designated as a family plot, even though the grave is to be marked only with a wooden cross bearing the legend 'George Frederick Clowes, 1838–1888'.

# Chapter 8

Ann has moved in with her son William and her daughter-in-law Lucy in nearby Percy Street. William hopes that in moving to other rooms his mother may not feel there is a close association with his father or rather his father's ghost or spirit. That is something that he and his sisters would not be able to cope with – his mother believing she is in communion with their dead father.

Despite these good intentions, though, Ann's behaviour becomes more and more extreme. Having always held a belief in the existence of spirits and the spirit world, Ann has now convinced herself that she is a spiritualist and a medium and that she can communicate with the dead.

The family in the rooms next to theirs in Percy Street is of a different kind. The father, Mr Symes, is a clerk to a barrister who often prosecutes cases at the Old Bailey. He certainly looks the type and William believes that he has seen him on occasions when he has reason to pass by the Inns of Court. Mrs Symes stops William in the hallway one evening to proudly proclaim that they are to have electricity installed. William smiles and compliments Mrs Symes on being so modern. Little is William to know at the time what effect this innovation will have.

Some weeks later work to install the electrical wiring commences. This becomes the tipping-point for Ann. She now is convinced that she is receiving messages from the spirits through the wiring being installed next door.

'I can hear you,' she exclaims one night as she is about to prepare for bed. 'Yes, yes, I can hear you. You want me to do what?' Then a moment's pause. 'How do I do that?' 'Oh I see. Well, I won't! You hear me, I won't. I'm going to kill you instead. I'll rip your wires out.'

Upon which Ann grabs a knife from the table and heads for the door to the hallway. William and the girls and Arthur, who is just visiting, are stunned and unable to move at first. As Ann pulls open the door, she sees Mr Symes returning home late. He sees Ann brandishing the knife and, as she slashes out, the back of his hand is cut. By this time William has been stirred into action and is able to grab his mother around the top of her body at the same time pinning her arms to her side. Symes backs away and pulls a kerchief from his pocket and tries to use it as a bandage to stop his hand from bleeding.

Ann is screaming and making the most terrible noise as William wrestles her back inside, shaking her from side to side until the knife falls to the floor.

Symes has moved to the doorway clutching his wounded hand with the other, and then starts shouting.

'She is mad. She is mad. The woman is dangerous and should be locked away. You mark my words, I will have her locked away and they will throw away the key.'

During all this commotion Arthur remains transfixed. Ann has stopped her screaming and collapses to the floor in tears. Jane and Emma, who with Arthur are also visiting, do their best to comfort their mother but at the same time are frightened of her.

Hearing her husband's voice above all the other commotion brings Mrs Symes out into the hallway. The door is still open and William moves to close it but before doing so he says, 'Mr Symes, I am so terribly sorry.'

'The police should be called and she should be taken away.'

'Please, Mr Symes, let me deal with this. My mother needs to be in a place where she can be cared for and safe. Calling the police will not help matters. Please let me handle this.'

# Chapter 9

Things are now set in motion. The doctor has consulted the Medical Board and they in turn consult the administrators of the Colney Hatch Asylum out at Friern Barnet. The paperwork is completed and Susannah Ann Clowes is deemed to be a threat to the public and to herself and she is to be admitted without delay as a pauper lunatic. The doctor is generous in spirit and with his time. All the family are present at his room from which he practises. Doctor French attempts to describe the position and the condition of their mother.

'The mind is a strange thing. There is so much that we do not know about how the mind works. There have been some advances I think that have improved our understanding of why the mind can go wrong but there is still so much we do not know. In years to come I think and I hope that we in the medical profession will learn more and what we now call "psychiatry" – that being how we are beginning to refer to the treatment of disorders of the mind – will make advances.

'If it is any comfort to you, Colney Hatch is the most modern and the largest place of its kind in all of Europe. It is wonderfully designed and set in open countryside and it even has its own farm. Not so long ago we just used to lock people like your mother away, as we do with common criminals. I prefer to think of Colney Hatch more as a modern institution offering care and accommodation as well as protecting the public and society in general from those that are dangerous. You should take a ride on the train to see for yourself. It will impress you!

'Please be assured that there is no better place for your mother. You will be able to go there and see her if you wish, and if my medical colleagues deem it safe to do so. Now I really must be on my way; I have many things to attend to. This matter has taken up quite a bit of my time as it is.'

Arthur stands to leave, as do the others. As the head of the family he thinks it is down to him to say something.

'We shall pray for her and plead that the Almighty will remove this affliction from her and cast out her demons. It is the Devil that is at work here and it is the voices of demons that she converses with and that torment her so. No matter what her sins and that she continues to lock the Lord from her heart, we will pray for God's forgiveness and her salvation.'

There is silence for a moment and it is Jane that sees the need to intervene.

'Doctor French, you have been so kind and generous with your time, especially when our mother has been submitted as a pauper patient, or to use that most horrible phrase "a pauper lunatic". I thank you on behalf of all of us.'

Doctor French smiles and nods his head as they all depart. Once out on the street Jane turns to Arthur.

'Brother! I do wish sometimes you would keep your beliefs and thoughts to yourself.'

'And you, sister, would do well to pay more attention to Scripture and to believe that there is nothing that cannot be put right through having faith and trust in God.'

Arthur turns for home wearily. His wife, Caroline, has known for some time that his mother has problems but does not know the details as Arthur will not talk of such things. Of the most recent turn of events, moreover, she is wholly ignorant. Arthur finds that he now has to tell her everything from the beginning, not just about his mother and her problems but about something else that he should have discussed with her long before now. To prepare himself, Arthur goes to his church for quiet meditation and to give himself some time to think about what and how he should tell things to his wife. It would also be easier if the two boys were in bed when he gets home.

As Arthur hangs his outdoor coat on the hook on the door Caroline starts to question him.

'You said you wouldn't be late this evening, my dear. I expected you home some time ago. What happened?'

'Let me get my coat off and sit down first, my dear, if you don't mind,' he says rather more harshly than he intended.

'There is no need to snap at me, Arthur. I just asked a simple question, that is all.'

'Yes I know. I'm sorry. Look, I have not told you this before because I did not know quite how to tell you ...' And he told his wife the sorry tale of his mother's attack on the legal clerk and her confinement in an asylum.

'That's terrible, Arthur. Why didn't you tell me of this before? I am your wife you know.'

'I find the whole matter very difficult to talk about and I feel so ashamed.'

Caroline senses that she should say nothing for the moment and there follows a few minutes' silence as Arthur gathers himself before he speaks again.

'There is something else that I need to tell you about. Now may not be the best occasion given what I have just told you about mother but also because you are just a few weeks away from your time. However, having made one confession perhaps I should now make another.'

Arthur looks up and smiles at his own attempt at a joke.

'No please, Arthur, let it keep for now. I have enough to take in as it is and I am feeling very tired tonight. I only stayed up because I was worried about where you had got to. Tell me your little secret another time. Goodnight, dear.'

# Chapter 10

Ann has been an inmate at Colney Hatch for some two months before she receives an interview and assessment from one of the doctors. She is seated in the doctor's office and there is no other person present. Ann is in the normal day clothes that she would be wearing if she was back at home. It is felt that unless patients are incontinent then they should be allowed some degree of normality in this totally unnatural environment. The doctor is a middle-aged man in a three-piece tweed suit and is sitting on the other side of a large desk from Ann. He looks up from his paperwork and smiles.

'You are Mrs Susannah Ann Clowes?'

'Ann, not Susannah. I hate that name.'

'I see. Well, I am Doctor Farmer and I am going to be your doctor for as long as we are both here. I like to get to know my patients, if that is possible. I would like to call you Ann, if that is all right with you?'

Ann nods her head.

'Is there any particular reason why you do not like the name Susannah? Has anyone ever called you by that name? Did your parents call you Ann or Susannah?'

'No just Ann. It's always just been Ann.' Her voice is hesitating and nervous.

'Very good. That's answered one question. Now, Ann, do you remember or do you know why you are here?'

'It's because I'm a spiritualist and medium, that's why. Do you know that the police are spiritualists? That's why they are so clever you see because the spirits are helping them.'

'What makes you think you are a spiritualist and medium, Ann?'

'Because the spirits talk to me, that's why, and sometimes I can feel their presence.'

'I see. And how and when do these spirits talk to you? You say spirits – does that mean that there is more than one?'

'Oh yes there is more than one and that is why I am a medium.'

'And how do they talk to you, Ann? Can you talk to them as well?'

'I just hear them. Sometimes they are clear and sometimes they are not. Sometimes they just make noises in the room to let me know that they are still there. They like to use the electricity wires to talk to me. That's when I hear them best.'

'And you can talk to them as well?'

'Yes of course I can. I'm a medium so of course we can talk to each other.'

'Do you remember the night when you picked up a knife and cut your neighbour, Mr Symes?'

'Yes of course I do. I'm not an idiot you know!'

'No one is saying that you are, Ann. Now can you tell me why you picked up the knife and attacked Mr Symes?'

'He's having the electric put in. I needed to stop him as my spirits were telling me to do bad things.'

'And what sort of bad things was that, Ann?'

'They wanted me to harm my children.'

'In what way did these voices want you to harm your children, Ann?'

'In a bad way. They want me to eat my own children.'

'Have you ever hurt any of your children?'

'No, never.'

'You lost a child once, though, did you not?'

'Yes. Poor little thing. It was sad, you know, to lose a child.'

'And what of your late husband, Ann? Did you ever try to harm him?'

There is no response and Doctor Farmer decides to bring the interview to an end. Ann is becoming increasingly agitated and nervous and her voice has trailed off almost to a whisper.

'I think we will finish things there for now, Ann. Come, the nurse is waiting outside to show you back to the ward.'

Doctor Farmer returns to his desk and starts to write up his notes. She is clearly very disturbed and a danger to society. This is to be the first of many such assessments. In later interviews she tells Doctor Farmer in a long and rambling manner that there were some papers held at Somerset House

154

about her coming into money and her having a castle up in Yorkshire. It quickly becomes clear to Doctor Farmer and to the Medical Board that Ann will have to spend the rest of her days in the asylum.

# SACRAMENTS

# Part I
# Matters of Faith and Family

# Chapter 1

Upon reflection Arthur decides to keep his own peace and not to tell Caroline about the big decision he has taken until after the baby, their third, has been born and Caroline is up and about again.

It is late one Sunday evening and Arthur has not long returned from the evening Mass. They are seated at the table and grace has been said before they tuck in to their evening meal. As Caroline starts to take the plates to the small sink and bring back pudding Arthur places his hand on her wrist and invites her to remain seated.

'Caroline, there is something that I have been wanting to tell you for quite some time. In fact, I was going to tell you the night I had to tell you about Mother being sent to the asylum.'

'Oh yes, I remember now – you never did get round to telling me. What is it, Arthur?'

'Well, my church is set aside from the Anglican Church that we were both brought up with, and the rites and the traditions of my church are so much closer to the Roman Catholic Church. But then you see it is set aside from the Roman church as well. That is why we are called the Old Catholic Church.'

'That is about as clear as mud to me, Arthur.'

'Very well. The Old Catholic Church is something that has recently been formed; it started off in Europe, you see … No, no let me start at the beginning. You see as I grew up and the more I read and the more I learnt and the more I reflected upon things, I found that parts of the Anglican tradition do not hold all the rites and traditions that give me the comfort I am seeking whereas the Catholic Church has traditions and rites that *are* much closer to my ideals and faith. But that left me with a problem, as I can't forget all of my Anglican background and teachings and turn to Rome.'

'Arthur, you're still not making sense to me.'

'Then let me explain further. About twenty years ago the Vatican Council conferred upon Pope Pius the Ninth the status of papal infallibility. He was an old man who had once been a Jesuit. Now Jesuits in the Roman Catholic Church are very certain of themselves and the Jesuit Order sets itself above others and consider that they have a stronger notion of infallibility and what that means.

'This ageing Pope went on a pilgrimage to Lourdes and whilst there he has said to have conferred in some way with the Virgin Mary. He is said to have told her that she was immaculate and Mary in return told him that he was infallible.'

'Are we going to get to the point soon, Arthur? I still have not had my pudding and I would like to do so before it gets any colder,' said Caroline.

Arthur ignored this flippant remark and continued. 'It was on his return to Rome that the Pope convened the Vatican Council. Now the majority of bishops comprising the Vatican Council are Italian and they do the Pope's bidding without question because the Pope is bound to pay all their expenses no matter what. Some of these bishops do not even have a diocese to attend to and are totally in thrall to the Pope. Anyway, the issue to be put before the Council was the issue of the infallibility of the Pope and all future popes to come.

'The Council met and there was a vote and there was a clear division on the issue. There were some delegates from outside Italy who were against granting the Pope the status of infallibility. Then there was a number who abstained and then there was an even smaller number, mainly Italians, who agreed to what the Pope was asking but with some conditions attached. Put all these factors together and the Pope was unable to get his own way.

'So, having thought they had won the day, those Council members opposed to the Pope's new dogma left Rome for home. Then the Pope turned the screws by calling for a second Council vote knowing that many of those in his way had left. The Pope then got his most powerful followers to put pressure on the remaining Council members. Those that were left in the Council were told to either vote in favour of instituting the dogma of papal infallibility or risk offending the person of the Pope. Well, that was enough and the Pope won the day.'

'That's fascinating, my dear, but what has all that got to do with you?'

'Well, despite my attraction to the Catholic Church, this whole concept of papal infallibility is something I can never accept, so there is no question of me ever becoming a Roman. This is where the Old Catholic Church comes in. We don't accept the concept of papal infallibility and we're not in communion with the Holy See, though we are in communion with the Anglican Church, although we have our own Catholic ways and traditions. So you see, I'm not betraying my Anglican background and traditions.'

'As always, Arthur, when you start talking about such things I find it very difficult to understand you. So you are calling yourself a Catholic but you are not a Catholic because you are in disagreement with the Pope being infallible. Is that what you are trying to tell me?'

'Well, that's a rather simple way of putting it – things are a little more complicated than that.'

'I will stick with simple thank you very much, Arthur. So why are you telling me all this?'

'God has called upon me, Caroline. I know now that I have a calling.'

'Will you stop talking in riddles, Arthur. A calling? A calling to be what or do what?'

'Our church has a Benedictine Order. I think that it may be my calling to take holy orders and to do God's work.'

'A monk!' Caroline was aghast. 'You think you can become

a monk! What about me? What about the children and your desire to have a big family. You're a husband and a father and you will not abandon us, and besides I have never heard of married monks. You mock me, Arthur. You mock me, our marriage and your family!'

'I'm not mocking you, Caroline and I have no intention of abandoning you. I do not think that I have yet proved myself as being worthy of taking up God's calling. I need to prove myself. I need to work hard and study hard and He will then tell me when I am ready. Now you must not upset yourself. Within our Order there is room for what they call working brothers. Such brothers go about their ordinary work, as I will do as a bookbinder, but we are there to offer spiritual comfort and support both within the workplace and in the wider community.

'Now as for us and the family nothing need change there. As I am already married and we have a family I can be accepted as a brother under the rules of our Order and our church. Now there may be times when I have to go away into retreat at our monastery in Yorkshire as I train and prepare to be accepted as a brother, if indeed that is God's will. Otherwise, things will be much as they are now except I shall spend more times at my studies and doing things in the community. For the time being I am to remain part of the laity. As I have already said, I do not feel as though I am ready yet for the next step.'

'Arthur, we hardly see anything of you as it is. Your sons are usually in bed when you come home. Sundays you are hardly ever here as you are at your church services …'

'I have said my piece, Caroline. Let that be the end of the matter. Now I am behind on my reading so let me get on with this before I retire to bed. On another matter, Arthur is now old enough at five to begin receiving more formal religious instruction. I shall be taking him to Sunday school every week starting this coming Sunday and I ask you to have him ready.'

Caroline knew that there was nothing to be gained from trying to talk to Arthur further on this matter. He would just get more and more agitated. She certainly did not fear her husband and in his own peculiar way he was an affectionate and considerate husband, but when it came to matters concerning his faith and religion she knew that she just had to accept whatever her husband wanted or decided upon. Besides, she knew that he had other things on his mind concerning the on-going condition of his mother. So now was definitely not the time, if indeed there ever would be, for confrontation. Arthur always ends up getting his way anyway, just as he did when he got her to sign up to the Catholic League of the Cross temperance movement to vow that she would never touch alcohol. This did not worry her unduly as she had never tasted alcohol in her life anyway but she was beginning to resent almost every part of her life being controlled so much by her husband.

Forgetting her pudding, as she no longer felt hungry, Caroline turned to the sink with the plates on the pretext of having something to do. There was nothing for her to do but she did not want Arthur to see that there was a tear in the corner of her eye and she completely forgot about the pudding. She need not have bothered, though, as Arthur was already looking for his place in the Bible to start up his reading again.

# Chapter 2

Birthday celebrations are called for on the occasion of Letty's eightieth birthday. What a remarkable woman she is. She has survived her 'husband' by forty years and her twin sons, George and Henry, too. She is now not only a grandmother but a great-grandmother as well. What is more, she is still enjoying reasonable good health and is quite robust for her age.

What is to be done to mark her marvellous achievement? It is her namesake daughter, the now-widowed Letitia Ann Lainchbury, who takes charge in her quiet and unassuming manner. She and her mother have always been so very close, so the family are happy for Letitia to take the task on and Letitia is happy to be doing something for her mother. Everyone is content when Letitia suggests marking the occasion, on the previous Sunday just two days short of her actual birthday, with a picnic out on Hampstead Heath.

Letitia did ask her mother whether she would like to take a train journey to Frimley to see what the place is like after all these years.

'No, child, thank you,' she replied. 'I once told your dear father that my life is now here in London and that remains the case. This is where all of you are – my wonderful family! I just so wish that my twin boys were still here to share things with us.'

With that option out of the way, then Hampstead Heath was soon settled upon. For this very special occasion Letty and her daughter would by arrangement be picked up by a hansom cab for the journey to the Heath. With the aid of a small set of steps Letty was sure that she could manage to climb both in and out of the cab. She said she did not like the look of those four-wheel 'growler' cabs anyway and has a fancy to ride in a hansom. The others, some fifteen in all, carry the picnic and refreshments and a special folding chair for Letty's use and comfort. Why, there may even be a few bottles of beer for the men. Freddy, to no one's surprise, brings a few extra bottles of his own.

Letty beckons her granddaughter-in-law Caroline over to her during the course of the afternoon.

'Caroline, my dear. That husband of yours, "Serious Arthur" as I call him, he called on me this morning together

with Little Arthur and Christopher. They were evidently off
to church and Sunday school. Nice of Serious to have called
in on his grandmother and to bring my two great-
grandchildren but nicer still if he could have joined us here
on the Heath and let church go for part of one Sunday at
least. He could always have gone to church this evening if he
thinks his immortal soul is in danger otherwise.'

Caroline covers her mouth as she sniggers.

'How long have you been calling Arthur "Serious Arthur"?
I've never heard you calling him by that name before,
Grandmamma.'

'Ah haven't you now? Well, I don't see much of you these
days. Hardly surprising with that growing brood of yours. You
should learn to say "No!" to him, my girl. That's your
problem. You'll be worn out before your time at this rate.
And here you are with another on the way within the month,
I would say. Am I right? How many is that you have now? And
what's with all these ridiculous names I hear they have. Has
all that religion turned that husband of yours soft in the head
just like his mother?'

'Oh Grandmamma, Arthur is a good man, you know,
despite his peculiar ways and I do love him so much.'

'Now answer my questions, my girl. I am an old lady and we
are here to celebrate my birthday. So indulge me, if you
please.'

'Well, there is Little Arthur and then there is Christopher
of course and you saw them this morning. Then there is
Little Carrie over there playing with the boy whose name I
can't remember. She's named Caroline Mary after me, you
know. Well, Little Arthur took his father's name so it only
seemed right I should do the same for our first daughter.
Then over there you can see Hilda. She's only five but look
how she is attending to her baby brother Aidan. Then with
this one here' – Caroline puts her hand on her belly – 'that
will make it six. As for their unusual names, well, Hilda is

167

baptised Hilda Faith so there is nothing really unusual about that and I didn't mind when Arthur suggested those names. He said that Hilda was a king's daughter who decided to become a nun and then ran a monastery and was later declared a saint, and he likes Faith as a name as his faith is so important to him. I didn't mind at all.'

Letty nods. 'And Aidan, he's the one with all the funny names if I'm right.'

'They are all saints' names, Grandmamma, from so many years back when the church was still quite young.'

'Then tell me.'

'He is Aidan Finian Cuthbert Chad.'

'Hah! I'm right – all funny names and names that no one who is right in the head would burden their child with. And what about the one you are carrying? Has that mixed-up husband of yours decided on the names of the next child?'

'Well, if he has, Grandmamma, he hasn't told me yet. I expect to expect the unusual for I am sure that he sees this as a way of showing to his church how devout and learned in respect of religious tradition and beliefs he is.'

'Tosh! Perhaps I should change his name from Serious Arthur to Pompous Arthur or Ridiculous Arthur. Is he still talking about becoming a monk?'

'Yes, Grandmamma, when he thinks he is worthy enough.'

'Hah, then he'll be "Arthur the Mad Monk" and he can take his name from his mother.'

Letty gives a wry grin to Caroline so as to show that she is only having fun at Arthur's expense and means no harm.

'I do hope I am not around to see it. Him dressed up like a monk, I mean. The last thing I want is for that pompous fool to be muttering words over my box. On that point I am being serious. Serious about having no Serious.' Letty has a little chuckle.

The remainder of the family are out of earshot and do not know what the two of them have been talking about but everyone is so pleased and happy that Letty seems to be having a good day out.

Caroline places her hand on the back of Letty's folded hands.

'I don't know if Arthur will be dressed up like a monk all of the time but perhaps he will some of the time. He intends to be what they call a working monk. Now if you will excuse me, Grandmamma, baby Aidan seems to be in need of attention.'

'I do like the way that you are loyal to your husband, Caroline. He is lucky to have you.'

Some weeks later the word gets to Letty about the names picked for the sixth child. Letty is reported to have said something along the lines of 'May the Saints preserve us!' and she then broke into a cackle at her own joke.

For indeed the boy was to be given, as Letty calls them, funny names. The latest addition to the family is to be baptised Gregory Ambrose Alban Bede after three more saints as well as after the most brilliant and learned scholar and historian of his age.

Arthur explains to Caroline his choice of names. 'I want these names because St Gregory was once described by Pope Leo XII as the "Doctor of the Church", St Ambrose is another ecclesiastical giant and one of the "Four Doctors of the Church", St Alban is the first British martyr and the Venerable Bede is a monk whom I greatly admire and is said to have had the most extensive library in the England of his age.'

Had she still been alive, Letty would no doubt have been further perplexed as to what 'Serious' was trying to achieve, or whom he was trying to impress or fool, when the seventh addition to the family arrived two years later. That unfortunate boy is lumbered with the names of an obscure fourth-century missionary bishop, another obscure abbot and bishop that almost no one had heard of, and of a Latin-speaking philosopher and theologian (he at least better

169

known), all three having been canonised and made saints by the Roman Catholic Church. The unfortunate has to endure the names of Aetherius Virgilius Augustine.

# Chapter 3

Arthur and Jane are returning from Colney Hatch to the station for a train back into London.

'Arthur, I don't think we have ever seen our mother so bad as she is today. I don't think I can stand to see her like this again. She makes no sense and I don't think she really knows that we are there.'

'This has been an education for me, Jane. I had no idea that so many people can be insane in so many different ways. To see some of those poor wretches and the state they are in is beyond my comprehension.'

'Then you admit that prayer to cast out demons is not the answer?'

'We must never give up prayer and hope that the Lord will hear us and intervene to bring our mother back to us, but you are right to chide me, sister, for what I said all that time ago. Yet there will always be the battle between good and evil, and men and women can be turned to evil if they either lose their way or do not know God.'

'Oh, Arthur, please! Not another one of your attempts at a sermon. I am upset enough as it is after visiting mother without hearing you try to preach to me.'

'Open your eyes and look around you, Jane. It is as plain as the nose on your face. Man can be corrupted if he turns away from or shuns God. You only have to think of Jack the Ripper and those poor women he butchered. Fallen women as they were, and even if they did break one of His Commandments, they did not deserve to die in such a manner. What is it, six or seven years, since he last killed but not because they caught him, no. It is because he is being protected so he can escape man's justice. Come the Day of Judgement, though, he will be facing God's justice and he will be cast down for eternity.'

'Arthur. Stop it! I do not want to hear any more. You sound like a pompous fool. It wouldn't surprise me if the Ripper was an insane religious fanatic who thought he was doing God's work by killing prostitutes.'

'That is a most evil thing to say. To break any of the Ten Commandments is to go against the word of God.'

'Not near the top of the list of ten, though, that Commandment "Thou shall not kill", is it?! Now I am going ahead on my own. Today has been bad enough as it is and you are just making things worse. Lord knows how that wife of yours puts up with you. You can make me so angry that at times I do not know what I am saying.'

'Do not take the Lord's name in vain!'

'Arthur! Shut up!'

# Part II
# Entering into Holy Orders

# Chapter 1

If only he had the wherewithal and the opportunity to do so, Arthur would very much welcome the opportunity to go into retreat at the monastery in Yorkshire for a week at least. Here, away from the distractions of work, family life and everyday living, he could contemplate and pray and find the reassurance he is seeking that now is indeed the right time to request that he be considered for admission into holy orders. It is not to be. Even if he could get permission to leave work for a week, Arthur could not afford the loss of his wages. The rent still has to be paid and the family needs to be fed. This is no easy matter as things stand and Arthur has noticed that at times Caroline takes the simplest and smaller portion of what is on the table so that the children and Arthur have the best of what is available.

Then one morning, with spring on its way after a long wet and cold winter, Arthur awakes with a feeling of absolute certainty and resolution. He must seek out his mentor and spiritual guide, Brother Cedric. Now is the time. Now is the time and he at last feels worthy of being able to answer his calling to God and to seek entry into the Benedictine Order.

# Chapter 2

Brother Cedric is a sage and philosophical man. He has watched Arthur and has seen over the years how hard Arthur has strived in his studies. Brother Cedric has no doubt about the strength of Arthur's faith yet he can see for himself that Arthur continues to have self-doubts about his worthiness to enter into holy orders even as a working monk. Brother Cedric keeps his thoughts to himself but it occurs to him that Arthur's faith and his desire to show that he is so learned and knowledgeable about Scripture and the saints serve as his crutch. Take this crutch away from him and Arthur's world may fall about his ears.

Nevertheless, when Arthur seeks Brother Cedric out and talks about at last taking his vows, Brother Cedric is more than happy to confirm that he will make a positive recommendation that Arthur be accepted into the Benedictine Order as a brother monk. He tells Arthur that he will that very night write to both the Old Catholic bishop at the seminary in Haberdasher Street here in London and to the abbot and the head of the order up in the monastery in Yorkshire.

As for Caroline, she takes this development in her stride. It has after all been a long time coming and she knows that this is what her husband desires. What perhaps Caroline does not realise is the extent of her husband's forthcoming solemn vow to carry out good works and how this vow will impact upon her and the family.

Arthur needs to be away for at least four days as his entry into the Benedictine Order and the grant of his Letter of Confraternity can only be done at the Old Catholic Benedictine Monastery at Painsthorpe in the county of Yorkshire. By making one of his days of absence a Sunday Arthur will only lose two and a half days in wages. The Order will pay for his third-class rail journey to Yorkshire and his accommodation at the monastery is at no cost to Arthur. In any event, he is to spend Saturday night in vigil in the chapel, partaking of neither food nor drink, in preparation for the ceremony at eleven o'clock on the Sunday morning.

Having spent the entire Saturday night and the early hours of Sunday morning in contemplation and prayer, it is with great joy that Arthur sees the first rays of Sunday's sun penetrate the gloom of the chapel. In just a few hours he will become a monk in the Order of St Benedict. He is to be the only new brother accepted into the Order on this auspicious occasion.

Abbot Ælred is to conduct the proceedings. Abbot Ælred has taken his name in honour of St Ælred of Rievaulx in Yorkshire.

Pride being one of the seven deadly sins, Arthur struggles not to feel proud of himself now that he is away from the monastery and he is journeying back home knowing that his Letter of Confraternity is in the satchel resting on his lap. He is now at last Brother Arthur. The train's rhythmic motion causes Arthur's mind to wander: *Should I have my Letter of Confraternity framed and hung on the wall at home, or should I seek permission to do the same at my place of work? After all, I am working monk and then people may come to me for help or spiritual guidance.*

As previously arranged before leaving for Yorkshire, when Arthur's train arrives in London he calls upon Brother Cedric before returning to his home and family.

'Welcome, Brother Arthur. All went well I trust. Did you give my regards to Abbot Ælred?'

'Yes indeed, Brother Cedric, and the abbot sends you his blessings. I have never been so far from home or away for so long ever in my life.'

'Well, of course you have not, Brother. Yet you know as well as most the long journeys and sacrifices that were joyfully made by the saints and so many others carrying God's message into the world. I think compared with their works your little journey into Yorkshire hardly compares!' Brother Cedric says with a cheeky smile.

'Now, Brother,' Brother Cedric continues 'we must talk further but not today. You should return home to your family. Call on me next Thursday evening. You must set aside your books and your studies now that you have joined the Order so as to spend more time carrying out the good works that you have vowed to undertake. In the East End in particular there is so much work for you to do both in terms of the practical and material as well as the spiritual.'

177

'Yes, Brother. Then Thursday evening it is. Good day to you.'

'Good day to you, Brother, and may God be with you and with your family.'

Arthur walks to his home. He looks upon some of the destitute and poor souls that he passes by. He thinks to himself: *Here I am at last, a Brother of the Holy Order of Saint Benedict and by the grace of God a loyal member of Christ's Holy Catholic Church. Can I ever be more complete?*

# Chapter 3

Each Sunday Arthur ensures that his sons and daughters – Arthur, Christopher, Aiden, Carrie, Aetherius (now known as Phil), Hilda and young Gregory – go with him to church in the morning. Carrie, Hilda and Gregory are then excused further church attendance but in the afternoon they must attend Sunday school. Arthur, always the favourite, is engaged to a young woman named Edith and has managed to talk round his father and is excused from further church attendance on Sunday after attending the first morning service.

As for Christopher and Phil, no such quarter is given. The two young men must accompany their father to further services at noon and again in the evening. This is a Sunday routine that Christopher and Phil dare not show signs of resentment about, despite losing almost the whole day to church attendance. Although from time to time the subject of heated discussion, Caroline stays at home with their youngest daughter who also bears the burden of being named after three saints – Althea Ethelreda Monica – but is mercifully called Elsie in everyday life.

Caroline's belly is again swollen. There is to be a further, and it has to be said (well, from Arthur's viewpoint anyway) welcome, addition to the family. This time, however, Caroline has a feeling that there is something different from the previous occasions when she has been expecting. She feels so tired and at first she put this down to the fact that it is now almost nineteen years since she had her first child, Arthur.

It will soon be the time for Caroline to get up and prepare breakfast, although these days she tends more to oversee Little Carrie. Seeing that her husband is now awake she turns to him.

'Arthur, I feel that there is something different with my pregnancy this time. I would like to see the doctor. Do we have the money to spare, please?'

'Different? Different in what way? I've certainly not seen you this big before but then you are getting older.'

'I don't rightly know, Arthur. I know that I am incredibly tired all the time but there is something else and it is worrying me. We have lost one baby before and I do not want anything to go wrong this time. Please can I go to the doctor, Arthur?'

'Very well. I try and set a little money aside for any eventuality. I was hoping to go to Painsthorpe for a few days as I have not been since I was accepted into the Order but if it will put your mind at ease then the money can be used to pay the doctor.'

'Thank you, my dearest. That is good of you.'

Caroline sees the doctor on Monday morning. It is then that she finds out that she is expecting twins. Arthur, as is his wont, returns home late as usual after visiting and carrying out his mission in the East End. As he slips into bed his movements are enough to bring Caroline out of her light sleep. She has been trying not to go to sleep as she wants to give Arthur her news.

'Arthur, the doctor has told me that I am expecting twins and he wants to be in attendance when it's time.'

'Twins! Twins! That is wonderful news. Two new souls for the glory of God.'

'I don't think God has much to do with it, Arthur. It is much more down to you. And, Arthur, there is something else.'

Caroline breaks off.

'Come on then, tell me. What else did the doctor have to say?'

'He says that for my sake and that of the expected twins that I need to drink something.'

'Well, go on.'

'He says I should drink at least a glass of porter every day. He says that he and many in his profession swear to the benefit that porter can bring to patients in their care.'

'Porter! I will not have that or any other drink in this house and I forbid you to bring the stuff in or to take it elsewhere.'

'But Arthur …!'

'No, woman. The answer is no. Both you and I signed the pledge years ago and nothing has changed or will change that. Now it is time to go to sleep and I will hear no more of this.'

# Chapter 4

Caroline's contractions are coming closer and closer together. After so many children she knows she is very close to giving birth.

'Carrie dear, go fetch the doctor; it can't be very much longer now.'

Carrie should have been back within ten minutes but it is almost half an hour before she comes through the door trying to catch her breath.

'What took you so long, child, and where is the doctor?'

'He is attending someone else, Ma, so I had to go there to

make sure he knows to come at once. He said he should not be very long but at his age he can only walk slowly these days. He told me to heat plenty of water and have clean linen or cloth to hand. He did not say what he needs that for. Should I go and get Father? It must be nearly time for him to finish work by now.'

'No, Carrie. Let your father be. It's the doctor I need now not him. In any case, he will probably be on his way by now to Whitechapel or to Stepney or to some other godforsaken place in the East End.'

It is almost an hour before the doctor arrives. By this time the sons Arthur, Christopher, Aidan and Phil are home from work. They are banished to the backyard where the tenants have at least somewhere to hang out the washing. Hilda is told to take little Elsie to her Auntie Jane and Uncle Henry and to ask to stay the night. Carrie is to stay inside and to help where she can.

One, then two, then three hours go by and it has now been dark for some time.

Arthur turns to Christopher: 'Come on, Chris. I'm not staying here all night; let's go get a nice hot pie from Old Mrs Bunce's shop.'

'What about us? We're hungry as well,' asks Phil.

'Can't help that,' says Christopher. 'You'll just have to go without. I've barely got enough to buy a pie for myself. Father takes most of what I earn.'

'Same here!' says Arthur. 'He's only just letting me keep a bit more of my wages since me and Edith decided to get married. It's as if he doesn't trust us with our own money but on the other hand I guess he's got to think about feeding and clothing you youngsters. Sorry, you'll have to wait here and wait until Father gets back as well.'

Arthur and Christopher then head off to the pie shop leaving Aidan and Phil in the backyard both hungry and thirsty and very bored.

Arthur and Christopher make short work of eating their pies with both of them not quite certain what the pies contain.

'You know, Arthur, you're very lucky.'

'How come?'

'Well, your Edith is very pretty and she has a lovely thin waist. It won't be long now before you are out of here, married and making a life of your own. What's more, I don't know how it is that Father no longer insists on you going to church three times a day on Sundays. The rest of us are fed up with religion. Once on Sunday morning, that's what you get away with, whilst the rest of us have to suffer. I wish I was getting married just to get away from all of this.'

'Well, then you'll just have to find your own woman, won't you? Mind you with that boyish face I suspect you will have little trouble in that quarter. You know Edith says that you and me look like two peas in the same pod. To be honest I don't know how me and Edith are going to manage. You don't get paid much making brass rulers you know and it's a very boring job but at least it is a job and I don't think I'm bright enough to do anything more challenging. I just wish I had half the brains of Father ...'

'Well, what good has it done him? Unless of course you want to be a religious fanatic and a monk. Would half of father's brain make you into a half-brother?' They both break out into laughter.

'That is an awful attempt at a joke. I don't know why we're laughing.'

It is just after eleven when their father comes down the stairs leading into the backyard. Aidan and Phil have been sitting at the foot of the stairs and are now very tired and very hungry. As they hear the familiar tread of their father's footsteps they rush to get up. Arthur and Christopher are now out in the backyard, too, continuing their conversation about this, that and the other.

'That doctor will not even allow me in my own house. He says your mother is having a hard time of things. We should pray together for your mother and the twins and that they will be born safely and well.'

It is sometime later before Carrie joins them all in the backyard. Arthur puts his hand on her shoulder, a rare sign of affection from him.

'Well? What is happening?'

'The doctor says you should come up now. Ma is exhausted but even so he has given her some powders as he wants her to have a long and undisturbed sleep.'

'And the babies? What about the babies?'

'It's a boy and a girl, Father, but the doctor says that the girl is small and weak. He is very concerned about her.'

'You lot stay here for a little longer. I'll tell you when you can come back up.'

Arthur ascends the stairs to find the doctor washing his hands and lower arms in the sink.

'Well, Doctor?'

'Mr Clowes, your wife is very weak – it has not been an easy delivery either for your wife or for me. There were some complications but that is over now. I have examined the babies. The boy looks in reasonable condition, although he is not as big as I would expect, not even for a twin. The girl is a different matter. She is frail as well as small. I have to say, Mr Clowes, that your wife is undernourished. This has made her ordeal all the worse. I recommended some time ago that she takes a glass of porter every day to help build her up during the latter part of her pregnancy and I say the same again now while she is nursing.'

'I will not have alcohol in this house and she will not take alcohol under any circumstances. That is my final word on the matter. I shall pray for them all and I will see to it that she eats better but no alcohol will pass her lips. Now I am grateful for all you have done and unless there is something else, then let me pay you and then I can see my wife and new babies.'

'Very well, Mr Clowes. I have given you my professional advice and if you chose to ignore that then I can do no more. Now given the time I have been here I require five shillings in payment if you please and then I will bid you good night as I have been ready to retire for some time now.'

The doctor dries himself and reaches for his coat and his bag as Arthur counts out the five shillings owing.

'I offer one further piece of advice, Mr Clowes. It may well be dangerous for your wife to bear another child. It is impossible to predict these things but your wife will soon reach that age when women are no longer able to conceive. Abstinence from alcohol is perhaps not the only thing you should decide to rule on.'

The doctor leaves, closing the door behind him. He shakes his head at what he perceives as the narrow-minded attitude of a religious fanatic. He sees the remainder of Arthur's family looking up from the bottom of the stairs to the landing.

'I think you can all go back up now.'

They all stand in the room that serves as both parlour and dining room, waiting for their father to come out of their parents' bedroom.

'All is well,' says Arthur as he emerges. 'Your mother is asleep as are your baby brother and sister. You can see them in the morning so off to bed with you.'

'But me and Aidan have had nothing to eat,' complains Phil. 'What about you, Carrie?' Carrie shakes her head. 'It's fine for Arthur and Christopher. They went off and bought themselves a pie each without a thought for the rest of us.'

'We only had enough money for the two of us,' pipes up Christopher.

'Enough!' barks their father. 'It is too late to be worrying about supper. If I can go without, then so can you.'

'Excuse me, Father,' says Carrie tentatively. 'There is still some dripping left in the basin. Could we please have some of that on the bread? It won't take a minute and you could have a slice as well.'

'Very well, Carrie, but make it quick. As for the rest of you, as late as it is you will quickly wash your hands and faces. There is no excuse to let standards slip. As I keep on telling you, we should always have in our minds that wise old Hebrew saying "Cleanliness is next to godliness".'

The girl is indeed not at all healthy and shows little or no sign of improvement over the coming weeks. Caroline is slow to regain her strength and remains confined to bed for over a week. She is at least able to nurse the babies, although the girl does not take as much as she should. Arthur sees the danger that the girl may perish without receiving the grace of being baptised and that her soul may then be lost in Purgatory. An early baptism is arranged for the twins.

Some things do not change and Arthur keeps to his perverse choice of baptismal names. For the boy there is a whole ragbag of names: Benedict, after the saint that founded his order; Theodore, a third-century Christian martyr; Laud, a former archbishop of Canterbury whom Arthur admires, and lastly the rather normal name of Charles which Arthur agrees to when Caroline pleads for her newest son to have a more common name.

For the girl her collection of names comprises: Scholastica, the sister of the Benedict who formed Arthur's Order and the founder of a nunnery who was later canonised; Theodora, a saint; and Helena, yet another saint.

Scholastica survives just a few days over two months. On the following morning after the burial service, none of the family travel with the coffin to the cemetery but Arthur makes the journey on his own by train to Finchley where his baby daughter has already been laid to rest in the family plot. Arthur needs the assistance of the clerk in the lodge gate to find the grave. The freshly-turned small mound of earth assists Arthur in finding the right place as the wooden cross that was set there last time to mark the grave of George Frederick is no longer there. Arthur assumes that after so many years the simple memorial to his father has become a victim of the elements. It is the first time that Arthur has visited the grave since his father was buried, so it is upsetting to find that the plot is now unmarked other than in the records of the cemetery kept in the lodge.

Now with the death and burial of his daughter, Arthur starts to think that this family plot should be marked with a lasting stone memorial where family names can be inscribed for all to see. This might also encourage visits to the graves so that people might both pay their respects and remember loved family members. As to when that may happen Arthur does not know. There is barely enough money coming in to feed, maintain and keep the family. Arthur leaves the graveside for the cemetery gates and starts the walk back to the station. The more Arthur thinks about things, the more determined he is to ensure that a lasting memorial is commissioned. Arthur stops in his tracks cursing himself for not thinking of it earlier. *Now why don't I ask the clerk at the gates if they can in the meantime arrange for a new wooden cross to mark the graves of my father and baby daughter? That could save a lot of bother.*

Arthur finds the clerk who is assisting someone else with directions to find a grave. He waits until the man is free before making his enquiry.

'How much? Just for a couple of wooden crosses! No thank you! I shall make my own enquiries upon my return to London. Thank you and good day.'

A now somewhat irritated and slightly guilty man makes his way back to the station. As Arthur is waiting for the train that will return him to St Pancras Station, he is fiddling with his train ticket in his hands. It is only then that he notices that the station name shown on the ticket and on the station platform has changed to Finchley (Church End) since he was last up this way. This makes him feel all the more guilty and ashamed for not visiting his father's grave before now. He could have at least replaced the missing wooden cross before now if only he had known the old one had disappeared. Arthur becomes even more resolved that he will somehow have a stone memorial erected. 'I might even then be able to ensure that there will be room for Caroline's and my own epitaphs to be added when the time comes.' He says this out loud and a gentleman standing nearby turns to give him the strangest of looks before moving further down the platform.

# Chapter 5

Arthur's mission in the East End is somewhat fluid and this is not quite to Arthur's liking. Arthur likes things to be done in a set and orderly fashion but then obedience is part of his vows. He has to get on with the task assigned to him. Arthur is just one more missionary seeking to fulfil his designated mission in the East End with its teeming mass of humanity in the most squalid part of all London. People are living the most desperate existence in overcrowded dwellings, in which sometimes extended or even different families have to share the same room with the crudest of shared sanitation facilities. Less than half of the children in often large families survive to reach early adolescence. Religion and God have little to offer and provide no comfort to these poor souls.

For so many years before Arthur arrived on the scene, the Church of England, as well as nonconformist Anglican offshoots, have sought to bring God's word to a populace so focused upon day-to-day survival and striving to hold their families together. Some said the East End was full of pagans.

If that is what they mean by non-religious people, then there is some truth in that. To others, the East End is an unknown, other than it is a place to be avoided. They are ignorant of the plight of people and are happy to remain ignorant. After all, the poor have only themselves to blame for being poor.

Murder, foot-padding, theft, extortion, prostitution, drunkenness seemed to many to be part and parcel of East End life, whether they be perpetrators, victims or ordinary folk trying to keep body and soul together.

There are some in the East End, however, who are well off and thrive. The owners of sweated businesses such as furniture makers, tanners and shoe and boot makers, garment producers and even matchmakers all who pay their workers less than a subsistence wage knowing there is always someone who will take their place. The brewers of the East End are also very rich, yet chose not to live there, though at least they provide some employment and on terms better than those in sweated labour. Things are no better in the docks. The fittest and strongest-looking may find casual work here and there but the pay is low and the work is irregular and hard. Then there are a different type of persons – the criminals and the runners of prostitutes – who also do well out of East End life.

Long before Arthur received his mission there has been an influx of the Irish into the area. At the beginning of the nineteenth century, many Irishmen, after fighting in the British Army against Napoleon, found themselves begging for food and looking for work in the East End, only to be joined by successive waves of their countrymen and women and children as they seek refuge from the scourge of famine and poverty that haunts their homeland. As bad as the East End is, it is better than life in Ireland. All this makes the overcrowding worse and makes it even more difficult for individuals to find work.

For the Irish in the East End and elsewhere, things

become even worse than just hard or difficult. As the incidence of rebellion and uprising in Ireland increases then resentment against the Catholic Irish in Protestant England increases. This resentment is extended even to second or third or even fourth-generation Irish, and not just to the new arrivals in England from the so-called 'Emerald Isle'. No one wants to give them work, not just because of reasons of politics or religion, but because the Irish are considered to be inferior to the English – an Englishman or woman should be given work ahead of any Irishman or woman.

Then come the Jews, who are fleeing persecution throughout Europe and in Russia. At least, the Irish speak some form of English whereas the Jews do not and their customs and habits are alien. They add to the rich patchwork of cultures and ethnicities that the East End has become. Because of the docks, there has always been a mixture of peoples from all over Europe and from further afield, from places such as India and China where Britain trades or has colonies. Indeed, the Chinese have their own 'quarter' almost entirely to themselves.

Another winter passes and, despite all the difficulties, Arthur throws all his energy into his mission, often leaving straight from work to go into the East End and then returning home only late into the evening when everyone is already asleep. Many will not venture into the dangerous East End unless they have some extremely important and essential reason to do so. Some of the 'enlightened' middle class, including women who teach at some of the impromptu schools established with the aid of churches or philanthropic patrons, have to be escorted to ensure their protection.

Arthur is convinced that he is under God's protection and that this will ensure that he will come to no serious harm; even if something were to happen it would be God's will as someone else might benefit from his own misfortune. Arthur maintains this view in spite of the fact that so many missionaries to the East End are attacked, not only for what they might be carrying about their person, but also for trying to convert people. Many of the Irish are lapsed Catholics but they will never betray their heritage and national identity by converting from the Roman Church. They might accept relief or aid from elsewhere, even from the Protestants, but they will not make such a break as to become Protestant. As for Arthur's mission, Arthur may be part of the Old Catholic Church but he does not recognise their Pope so he is not a real Catholic.

It would have satisfied Arthur's pious outlook to have converted people but he finds no joy there. Those Irish that do have a thought for religion hold their priest in awe, even if they do not attend Mass. He certainly would not find any joy in trying to convert among the Jewish community, or the Chinese, or from the criminal underworld and its associates, or from the fallen women who sold their bodies to survive, or from all those others whose sole goal in life was to ensure that they had food and clothing for themselves and for their families. If Arthur is to make any difference at all, then he needs to try and help people and not to convert them. This is his mission but he never, ever gives up hope of one day finding at least one convert.

# Chapter 6

'You always have been father's favourite, Arthur. Whether it's because you are the eldest or because you carry his name or a bit of both, I don't know. Or maybe he feels guilty as you were conceived before Mother and Father were married,' says Phil.

'I'm sure that's not true … well the first bit of what you say. He loves us all but perhaps doesn't always show it. There is no cause to be jealous, Phil, I am no different from any one else of us.'

'Well, it does not feel like it from where I'm standing and I know some of the others feel the same way as I do.'

'And which others might that be, Phil.'

'That's for me and them to know, Arthur. And another thing where it's all right for you. You got a proper name; and so did Christopher, him being named after Grandfather Wright, and even Carrie got our mother's names but as for the rest of us we get lumbered with a mouthful of saints and church-related names. Every time I have to give my names I see people smirking or even sniggering.'

'My, you are in a mood this evening, aren't you? Still, we all call you Phil so it can't be that bad. Even Father does that.'

'I don't mean to spoil the evening, Arthur. Anyway, on to other things. So you and Edith have fixed the wedding day, have you?'

'Yes. For the end of September. I wish it could have been earlier and we could be more certain of fine weather but it has been so difficult to find the money to set up home even with father's help, which, before you ask, is most unexpected as I never asked him for a penny.

'Remind me again about Edith,' asked Phil.

'Well as you know, Edith has a good job and an income as a school secretary. Her parents are not very keen on our match as they think she could have done better than me – they probably think she could have married a teacher instead of someone who works with his hands making stupid rulers made out of brass. Still, she won her parents round in the end and I think they have at last accepted me, even if with no great enthusiasm. This probably is because Edith's elder sister, Caroline, will soon be forty and has been left on the shelf and they don't want a second spinster daughter on their hands. Mind you, for once I think that father's taking of holy orders has worked in my favour. It at least shows to my prospective parents-in-law that we have been brought up as a very religious family and – how does Edith put it? – oh yes, her parents have decided that father being a Benedictine monk has a certain cachet. That seems to at least make it just slightly easier for them to accept that their daughter is marrying below her station. Mind you, Edith expects that her parents will probably describe me as someone who does something in engineering.'

'And how will you manage after you are married?'

'Regrettably, we will not be able to afford to go away after the wedding and we will no doubt have to wait to start a family so that I can pay Father back and buy all the furniture that we need. We need both incomes to start off with as Edith will have to resign her position once we start to raise a family.'

'And how much did Father lend you and what on earth is a *cachet* when it's at home?'

'Oh, not that much, just enough to pay the rent in advance and to buy a few things. Nothing new, of course; it will have to be used things that we buy for now. As for what a cachet is I had to ask Edith the same question. Evidently it's French and something with cachet has quality. Edith thinks her parents don't really understand the word and when it should be used, but they are always out to try and convince people that they are sophisticated in some way or another.'

'Seems to me that everyone likes the French these days especially after Blériot flew his contraption over the English Channel. It should have been done by an Englishman first. It is not called the English Channel for nothing.'

Arthur laughed. 'Well, has Chris told you I've asked him to be my best man and one of the witnesses? He is the next oldest brother so I have known him the longest. I hope you don't mind.'

'No, Arthur, I don't mind. He's not the oldest brother though. Father is!'

They both start laughing.

'All these jokes at Father's expense are not that funny, you know, but I always seem to end up laughing at them. He would give us a right blast if ever he got to hear what we are saying about him. Probably mean double church attendance for months for being so wicked.'

'Oh no, please!' pleads Phil.

The weeks pass quite quickly and the weather has been fine and not too hot. Not like the previous year when for weeks on end summer nights were far too warm and it was so difficult to sleep. Having heard her mother say it once Carrie would time and time again say 'You can stir the air in here with a stick'.

It is the morning of the wedding. As is usual there is not room enough for everyone around the table to take breakfast at the same time and it is normal for Caroline, with the help of Carrie, to ready and to dish out breakfast. Carrie has been out early to get a fresh warm loaf from the baker and as a special treat this morning everyone is to get a boiled egg. The large teapot has been filled. Grace has been said. Everyone is in a happy mood, although Arthur is very quiet and just smiles or nods occasionally when remarks are made about him and his bride.

As soon as room becomes available at the table, Caroline and Carrie start to take their own breakfasts. Arthur the father and Arthur the son remain seated and the others start to get themselves ready and dressed to leave for the church, even though there is still over three hours to go.

Carrie has almost finished eating her now hard-boiled egg; she's disappointed that it is not runny like some of the others served up. She turns to her brother Arthur.

'Arthur, I think it is ever so romantic that you and Edith have known each other for all these years since Sunday school and now you are getting married to each other. I hope that one day soon I am so lucky as that.'

'What do you mean by that, Carrie?' asks her mother. 'Is

there something going on that me and your father should know about?'

'I am still friendly with Fred, you know that. We have known each other for some years now but I would never dream of seeing him or walking out with him without asking for your and father's permission, Mother. I like to think he will show more interest in me soon, though, and not just think of me as a childhood friend that has grown up.'

'I know young Fred Howard,' says her father. 'You tell him from me that should he wish to walk out with you then it is me that he comes to see first.'

'And what would you say, Father? Would you frighten him off?'

'Don't take that tone with me! I am your father and this is my house. I do not have anything in particular against young Mr Howard but he comes to see me first – is that clear?'

'Yes, sorry, Father.'

'Now that's settled,' Caroline interrupted, calming the waters, 'let's all start to get ready and dressed. I can see you are rather quiet, Arthur. Getting nervous, are we, son? Well, don't be. This is a happy day. The first of my children getting married. Why don't we all get a move on and go for a little walk around the park? Maybe that will help you to relax a bit, son.'

'Yes, Mother. Thank you, I should like that.'

'What are they like, Arthur? Edith's parents, I mean,' asks Carrie.

'They are somewhat different from us, Carrie. They look at things in a different way from what we do and I do not always find it easy to talk to them, but things between us have improved.'

'Well, I think it is very odd,' says Caroline. 'Here we are on the day of the wedding and neither myself nor your father have met them. A fine state of affairs, if you ask me.'

'Now be fair, Mother. You were both invited to tea; it's just

194

that Mrs Tickner was what they called "indisposed" so the invitation to tea had to be cancelled.'

'Then they could have invited us again but they didn't, did they?'

'Well, as Shakespeare's Lady Macbeth says, "What is done is done,"' says Arthur senior.

'I did not know you read Shakespeare, dearest. I thought you had no time for such things outside of your religious books, and the Bible of course.'

'I used to read more widely when I was younger and I did occasionally enjoy some of Shakespeare's works before I found my vocation. Now your idea of a walk in the park seems a good idea to me so let's get ready.'

The wedding ceremony itself goes smoothly with a congregation of around twenty people. The weather remains dry with some pleasant autumn sunshine just now and then blocked out by scattered clouds. Edith looks such a beautiful bride in her white dress that shows off her slim but well-proportioned figure to great effect. Her mother even lends Edith her prized three-string necklace of pearls held together at the front by a cameo-type brooch. Ladies should always wear a hat but Arthur is far from convinced that the wide-brimmed, two-toned blue confection together with its nest of artificial flowers on top is a good choice, but then what does he know about ladies' fashions and hats in particular?

Arthur's suit looked well enough when he put it on earlier but he knows that, even though it is in good condition, that it has been worn and owned by someone else before him and does not have the same sort of cut as the suits worn by members of the Tickner family. He is also slightly conscious of a slight scuff at the front of one of his shoes. Nevertheless, he keeps such thoughts to himself and is more than happy to pose with his beautiful bride for the photograph that is to be taken in the garden at the Tickner house when a photographer turns up as booked.

Caroline has some limited success in holding conversation with Mrs Tickner but the same can certainly not be said in the case of Mr Tickner and Arthur senior, particularly when Mr Tickner picks up a small glass of sherry from the tray offered by their maid. The poor girl is not to know of Arthur's strong convictions against alcohol and he rather unnecessarily waves her away before starting to lecture Mr Tickner on the evils of drink. To his credit, Tickner listens for almost a full minute before excusing himself on the pretext that he must attend to his other guests. He has some respect for Arthur's view but does not see that the occasional small glass of sherry on the occasion of the marriage of his daughter is likely to put his immortal soul in danger. Moreover, he dislikes being told what to do in his own house and in front of other members of the Tickner family and invited friends.

As to the remainder of the guests, the two sides of the new-joined family keep pretty much to themselves. Carrie is most impressed with some of the dresses and hats belonging to members of family or friends of the bride. She hopes that someday she will own dresses and hats of such a quality and be up to date in fashion (though little does she know that even the TicKners are some way behind the times).

As soon as the happy and glowing bride and groom depart for their new home and the start of a new life together most of the guests leave, including all of Arthur's family. Edith had invited some close friends and colleagues from her school but Arthur had decided against inviting the few close friends that he has outside of the family. He thought it unlikely that they would feel at ease in such company and surroundings. He was exactly right on that account.

As they lay together that evening in their very own bed for the very first time Arthur turns to his bride.

'It may take a little while before we can afford it, my love, but I do want to take you away for a few days by the seaside to

196

make up for us having to remain here tonight of all nights. For the moment it's back to the works for me on Monday and back to the school office for you on Monday as well.'

'Well, it may take quite some time before we can take a holiday, my dearest.'

'Not that long though, surely?'

'I'm afraid it will, Arthur. You see there is something that I have to tell you.' Edith falls silent.

'Well, come on then, you silly goose. We are married now, so tell me. What is it?'

Arthur feels Edith's body tense beside his.

'I'm sorry, my love, but I fear that some of our plans are in jeopardy. You remember that afternoon some months back when we went to the house whilst my parents were visiting up in the West End?'

'Of course I do! How could I ever forget! Now why don't you cuddle up closer to me? We have all the time we need now and no fear of being discovered.'

Arthur slips his hand around Edith's slim waist and slowly but gently moves his hand upwards.

'No, Arthur. Please not just now. You see what I have to tell you is very important.' She pauses and breathes in deeply. 'Arthur, I am going to have your baby.'

'You're having a baby? Are you sure? It can't be. We were only together briefly and just that once when your parents were away from the house!'

'Don't be angry with me, my love. Maybe it is meant to be and just that once is enough. I have yet to see the doctor, Arthur, but yes I am certain. Apart from the obvious indications, I am now being sick in the mornings. It has not been easy at home to ensure that no one hears me.'

'Why haven't you told me before?'

'I was scared, Arthur. Not scared of you, of course, my love. You are the kindest and most considerate person I have ever known but I was scared all the same. Perhaps scared that you

197

might think that I have trapped you into marriage. I don't know.'

It is Arthur's turn to be silent for a while. He then presses his cheek close to hers and speaks to her gently.

'You must never feel that there isn't anything that you can't tell me. I must admit to this being a big surprise. For some married people it can take ages before they have a baby. Obviously not for us!'

'Are you disappointed, Arthur? What about our parents? How do you think they will react when we have a baby so soon. I won't be able to hide the signs for very long no matter what clothes I wear or how tightly I bind myself. Then there is my job. How will we manage without my income? Oh Arthur, what are we going to do?'

Edith starts to sob.

'The most important thing is us, my love. Me, you and now our baby. We will manage somehow and we are no different from many others. As for our parents, well, I tell you my parents had knowledge of each other before they were married. In fact, it was just a few months after they were married before I came into the world.'

Edith lifts her head.

'Your father was messing with your mother before they were married? Him! With all his religion and all that, he was messing with your mother?'

Edith starts to giggle.

'That old hypocrite!' she blurts out.

'I doubt if you are the first one to call him that. Now with you talking of messing, why don't you come here? It is our wedding night after all.'

Later Edith suggests that they should take the train for a day out at the seaside. If not next weekend, then the weekend after, before the weather turns wet and cold. A day out and the train tickets may be more than they can really afford at the moment, but this is something they will do as there is unlikely to be an opportunity to do so later, particularly when Edith has to give up her employment to tend to and nurse their baby.

# Part III

# Peace at Last

# Chapter 1

The Colney Hatch Asylum is filled to capacity with lunatics and the pauper insane. Even the five additional dormitories provided for chronic and infirm female patients are filled to capacity.

It is just after five o'clock on the morning of 27 January 1903 when the asylum's steam siren sounds. A fire has started in one of the blocks in the annex. The fire spreads at a terrific rate throughout the mainly wooden dormitories, which are constructed out of timber frames covered in match-boarding; a strong wind fans the flames.

The shrill sound of the siren wakes the residents of New Southgate, Barnet and Edmonton and many swarm into the streets. There they can see that a massive fire is already in progress.

The asylum's own fire unit is totally ill-equipped and undermanned to combat a blaze of such magnitude. There are fewer than a dozen people within the asylum walls who have received any degree of firefighting training. There are also problems with the lack of water to fight the fire. The Hornsey Fire Brigade joins the scene and is unable to get their steamer into action to help fight the blaze. That is until the brigade manages to dam a brook some 400 yards away and down the hill from the raging inferno so that the now backed-up brook provides a water supply for the steamer. As the corrugated-iron roof and the wooden walls of each building collapses, flames shoot up into the air sending out a shower of sparks that accelerates the progress of the fires already under way in the neighbouring blocks. Some witnesses later said that the iron frames intended to make the structures more rigid glowed white in the heat.

A number of the local residents scale the wall at the rear of the asylum in order to render assistance but their help is refused by the firefighters and by the staff. When the brook has been dammed and the fire brigade and asylum staff are finally able to use their hoses on the flames, it is far, far too late. Within half an hour of the discovery of the outbreak of fire, all five blocks in the annex and the doctors' accommodation block have been totally destroyed.

Dawn breaks and while some of the firemen continue to play water on the still-smouldering remains others begin the gruesome task of searching through what remains of the buildings. The corrugated-iron roofing and even the bedsteads are seen to have melted in the intense heat. Most distressing for the searchers is the sight of charred human remains. Some of the remains show that groups of people have huddled together as the fire swept through the blocks, either because they were physically unable to get themselves to safety or because they were so confused and panic-stricken they could not help themselves.

Susannah Ann Clowes is being held in the main body of the asylum but she, like many other patients, is traumatised by the catastrophe and what she has seen.

It is later reported that the fire started in the block set aside for insane Jewish women but in all some 600 women were being held in the now-destroyed so-called temporary accommodation block. The nursing staff experienced great difficulty in trying to get some of the panic-stricken inmates to safety and many of the inmates prevented the staff from trying to save the other patients.

It transpires that some of the insane escaped the fire by scaling the asylum walls, thus making the job of the authorities as they seek to determine who has perished even more difficult. By the time the debris from the fire has been thoroughly sifted through, fifty-one bodies have been recovered.

When the news reaches London, Arthur and William are amongst the many relatives that besiege the asylum trying to find out if their relatives are amongst either those who have perished and could be identified or amongst those numbers who can't be accounted for. To their considerable relief, even though it had been so many years since any of the family has visited her, Arthur and William are assured that their mother is safe.

# Chapter 2

Ann's behaviour becomes more noisy and erratic. She experiences delirium and hallucinations. Her spirits and voices are forever with her and at times she can be quite spiteful. The one thing the staff are grateful for is that she continues to keep herself clean.

One Saturday morning she is found waving one arm over her head and when seen by the doctor on duty she is diagnosed as having suffered a small brain haemorrhage. There is little that can be done for her other than to keep an eye on her condition. As the family have not visited her for such a long time, the authorities at Colney Hatch Asylum took no action to notify the family of her change of condition. Thirteen days later she is dead.

The family is then of course notified of her death so that appropriate arrangements can be made and so that no costs in relation to her burial are incurred by Colney Hatch. The evening of the day on which they receive the news of their mother's death, the brothers and sisters gather together at William's lodgings. Arthur takes charge of the proceedings.

'Come. We have things to discuss but first of all I should like to lead you in prayer for our dear departed mother's soul and in sure knowledge that she is now at peace.

'We pray, O Lord, that you will now take into your keeping the soul of our mother, Susannah Ann, who has been baptised in the name of Your Son and Redeemer Jesus Christ

Our Lord. We pray also that she will at last in Your keeping find peace and release from her torments. Amen.'

They all respond with 'Amen' and then Arthur continues.

'There is no denying that we became strangers to our mother as her torments became worse. Nevertheless, she is our mother and we should try now to do what is best for her. It does not make for pleasant reading but I have here a copy of the death certificate sent to me in incredible haste by the authorities at Colney Hatch and I will give you the brief details. Our mother Susannah Ann Clowes is described as a pauper patient who on 19 February 1909 died following a brain haemorrhage after suffering from chronic mania for eighteen years.

'Our mother is at peace now and with our Lord, so I say that we should not mourn for her. I say that it seems only right that she should be laid to rest beside her husband and our father and my poor little daughter, Scholastica. It is now some nineteen years since our father was laid to rest at Finchley and I now say that it is time that the grave is properly marked and that we find the money to pay for a memorial to be carved in memory of both our parents. This may go partway to relieve the dishonour of her being deemed a pauper patient. Let us the family now do something to restore her dignity. Is that agreed?'

There are a few moments of silence as one or two of those present nod their assent.

'Fine, then we will each of us set aside a certain amount of money each week until there is enough there for me to commission a memorial for the grave. It will no doubt take some time to find enough money. It may even take a number of years but we shall do this.

'As for the burial service and her interment, this is something that I can arrange. There's a small chapel at St Pancras Cemetery, and I shall arrange for her to be taken there from the asylum and for a service to be performed.

Then as she is placed into the earth I shall offer prayers for her soul's safekeeping. I will let you know the details of the arrangements as soon as I know.

'One final thing, and I am sure you agree with me on this as well, we shall say nothing outside of the family about our mother and what has happened to her.'

Jane interrupts impatiently. 'She has been locked away for all these years, Arthur, and I doubt whether there is anyone but our immediate family who remembers her. And tell me, Arthur, what have you told Caroline about all this? She is your wife after all,' asks Jane.

'She knows all that she needs to know. Nothing more, nothing less and I thank you not to pry into matters that are no business of yours, sister.'

There is no dissent from Arthur's proposals, which in any case are more in the nature of demands than suggestions. On the other hand, no one can fault his reasoning.

The siblings spend the remainder of the evening catching up on other family matters and it is Arthur who is first to leave William's house. With Arthur gone, Jane catches William's ear.

'I see our brother is his normally charming self this evening. I am not denying that it is good that he has taken on the role of making all the appropriate arrangements. I just wonder if after all this time he now has slight pangs of conscience about what he said at the doctor's surgery all those years ago about our mother being possessed of demons and her being sinful?'

'Maybe he does, Jane, but he is too full of himself ever to admit to him being wrong.'

'Too right there. Anyway, I must be getting home or that husband of mine will be wondering where I have got to. I'll just say goodnight to everyone and then I am off.'

The remainder soon follow Jane's lead, leaving William and his wife Lucy in peace.

'I like Jane, you know, Billy, but as for that brother of yours he's another story. What a peculiar kettle of fish he is. All pious and so full of himself he is. Didn't stop him though having his fun with Caroline before they were wed, did it? What was it just four or five months after they were married when Arthur came along. There's a word for people like that but I can't remember what it is.'

'Hypocrite.'

'Hypocrite, that's the word. And you know it wouldn't surprise me if he has a little bit of your mother inside his head. Oh my dear, I'm sorry! I didn't mean it like that – it's just that Arthur gets my goat.'

'"Gets my goat" – where on earth did you pick that phrase up?'

'It's something my friend Jenny picked up from overhearing two Americans in conversation. I think it means bloody annoying.'

'Why can't they speak English? Well, anyway, Arthur will never change now, Lucy. He has always been both complicated and serious and never easy to get along with. I was never sure just what he was thinking and then he got religion real bad and I gave up trying to work him out. That wife of his must be a saint to put up with him. Anyway, at least he is going to take care of the arrangements and we should be thankful for that. Now it is late and I'm feeling tired and I can see you are as well. Leave all the plates and stuff until the morning and let's just get to bed.'

# Part IV

# A Country Girl Comes to Town

# Chapter 1

A village out on the Fens, when compared with places such as Clerkenwell and Holborn, or indeed anywhere else in England's capital city or other cities and large towns, is so different that they cannot in fact be compared.

From childhood almost everyone in Swavesey was destined, in some way or another, to be connected to the land unless they decided to leave the village. To work the land or to go into service for someone who owned the land was to most the sum total of a young man's or girl's prospects once they left school.

Some young men might strike lucky and find work to become a mechanic at a garage or even on one of the larger farms but there again it was only the rich farmers that had cars and even as a mechanic on a farm maintaining and repairing agricultural machinery and equipment you were still tied to the land and its fortunes. The baker, the butcher, the grocer and the ironmonger would not be there if not to support this agricultural community. It is often the case that these businesses are handed down through the generations, so job prospects in these places for someone outside of the family that runs the businesses are very limited.

The navigation drain from the river Ouse and the docks in the village itself have fallen into disuse and silted up many years ago. The navigation was once used by the typical flat-bottomed fenland barges of the time to bring in coal and building materials and were in turn used to take out goods such as the locally grown grain and eels netted from rivers.

Some things have not changed, though, and even nowadays carters carrying produce from nearby farms, or just carrying other materials for delivery, watered and rested their horses at the site of one of the disused docks now known as Swan Pond. For indeed the former dock is now only a pond. The carters, as they did when the docks were active, still 'water' and 'rest' themselves at the adjacent Swan with Two Necks hostelry.

The lifeblood of the village was now the railway and Grace's cousin Steve knew he was indeed a fortunate young man to have found a job as a porter with the Great Eastern Railway at the village railway station. Early each morning Steve would start his day by sweeping down the platform and then when the milk train arrived he would unload the empty milk churns and then load the full ones with fresh milk from the local farms to be sent by the milk train either to St Ives or to Cambridge.

For Grace, things were to follow a familiar pattern for a young village girl and the daughter of a labourer on the land. She left school at the age of fourteen and was fortunate enough to be able to enter into domestic service at the Old Manor House opposite the church dedicated to St Andrew. Her days followed a regular routine with hardly any day being different than any other day.

One Monday morning Grace left home, a simple wattle-and-daub cottage with a thatched roof, adjacent to the green now known as Market Square. The green was in fact the site of the larger of the two docks that had been filled in all those years ago. It was a short walk for Grace to her destination – across the green, a turn right into the main road running the length of the village and past other thatched cottages similar to her own family's, and then onto that part of the village known as Church End. Ahead of her lay the church itself and the Manor House and beyond that, in the aptly named stretch of the road called Station Road, the level crossing and railway station with its two platforms where her cousin Steve was already at work and the first of the day's passenger services into St Ives and Cambridge were beginning to come and go.

It is still dark when Grace sets out to begin her day one morning in March yet it is not as cold as some mornings of late because the wind is coming from the south-west. The wind is blowing very hard but at least it is far more bearable than one of those winds that comes straight off the North Sea or when the wind blows down from the north. That sort of wind can cut through a person no matter how many layers of clothing they have on for the land on the Fens is so flat there is no protection or respite from the full force and effects of the weather. Despite the hard-blowing wind it is at least dry and Grace is glad of it. Starting work in wet or damp skirts is most uncomfortable particularly as she is forever bending down as she goes about her morning cleaning duties.

Luncheon has been taken by the master and the mistress, Mr and Mrs James Norman, and Grace has brought all the things from the dining room back into the kitchen. Cook, Grace and the other day maid, Mary, having had their own lunch comprising mainly of the leftover vegetables, have started the next chores of the day. As Grace washes the dishes, Fred Woodruff the gardener and general outside labourer bursts through the kitchen door.

'There's a fire down the road! Everything is going up in flames. Drop what you are doing – we must go and see what we can do. Grace, it looks as though the whole village including your house will soon be up in flames as well!'

Fred has the wits to pull Grace's coat off the hook by the kitchen door and does the same for Mary. Running as fast as they can, whilst trying to put their arms through their coat sleeves and then pull their coats over their shoulders, the two girls quickly make their way back into the main part of the village. One of the small cottages in Taylors Lane and its outbuildings is well ablaze and the sparks from the fire have set light to the roofs of the thatched cottages next to Swan Pond. The flames are already several feet high.

Grace heads for her own house where she can see her mother struggling to pull what contents she can from inside the cottage. Her younger brothers and sisters are standing together on the far side furthest away from the fire and activity. Her mother sees Grace running towards her.

'Grace, inside quick. Leave the big and heavy stuff; just grab hold of what you can.'

Some of the older men are helping families who are trying to save what they can from their threatened homes by taking their belongings away from cottage doorways to the relative safety of the green. As more and more of the younger men arrive having abandoned their work in the fields, they bring the elderly and bedridden still in their homes first to safety and then help them away from the scene. Some poor wretches are clutching pathetic bundles, all that they have left save the clothes they are wearing. A number of the men take off their overjackets to put them around the shoulders of these wretched souls. One particular show of bravery occurs when three of the younger men enter the already alight cottage of old Francis Rockcliffe and his invalid wife Edith and manage to bring them out just before their dwelling collapses and is totally engulfed in flames.

The antiquated village hand fire pump is on the scene and some of the men are trying to connect the hoses so that they can use the water in Swan Pond to play on the flames as they are having so much difficulty from getting water from the public supply. There is then a crashing sound followed by a roar as the roof of first one and then another of the cottages around the green collapses, causing a further escalation in the fire's intensity and more sparks to fly off and land on the thatched roofs of other cottages. It takes but a moment for flying sparks to cause the thatch in yet more homes to start to flame.

Attempts to bring the old Swavesey fire pump into service are abandoned and it is left useless and unused in the middle of the road. The heat and intensity of what is now several fires is far too much for this second-hand hundred-year-old piece of equipment and, even if they could get it working, no one could get near enough to tackle the flames what with the feeble and inadequate capacity of the pump.

The village constable, PC Bill Plowman, returns to the scene and makes the point of telling anyone who will listen that he has sent a telegram to St Ives asking them to send their hand pump; he has even telegraphed Huntingdon requesting assistance from their steam-pumping engine. It is obvious to one and all that before any assistance arrives the fires will have consumed everything and that only smouldering ruins and ruined lives would remain. The only jobs left to be done by the men and machines from St Ives and Huntingdon would be to damp things down to ensure there is no danger of even more fires starting up.

It is some twenty or so minutes after Grace has arrived on the scene yet already there are at least twenty of these simple cottages and homes fully ablaze. Only those houses made of brick and with tiled roofs are saved from the inferno.

People are in a daze and perhaps the reality of events has yet to sink in. Others are already in a state of shock. It would be dark soon and people's urgent needs must be attended to. The likes of PC Plowman, Mr and Mrs Norman, and the vicar, the Reverend Sharp, are those that not only tend to show a degree of organisational ability in times of crisis in small communities such as Swavesey but are the type of people that others look up to and respect. Indeed, the vicar was one of the first helpers on the scene as he could see what was going on from his study window up at the vicarage.

Some who have lost their homes have relations nearby either in the village itself or in some of the neighbouring villages that can offer food and shelter. The fact that things will be cramped and uncomfortable is not a matter for consideration. Mr and Mrs Norman offer what shelter they can and even the church is made available as a place of refuge until other arrangements can be made, as indeed is the case with the village school.

# Chapter 2

The following day Swavesey is visited by newspaper reporters. Not just by the expected local paper reporters from Cambridge, St Ives or Huntingdon but also from the nationals such as the *Daily Mirror*.

The reporting proves to be extensive with the Daily Mirror being just one such instance of the national press taking an interest in the tragedy. *The Mirror*'s front page is given over entirely to a collection of five photographs showing the scenes of devastation and the plight of the inhabitants. Some villagers are shown carrying pieces of furniture down the street to some place of safekeeping – all that they have managed to save before their homes were engulfed in flames. Other villagers are shown in a state of despair standing next to their ruined homes that now comprise nothing more than heaps of debris. Individual tragedies are reported and explained, bringing the tragedy home to readers. There are photographs of Mr and Mrs Wright with their sole possessions now contained in just two small trunks and another of old Samuel Wilderspin who at the age of seventy-eight has lost not just his home but all his life's savings as well.

At the final count, it is reported that some sixty-three people, from twenty-two families, have been rendered homeless, and that a total of twenty-eight dwellings have been destroyed as well as a number of outbuildings. An appeal is launched to help relieve the plight of those devastated by the fire and the Reverend Sharp is proposed as one of the trustees. As tragic as the fire and loss of homes is, of greater importance to both the villagers, and to the readers up and down the country, is the miracle that there has not been one single loss of life.

As he is walking to work for his job as a delivery driver one morning, Phil Clowes' attention is caught by the arrangement

216

of photographs on the front page of the *Daily Mirror* and the headline:

## DEVASTATION CAUSED BY VILLAGE FIRE WHICH HAS LEFT MORE THAN SIXTY PERSONS WITHOUT A HOME.

Phil is not in the habit of buying a paper, as even at halfpenny a time the halfpennies do add up and his wage as a delivery driver does not stretch very far. In fact, even though Phil would be more than content to attend church less times than he does, he has to go to the Sunday morning and evening service at a church nearby where he earns a few extra coppers working the bellows for the church organist. This way he can keep his father happy and earn a few pennies at the same time.

Phil brings the newspaper home with him that evening and leaves it on the table. When his father comes home having performed his mission in the East End after work, his father picks up the paper.

'Who bought the paper then? Was it you, Phil?'

'Yes, Father. I just wanted to read more about the story of the fire. The paper is saying that it is a miracle that not a single life was lost.'

Glancing at the photographs of the after-effects of the fire, Arthur agrees. 'Well, indeed. Something else to thank the Lord for. All we can do now is hope and pray for another miracle and that these politicians see sense and things in Europe can settle down. It needs just one spark in the wrong place and at the wrong time and just like this village Europe will be up in flames and brother man will be fighting brother man.'

'Do you think things are getting that bad, Arthur?' asks Caroline.

'I fear the worst, my dear. I fear the worst. We may soon be at war. We have a duty to our country, of course we do, but we also have a greater duty to God and God's Commandments and he tells us that thou shall not kill. If it comes to war I would hate to think that any of my sons would be taking up arms against their fellow man.'

# Chapter 3

For the homeless Harry and Kate Holmes and their children – Grace, Albert, Henry, Gladys, Jane and baby Bill – things need to be arranged until such time as they could find and rebuild a home of their own again. The family has to split up, with Harry staying with his brother and his family. Grace is provided with accommodation at the Manor House courtesy of Mr and Mrs Norman. Jane, who would soon be leaving school, is with one of her aunts and Kate, with the remainder of the children, moves back in with her father and mother.

Although she would never have wished for such a sad and tragic state of affairs, Grace starts to think that the turn of events might bring about a change in her life.

It is now almost three months after that fire back on the third of March and it being a warm spring Sunday afternoon the family has found a spot to sit down and catch up with each other. For some days now an idea has been growing in Grace's head. She waits for her moment to speak.

'It is going to be some time now before we can be under the same roof again. Mr and Mrs Norman have been so kind to let me stay with them but I think they want their house back to themselves. So I have been thinking.

'I am turned seventeen now and I have been in service with Mr and Mrs Norman for three years. I would like to see London just as Aunt Amy is doing. Would you let me go to London if Aunt Amy can find me a position? Even if Aunt

Amy and Uncle Bill have no room for me, then I could find somewhere nearby. Maybe one of the special boarding houses for girls or young women in service or maybe I can find a live-in position near to Aunt and Uncle. So you see, it's not as if I will be in London on my own. I really would like to see more of life than Swavesey, or what remains of it, and the other villages hereabouts. What do you say? Will you let me go? I can always come back home if things do not work out for me in London.'

'You have a good position up at the Manor House, Grace. There is many a girl who wishes they were as fortunate as you, Grace,' says her mother.

'I know that and I am not ungrateful but every day is the same and so will the next day be the same and the day after that and the day after that. Then if I do stay here and marry – and I have to say there is no one here that appeals to me in any way – and have a family of my own then that's me done. A country girl who has seen nothing of the world beyond these few parishes and the occasional trip in to Cambridge or St Ives on market days.'

'You have grown into a very pretty young woman, Grace. I would worry about you,' says her father. 'Just look what happened to your Aunt Amy! She left the village under a cloud having a child out of wedlock.'

'Harry Holmes! How can you say such a thing to your daughter and in front of all the others as well. You should know your own daughter better than that, so don't bring Amy into it. She made a mistake but she is married and now has two girls of her own with Bill. Grace, as far as I am concerned, and provided your Aunt Amy promises me to look out for you, then you have my blessing to try things in London. I am sure that Mrs Norman will give you a good reference and no doubt your Aunt Amy will help you to find a position. Why don't you write to her and see what she has to say? Harry, do you have anything useful to add?'

'No, I suppose not.'

'Good! That's settled that. Now I wonder if the Normans will be willing to take on Jane when she leaves school in a few weeks' time?'

Within the week a reply comes back from Aunt Amy and Uncle Bill. Of course Grace can come and stay with them for a few days. They are just so relieved that no one was killed or seriously injured in the fire. In the meantime Amy says that she now has another baby girl that they have named Gwen. Anyway, Amy will make enquiries at various agencies. Amy then goes on to say that it is more likely that Grace will find a good position as a young woman with good references and experience of being in service rather than as just another raw girl from the country who will have to be trained and shown what to do. She may even get a little more pay given that she has some experience and an expected good reference.

Although Grace is a little sad to be leaving her parents and her brothers and sisters behind, she is excited about leaving village life for London. In order to get the cheapest fare to the capital possible, Grace takes one of the very first passenger services of the day to Cambridge. She sees her cousin Steve on the platform and they are able to talk briefly until the train arrives, parting with a kiss on the cheeks.

'Goodbye, Grace. Look out for yourself in London, won't you? Give my love to Aunt Amy and to Uncle Bill. You'll be back before you know it. I promise you!'

'No fear! Bye, Steve, and you take care too.'

Grace finds herself a seat in an empty compartment. With the lighter mornings she is able to look out of the window across the all-too-familiar fields and meadows as the train with its small engine and three carriages slowly pulls out of the station and gradually picks up speed. It makes its way down the line stopping at other small station stops along the way before arriving in Cambridge. Grace has seen the large express trains to London at Cambridge Station on her occasional visits on market days. This time, though, she is to ride on one herself, knowing that Aunt Amy will be there at Liverpool Street Station to meet her and to take her back to her aunt's home close to King's Cross.

Grace is so excited that she nearly forgets that she has not had breakfast but then her stomach makes a noise to remind her. She then opens her package of bread and cheese while she waits to board the train that will whisk her to the capital of the British Empire.

As the train makes its way to London, passing first through a flat landscape of fields and pastures, there is little to bring Grace out of her reverie as she wonders again just what London will be like. Then as the train nears London and the country scene starts to give way to the sight of more and more buildings Grace takes more interest in the progress of her journey and the view from out of the window. She becomes somewhat disappointed when she sees how closely packed together are the houses alongside the railway line and how dirty everything looks. As the train starts to slow and pull into Liverpool Street, her disappointment is but a temporary thing and she becomes excited, even if this is tinged with a degree of nervousness about what lies ahead of her.

The train is full; indeed, if she had not boarded at Cambridge as soon as the announcement that the train was ready for boarding, she would not have found a seat by the window. She knows that Aunt Amy will be there to meet her but nevertheless with all the people leaving the train and making their way to the exit she becomes worried that she may not see her aunt. There she is! Close to the barrier at the end of the platform with what must be the new baby tucked inside the shawl she has tied around her neck. Then Grace sees a young girl clutching her aunt's skirts.

'My, my Grace, haven't you grown since I last saw you?! You are going to turn more than a few heads; I can see that coming. Here is my eldest, Laura – she's six – and here's tiny little Gwen. You will meet Lily my middle one when we get home. My neighbour is looking after her.'

'Hello, Auntie.'

'Come. Let's get you home. We walked here from home but we'll take the Underground Metropolitan Railway back. Much quicker than the bus and quite an experience for the first-time visitor to London. Besides, you have your bags with you and we are just a short walk from the station. This is the first time you will have been on the underground railway as well, isn't it, Laura?'

Laura, a bit shy in front of Grace, a stranger, merely nods her head.

'Then,' Laura's mother continues, 'when you are settled and I have seen to the little ones, we'll have a cup of tea and you must tell me about how my boy Henry is getting on, the fire and how people are coping and all the other gossip. That's a big difference between Swavesey and London. You know you can pass people in the street here and not know who they are and they may even be living just two minutes around the corner.'

# Chapter 4

For her first two weeks in London Grace stays with Aunt Amy and the family. She also finds, with Amy's considerable help, a position as a day maid with Mr and Mrs Prior in nearby Islington.

Grace and the cook, Mrs Thomas, are the only persons employed in the household, yet Grace finds that Mrs Prior is not over-demanding and, from stories Grace hears from Aunt Amy, who has been in service herself, she believes herself very fortunate to have found such considerate employers. Mr and Mrs Prior do not require her to bob or curtsey or call Mrs Prior 'Madam', and in company Mrs Prior does not demean or berate her servants as some mistresses do. Not at all. Mrs Prior is considerate at all times whether she is entertaining or she and Grace are on their own.

The two daughters attend a private school nearby as day girls. So, apart from early morning and late afternoon and evening until dinner is served and on Saturdays, Grace sees little of the girls, and when she does they are as pleasant and polite as their mother and do not treat her as a servant to be used but as a person. Grace has all day Sunday to herself.

The rooms occupied by Aunt Amy and Uncle Bill are not big enough to accommodate three adults as well as the children and Grace does not wish to impose on them any further. Mrs Thomas the cook is from Wales and she and her husband attend the local Welsh chapel every Sunday without fail. Mrs Thomas suggests to Grace that she should find accommodation at the Morton Temperance Guest House that specifically caters for young single women who are in service. The house is overseen and run by an unmarried friend of theirs who is also Welsh and attends their chapel. She acts as a sort of matron to the young women who are, as Mrs Thomas puts it, 'in her care'. Grace is very open to this suggestion as it was something she had been thinking about, or something similar, when she was still up in Swavesey. Nevertheless, Grace decides first of all to tell Mrs Prior of her intention. Mr Prior has left for his business and the two girls have left for school when Grace approaches Mrs Prior.

'There really is not enough room for me with my aunt and uncle. Mrs Thomas has suggested that I find a room at the Morton Temperance House where a friend of hers is the Matron. The accommodation is quite nearby so it should not affect my work here in any way.'

'Well thank you for telling me of your intentions, Grace. I must say, however, that I do not much like the idea of your returning to such a place in the evenings and your spending the evenings alone in your room or being tempted to venture outside. We are very happy, Grace, with your work and the girls like you as well. Before you make any arrangements let me speak to my husband this evening. If he is in agreement, would you like to take the bedroom at the back of the house and live in with us? As you well know, some evenings my husband has functions to attend in connection with his business and I might welcome some company. What do you say to that?'

'Oh that would be absolutely splendid and most kind of you. I don't quite know what to say.'

'Then just say yes, Grace. I have a feeling that we might become good friends.'

The following evening Grace collects her belongings from Aunt Amy's and moves in. As the weeks pass into months, Grace begins to feel she is one of the family. Sometimes of an evening, if Mr Prior has gone out and when the girls have gone to bed, Grace and Mrs Prior will sit together rather than Grace spending the evening on her own either in her room or in the kitchen. Grace may sometimes attend to some sewing or embroidery whilst Mrs Prior reads, but on some evenings they will chatter away most of the time. After a few months, as they become more accustomed to each other's company and when they are on their own, Mrs Prior encourages Grace to address her as Emmie. The friendship grows.

# Chapter 5

Some six months have gone by since Grace came to London. Grace's aunt and uncle, Amy and Bill, are sitting at home one evening and the girls have gone to bed.

'You know, Bill, I think we should introduce Grace to a young man. She is such a pretty girl and I think it better that we should try and find someone suitable for her rather than she run the risk of meeting up with a bad lot.'

'And knowing you as I do, I suppose you have someone in mind?'

Amy smiles back.

'Am I going to be told who it is?'

'You remember that nice lady from Laura's school? You know the one – the secretary who kindly brought Laura home when she took sick one day. Well, before you came home from your finishing your milk round, we got to having a little chat, it being coming up to her lunch break and all. I see her most days when I go and collect Laura after school has finished and sometimes in the mornings as well when I take Laura to school.

'Despite our differences of background and where we come from, Edith – that's her name, you know – and I have become quite firm friends. She is interested in what life is like back in Swavesey, after she read about the fire and all. I think I should ask her and her husband for tea one Sunday and ask her if she could bring her brother-in-law. She speaks about him so highly. By all accounts her husband's family are very respectable and the father is all tied up with religion and all. Now I am not that bothered with religion as you well know but it seems to me that it is no bad thing for Grace to be introduced to someone with such a background.'

'You sure you want to bring them here. It's not exactly Buckingham Palace.'

'They can take us as they find us.'

# Chapter 6

The following afternoon the two friends meet at the school gates. Edith was on gate duty.

'Hello, Edith. I was hoping to catch you this afternoon.'

'Hello, Amy. Is everything well with you? Why in particular are you looking for me this afternoon?'

'Everything is fine, Edith. Thank you for asking. Edith, I was wondering if you and Mr Clowes would do us the honour of taking tea with us one Sunday afternoon? My niece Grace has been in London for a little while now and both Bill and me would like to introduce her to someone whom we know we can trust. Grace is such a pretty young woman and we were wondering whether you could bring along that brother-in-law of yours that you sometimes talk about.'

'That is a very kind invitation, Amy. Is Grace also from Swavesey?'

'Yes she is. She is from one of those families that lost their home in the fire. That is one of the reasons why she came to London looking for work. She is now in service with a very nice family. Well, that is how it started out but so unusually they have adopted her in some kind of a way and she is not treated as a servant at all. I hope the fact that she's only in service doesn't present a problem.'

'Oh I shouldn't think so, Amy. Let me talk to my husband, and my brother-in-law of course, and I will get back to you as soon as I can.'

'That is very kind of you, Edith. Thank you very much.'

'Not at all, Amy, not at all. My, it looks as though it is going to start to rain any minute now. That seems to be the last of the children accounted for, so I suggest we both head off home quickly and try to avoid getting wet.'

The following Monday morning it is Edith who is looking out for Amy bringing Laura to the school gates. Edith is pleased to tell Amy that she has spoken to her husband,

Arthur, and he in turn has spoken to his brother, Phil, and that they are free to come to tea the following Sunday afternoon.

Amy has arranged for her neighbour and good friend to look after Laura and Lily for the afternoon and the baby is asleep in her crib in the main bedroom. Nevertheless, the parlour room that serves also as the room where the family eats and sits of an evening, is rather too small to accommodate six adults comfortably. With introductions complete, it is Edith that takes the initiative while tea is being poured and the cups handed round.

'Phil, Grace is from Swavesey. Her family is one of those that lost their home during the fire. You remember the fire, don't you? Of course you do, silly me! Why, you brought the newspapers that reported the story, didn't you?'

That is the start of a conversation between Grace and Phil. The others leave them to it and talk amongst themselves. It is getting towards the evening.

Edith finally thinks that they have matters in hand and smiling says, 'Amy, you, Bill and Grace must come to us for tea. Phil, you will come of course, won't you? How about next Sunday or the Sunday after that?'

'We will be delighted, Edith, thank you, Bill and me have already made other arrangements but I am sure that Grace will be delighted to take up your invitation. Won't you, Grace?'

'What a shame you and Bill are unable to make it but we will be happy to see Grace and Phil and we'll see her safely back afterwards.'

The friends' stratagem has paid off and the die is cast. Phil and Grace are at ease in each other's company and it is not long before they are walking out together and Phil is able to show Grace some of the sights of London. Sights that a country girl sometimes finds it difficult to take in.

Amy is delighted that her plan is working out.

# Part V
# The Coming of War

# Chapter 1

Arthur Clowes, in part through his concerns that a new and bigger conflict in Europe could inevitably pull in Britain but also because of his deep religious convictions and his belief in the sanctity of life, took a far greater interest than most men in European affairs and what politicians, leaders and rulers might be up to. Nevertheless, Arthur is only as informed as it is possible for any ordinary member of the public to be by reading the newspapers.

Brother Arthur is as ignorant and unknowing as everyone else about the recent behind-the-scenes attempts by politicians and rulers to prevent tensions boiling over as a consequence of the collapse of the Ottoman Empire. The difficulties are as a result of a dangerous mix arising from the various highly nationalistic claims and ambitions of powers such as Austria-Hungary, Serbia and Russia in that fairly distant and forgotten region of Europe known as the Balkans.

The ordinary man in the street has little or no notion of the extent to which the Government and the Establishment controls the press and thereby what is being reported or what appears in newspaper leader articles and in editorials. It is all so far, far away as well, so anything of this nature that does appear in the newspapers may not be read by those readers who are rather more interested in stories and news about events at home or elsewhere in the Empire.

Then there are so many people who do not buy a newspaper at all because, as far as the ordinary man and his family is concerned, life is about trying to find work and to earn enough money to feed, clothe and house themselves and they certainly would not break this habit because of hearing of events in Europe. Anyway, isn't it for the Government to look after such matters in remote and foreign lands? Moreover, when not all men, and certainly no women, have the right to vote, why should they be interested in what the Government is doing or not doing in relation to affairs in foreign lands?

It is only following the assassination in Sarajevo of Archduke Franz Ferdinand of Austria, the heir-apparent to the Austrian throne of Emperor Franz Joseph, and of his German-born wife, Sophie, Duchess of Hohenberg, that articles start to appear in newspapers. It is only then that British readers are alerted in detail about the risk of nations going to war as a result of the complex nature of European treaties and mutual-assistance pacts. Britain, too, is not without her obligations to come to the aid of others.

There then occurs a relatively minor incident in which some Serbian boats carrying reservists cross over the demarcation line on the river Danube and into Austro-Hungarian territory. Warning shots are fired by the Austro-Hungarian side to warn the Serbs off. The incident itself comes to nothing, but Austria's politicians and court officials, who want revenge for the murder of the Archduke and his wife and who believe this is what their emperor wants as well, seize on it as an excuse to declare war on Serbia. Germany then sides with Austria-Hungary, and then Russia – or rather its absolute monarch, the Tsar, in his country's name – sides with Serbia. As a consequence of this, because of what is called a 'Secret Treaty', France is compelled to side with Russia as a result of Russian mobilisation. Then just three days later Germany declares war on France. Europe is cast into the abyss.

Arthur arrives home early one evening, having decided for once not to undertake his evening's work in the East End. The newspaper he has been reading during the course of the day is now before him on the table neatly folded but in such a way that everyone can see the front-page headline. Grace has been said but most of the family are not concentrating on their evening meal but on what Arthur has to say.

'This is the most appalling turn of events. It is as I feared. The wrong type of spark in the wrong place at the wrong time is leading to Europe going up in flames. Not in my wildest imagination – or should I say nightmare? – did I think things could ever get this bad though. The European alliances are pitting so many countries against another set of countries and now all over the Continent brother man is against brother man. Now France and its allies are against Germany and its allies and Belgium is being threatened by Germany. It is inevitable now that Britain and her Empire will become involved. It will take a miracle to turn these events around.'

'If it is to be war, then you boys must promise me that you will do nothing rash. Phil, Aidan, you are lorry drivers. The army will need lorry drivers so you may be able to serve your country without taking up arms and killing. We are not there yet, though, so I ask that you bide your time.'

'What do you mean by not doing anything rash, Father?' asks Aidan.

'This has happened in the family before. There is, or rather I should say there was, a distant cousin of yours – he was called Arthur as well. Well, your cousin Arthur decided he needed adventure so without the knowledge of his father – that will be your great-uncle Frederick or Freddy as he was called – young Arthur enlisted in the army and went off to what was then the Cape Colonies to fight against the Boers. The only adventure he saw, apart from a sea journey, was a bullet in the back from a Boer sniper. Other than being drilled and being shown how to shoot he never saw the action he was hoping for. A young and foolish man and a waste of precious life!

'There may be plenty of young men such as those I encounter in my mission in the East End who are out of work and so desperate that they may see joining the army as a solution to their problems. Then there will be those young men that want to fight for King and Country. You are different from the likes of such young men and none of this is going to happen to you two. Do you hear me!'

Both Phil and Aidan just nod their heads in response. Caroline looks worried.

'What about Chris and Arthur?' she says. 'What with them both being married and Arthur having a young family to support. What will become of them? I don't want *any* of my boys to go to war and be injured or worse. At least, Greg and Ben here are far too young to fight.' She glances with maternal anxiety at her two youngest sons. 'It's time you were in your bed, Ben. Off you go!'

'Quite right!' Arthur replies. 'I will speak to them both tomorrow. No one knows how long this crisis will continue. Hopefully, if there is to be fighting it could all be over before Christmas and then we can celebrate the birth of Christ in peace and not when there is war and fighting going on.'

'Who are the Boers and where are the Cape Colonies?' asks Elsie. 'I have never heard of a cousin called Arthur before. We never seem to talk about our family ... well, except Mummy's family. Why is that?'

'Just finish eating your supper, Elsie, there's a good girl. There was a war that ended the year before you were born in a place a long way away in Africa. That is all you need to know. Ben! I said it's time for you to be in bed. Off you go this instant. Now let's change the subject to something nicer. When are you next seeing Grace, Phil?' asks Caroline.

'Next Sunday as usual. We seem to be quite taken with each other. When I can find enough money for the train fare Grace has promised to take me to Swavesey when she next goes home for a visit. Grace thinks it will be fine for me to stay with her widowed uncle and her cousin. It seems that there is already some building going on to replace the cottages destroyed in the fire.

'I've never seen the country or been on a train. I am looking forward to Grace showing me what life is like in the country. Grace tells me that there are places where you can stand and not see a single building for as far as the eye can see. Grace has told me about the river nearby and of the open fields and the meadows and of what the local people call the big sky.'

'Grace this and Grace that. Quite taken with her, aren't you, brother?' teases Aidan with a grin.

'I like Grace. She is very pretty,' says Elsie.

Phil continues as if no one has interrupted him.

'You know Grace has told me about her employer Mrs Prior and how, when Mr Prior is out for an evening, they will sit together and keep each other company. Mr Prior is an army reservist lieutenant. Do you think he will have to go and fight if war does break out?'

'I thought we were going to keep off the subject of fighting. Elsie, come help me clear the table, then Carrie can wash the plates and you can dry things.'

Germany refuses to recognise the neutrality of Belgium, and the headlines of the evening papers the following day trumpet that Britain is now at war with Germany.

# Chapter 2

At the time of the outbreak of war the British regular army comprised fewer than 200,000 officers and men and many of these were not fighting men. For Britain to launch its Expeditionary Force all the fit and able-bodied reservists need to be mobilised. This includes a certain Lieutenant Prior. It would be some months before an Expeditionary Force can be fully mobilised. In the meantime it is the duty and task of the regular army and some territorials to prevent Germany's advance.

Lieutenant Prior is called up, at first, he thinks, to assist with the preparation of the anticipated Expeditionary Force. He is told to report to a location that he should not even tell his wife Emmie about. He does not know quite when he will be back home, even for a short visit. In truth, he has soon embarked on a ship to France, for the Expeditionary Force is to see early action.

Emmie and Grace are sitting in the parlour one evening a little more than a week after Emmie's husband has reported for duty.

'Grace, I have a mind to take the girls and to go and visit my sister down on the south coast for a few days. I feel in need of a change of scene, and with Robert now away it will be good to get away from the house – for a little while at least. You can stay here of course. Perhaps a few days to yourself will allow you to see or do some of the things you don't usually have time for. Why, you could even go home and visit your family if that is what you want to do.'

'Yes, I would like that and I have promised Phil that I will take him back home to Swavesey sometime. Perhaps now is as good a time as any given all that is going on – that's if his employer can release him for a couple of days, of course.'

'So you and your young man are getting on famously, are you? Will we be hearing wedding bells sometime soon?'

'I'm far too young to think about marriage, well for the time being anyway. So, we will just have to wait and see what happens. I don't think either of us is in a particular hurry right now.'

'Can we try and make our arrangements for a fortnight's time? Phil works in the morning only on a Saturday, doesn't he?'

Grace nods.

'Then you can travel on the Saturday afternoon and even if Phil can only take one day off from work then you can travel back to London on Monday afternoon for him to go to work the following day. I shall probably stay with my sister until the Wednesday so you'll have time to make sure that everything is ready for our return home, if that suits you. I think this is an excellent plan!'

Emmie looks even more serious for a moment.

'I need you here with me, Grace, and I will need you with me even more when Robert has to go and fight.'

The plan falls into place. Phil obtains a leave of absence for one day, without pay of course. As soon as he has returned his lorry to the yard at the end of his Saturday-morning deliveries he makes his way as quickly as he can to Liverpool Street Station where Grace is waiting for him. Soon he is captivated by the view from the train window as he continues to question Grace about life in the country and about things in Swavesey in particular. His companion playfully tells him to be patient and to wait and see – and at that moment Phil realises just how much he feels for this beautiful and fresh young woman. He admits to himself that she is the one.

Phil has obviously heard about Cambridge and its fine university and feels it is such a shame that there is no time for him to see the place. The branch-line train for Swavesey and St Ives is due to leave within twenty minutes of their arrival in Cambridge and the railway station is not at all conveniently located to allow even a fleeting glimpse of what Cambridge has to offer.

'How many station stops, Grace?'

'Just the four, Phil, then we get out at Swavesey. You may be disappointed. There is not much to see. It is all very flat around here.'

'Will your cousin still be working at the station when we get there?'

'Why? Do you think you need a porter to carry that little bag of yours? You townies are all too soft. Just you wait until Monday and I will show you how a man can cut a field with his scythe in no time at all.'

They smile at each other at Grace's little jibe.

'Steve must be close to finishing work by now but I suspect that he will wait for this train to arrive, knowing that we intend to be on it. You know I didn't think I would ever miss this place but I do. It will be so nice to see everyone again. Tomorrow morning I will take you for a good long walk down along the river and along some of the pathways. That is unless you want to go to church in the morning – it is a Sunday after all.'

'Forget the church! To be out of father's sight is all the excuse I need to miss church for one week at least.'

'And, Phil, just one more thing. You are staying with my Uncle Ned tonight. Whatever you do, don't take up his offer of some of his carrot or marrow wine. You're not used to it. A few glasses of that and you will be flat out on your back and fit for nothing the following day and our little stay here will be ruined. I have seen full-grown men bouncing off the walls of buildings after they have been on Uncle Ned's evil brews. Ah, there you go! We're on the move at last.'

Phil receives a warm welcome from one and all, yet he is slightly surprised at people's lack of curiosity about what life in London is about. They just do not seem interested in much other than the way of life that they have.

The following morning is a bright one as it has only just turned into September and Phil and Grace go for their walk. As they walk arm in arm, they pass a particularly attractive thatched cottage in Black Horse Lane that Phil insists on staring at for quite some while.

'That will do me,' he says to Grace.

They continue their walk down through some fields and meadows passing the old windmill and they eventually find themselves at the riverbank where they sit down and rest a while. It is here that Phil, as he lies on his back, discovers what the local people mean by 'the big skies' hereabouts. Being so close to the river, that is known to flood on occasions, the land has not been worked. Lush reed beds eventually give way to the greenest grass that Phil has ever seen. Apart from the odd small tree, there is little for the eye to catch and that makes the huge expanse of blue sky, with just the occasional tuft of cloud, appear all the more amazing. Even from Primrose Hill on the brightest of days the London skies seem so dirty and so much smaller what with the plumes of smoke from the tanneries, breweries and other works and the shapes of buildings imposing themselves on the skyline. Phil lies back resting his head on his hands and tries to take this incredible sight in. It is not too long though until he finds his gaze is concentrating on Grace sitting beside him.

Time passes for Phil all too quickly. He has fallen in love with the place and with a certain country girl – his love for the latter is now a matter of unwavering certainty. Before he knows it, and much to his disappointment, they are back on the train for the return journey to London.

# Chapter 3

News is coming through that things are not going well with the war and all thoughts that things will be over by Christmas are dashed. Robert Prior writes to his wife to say that, following a reverse and the decision to retreat from Mons, he has been promoted to Captain. He does not tell her that this is because his previous captain has been killed. Robert jokes that, now he is not that far from Paris, he will at last be able to enjoy a good meal with a bottle of wine at the weekend. What Robert does not tell his wife either is that the German Imperial Army has now reached the outskirts of Paris and that he expects to be in the thick of things. Yet just several days later reports appear in the newspapers that the French and British armies placed along the banks of the Marne have halted the German offensive on Paris and that the German army has retreated.

Anxious to hear from her husband, Emmie looks forward to each postal delivery with a sense of nervous anticipation. At last a letter arrives but she quickly notes that the address on the envelope is written in something like her husband's hand but not his normal, strong handwriting style. Robert tells her that he has been injured. Nothing serious, just a scratch really, and that he hopes to be patched up and sent back into action very soon and that the great news is that the Germans have been pushed back some forty miles.

Robert Prior was indeed to return to active duty soon as the war develops into what becomes known as trench warfare. By this time those who were among the first and original combatants sent out to France at the outbreak of war as part of the regular British Army have all but perished.

Things back on the home front are changing as well. The Government has put British industry on a war footing. To Caroline's delight, her sons Arthur and Chris (one being a metal machinist and the other a woodworking machinist) are regarded as too important to Britain's industrial war machine to be sent to fight. As Kitchener continues to exhort men to fulfil their patriotic duty and join in the fighting, they start to receive bad looks in the street as much as to say 'Why aren't you over there fighting?'

Both Aidan and Phil are differently placed than their brothers. They are just lorry drivers and Aidan is still quite young even though he is a driver. However, their father continues to tell them not to do anything rash such as enlist in the army. Towards the end of the year Arthur uses his religious convictions as good reason to join the newly formed No Conscription Fellowship.

# Chapter 4

There is a knock on the door and Grace opens the door to the street and to the effect of a chill March wind blowing from the north. It is the sight that everyone on the home front does not want to see at their front door: that of a messenger boy in his uniform together with his bicycle.

'Does Mrs Prior live here?' asks the boy.

Grace merely nods and the boy hands over the envelope. She knows what this means. She quietly closes the door and goes to her mistress and friend who is sitting in front of the fire in the parlour and reading a book. Grace enters the room and Emmie looks up from her book. Seeing an envelope in Grace's hand, and knowing it is not the time for a postal delivery, all colour drains from her face.

'Oh dear God, Grace. Is this what I think it is?'

'He may be just badly injured. He was injured before.'

'Open it for me, Grace. Open it and read me what it says.'

'It is from the War Office … Oh Emmie! I cannot read this … It says that Captain Robert Prior was killed in action at … some place that I can't pronounce, on the tenth of March … It sends you the sympathies of the Army Council, but it's not even signed. The tenth of March – why, that's almost a week ago! Oh Emmie, what can I say to comfort you?'

There are tears in Grace's eyes as she cradles Emmie's sobbing head. The War Office notification letter lies face up on the carpet floor. The girls are due home within the hour. How are they to be told of their father's death and that they will never see him again?

A few days later another letter arrives addressed to Mrs Robert Prior. It is from the Secretary to Sir John French, Commander-in-Chief, British Expeditionary Force, in which, on behalf of his Commander-in-Chief, he expresses his sincere regrets and offers his sympathies over her husband's death. He goes on to say that she should be proud of her husband who was shot and died instantly whilst leading his men in the offensive at Ypres in Flanders. Her husband's body has been interred in a special cemetery so it may be possible to visit the grave once hostilities have ceased and the war is won.

Needless to say, such a letter is only sent to the widow because of Captain Prior's class and social standing and because he was an officer. The Secretary to the Commander-in-Chief, too, is only writing because the late Captain's senior officer lies in hospital badly injured and therefore is unable to perform such a duty himself.

Emmie Prior's world has been turned upside down. She and Grace are drawn ever closer together over the following months. All things considered – and there was a lot of crying – the girls show a remarkable resilience in the face of the loss of their father.

# Chapter 5

That first December of war was wet and miserable in London. The build-up to Christmas in the Clowes household was, as usual, slightly different from that of other families. Rather than looking upon Christmas as a holiday just for enjoyment, the accent is upon the need to celebrate Christ's birth at a time of war when it should be a season for peace and goodwill to one's fellow man.

With little discussion it is agreed that the family will not this year exchange even the simplest of gifts. Whatever they could afford, which was not a great deal, would go towards either buying the wool to knit things or making things up from material to go as gifts to soldiers and sailors away from their families. Although Arthur is averse to war and to fighting, he sees this sacrifice as part of his Christian duty.

For Phil it is a particularly busy time as he takes the opportunity of earning just a little more money by working the organ bellows at carol services as well as at his normal times of attendance. This, together with the expected requirement of him and other family members to attend church services at this special time of the year, means that there is going to be little opportunity for him and Grace to spend time together. As for Grace, she will not return home for Christmas but she will spend her time with Emmie Prior and the two girls. For the latter, this is a time, as will all Christmases to come, when they will most deeply miss a husband and a father.

Strange stories begin to circulate back home in Britain – stories how, in certain parts of the western front, in the run-up to Christmas, British and German soldiers cease hostilities in order to recover and bury men lying in no man's land between the opposing trench systems. Some poor blighters are still lying in shell holes full of water or strung up on the barbed-wire barriers where they were gunned down. Then there are stories of carols being sung in the British and German trenches. Stories of German Christmas trees being hoisted onto trench parapets. Stories even of fraternisation between British and German troops as a heavy frost makes the muddy condition of the trenches more bearable and soldiers on both sides leave their trenches and come out into the open.

But there are other more terrible stories, how in other places the coming of Christmas changes nothing. The killing continues as snipers look to pick off men and yet more families lose a volunteer father, a brother or a son. Arthur knows from his mission in the East End that many such 'volunteers' are left with little choice. They either join the army or they receive no more poor relief! What choice do they have? Some are even Irish and do not wish to fight for

Britain and the Empire at all, but circumstances leave them with no choice but to be part of the British Army.

Despite their father's strong views, both Phil and Aidan feel under immense emotional pressure not to continue to sit the war out. The Government, and Lord Kitchener in particular, continues to press, with only limited success, for more men to join the army in ever-increasing numbers. As the wet new year advances, both Aidan and Phil see occasions while they are about driving their lorries where young women accost men in the streets and hand them the dreaded white feather to shame them into doing their duty to go and fight for King and Country. There is more and more public discussion about the army's need to introduce conscription with the Government suggesting that conscription should be limited only to single men and widowers without children. The intended passing into law of the National Registration Act with the purpose of recording details of everyone who might be eligible for service also influences Phil and Aidan's thinking. The two brothers need to decide what they are going to do. Not a discussion they can have at home.

'We need to find a way around this problem, Aidan. It matters not a jot what father says or thinks anymore. If we are forced to enlist then we could be sent anywhere. I just wonder that, because we are lorry drivers, if we went to the Recruitment Office then they may be able to take into account what we can do rather than just put a rifle in our hands. I think in your case it might be easier as you are under twenty and still what they call a teenager and teenagers aren't supposed to be sent to the front to fight. Though you're not a teenager for very much longer, are you? Just one more year and a bit. Why don't we go together and see what they say?'

'Agreed. We will just have to face Father down. What will you tell Grace?'

'I think it's best not to tell Grace until after the event. It is nearly the weekend, so why don't we go to the Recruiting

Office on Saturday afternoon. Until then, and until we hear what they have to say, we say nothing to no one. I am seeing Grace on Sunday afternoon anyway. Let's get home. I can do with something to eat.'

The brothers meet up at the Recruiting Office on The Strand a little before two o'clock on Saturday afternoon after they have returned their lorries to the yard.

'Ready?' asks Phil.

'As ready as I ever will be.'

The office is fairly empty. The levels of volunteer enlistments has slowed of late and there are only two other civilians and three men in uniform, one obviously having lost his left arm. Each of the civilians is being attended to by one of the soldiers and a sergeant seizes upon them as soon as the two brothers enter the door.

'Welcome, lads. Come to serve your country! That's what we like to see.'

'Well, actually, Sir, we were hoping first just to ask one or two questions if we may,' says Phil.

'Officers are Sir. I'm a sergeant!' he barks. Then in slightly softer tones, he adds, 'What is it you want to know?'

'Sorry, Sir, I mean Sergeant,' begins Phil. 'My brother and me are lorry drivers and we were wondering if it might be possible if we are to sign up to find positions as lorry drivers in the army. The army must need lorry drivers, don't they? My brother here has been driving a delivery lorry for over a year now and he has yet to turn twenty. I've heard that men under twenty-one do not go to the front to fight but we both want to serve our country. Me, well I have been driving lorries for something like seven or eight years now' – he hopes the sergeant will be impressed with this slight exaggeration – 'and I know my way around an engine if my lorry happens to be playing up. So I would like to keep to driving a lorry if I can. I am sure I would be useful to the army.'

'The army will tell you what you will be good for, not you.

245

As for you' – the sergeant touches his stick against Aidan's chest – 'so you are not old enough to fight, are you? Well, we won't be sending you to the front line to fight just yet. And you' – this time the sergeant touches his stick against Phil's chest – 'you are not the biggest specimen of manhood I have seen but you are a damn sight better than some that I have seen. Why have you left it so late to come and enlist?'

'Well, Sergeant, my father has very strong religious convictions and ...'

'A bloody "conchie", is he? Bloody conscientious objectors! I would line them all up against a wall and shoot the whole bloody lot of them.'

'It's not like that, Sergeant. He is fifty years of age and I am sure of no use to the army, but you see he is a lay brother of the Benedictine Order of the Old Catholic Church and he has taken vows to keep God's laws so he does have strong views against killing.'

'You two are sons of a Catholic monk. Now I've heard it all. Bloody Catholics and bloody Irish stirring up trouble in Ireland when the country and the Empire are at war.'

'No. no Sergeant. He is not a Roman Catholic but an Old Catholic lay brother; there's a big difference ...'

'Don't interrupt me, lad. You do that when you are in the army and you will cop it. Now, I don't make the decisions but I am sure' – he puts an arm over their shoulders – 'that you, me and the army can come to some sort of understanding if I write the right words down. So, what do you say? Enlist now and things will be as right as nine pence.'

Rather swept away by the sergeant's words and his force of presence Aidan and Phil look at each other and nod.

'Capital, capital,' says the Sergeant. 'Now let's get this paperwork sorted out and all you need do then is pop into that room back there for a short medical examination and within a day or two you will receive instructions on where you should report to.'

Half an hour later they are back out on The Strand.

'Well, that's torn it, we best go home and face the music. I wonder what Father is going to say? He is going to be livid, I bet,' says Aidan.

'You know it is about time we stopped being afraid what father might think or say. We are grown men now. Chris and Arthur have had the sense to fly the nest and get away from him and now *we* can as we are joining the army. I'm more frightened of what I am going to tell Grace tomorrow and what I am going to ask her.'

'Going to pop the question, are you? Good for you and good luck. I'm sure she will say yes.'

'Just keep that to yourself for now, Aidan.'

As it turns out that night things are not that bad. Father is expected home late as usual from the East End so they break the news of what they have done to the rest of the family, putting things in a reasoned way and explaining why they have done what they have done and why they have done it now rather than wait for conscription to be introduced. Caroline takes things well and does not argue the point.

'I think it best if your father hears it from me first. I actually think you have both done the right thing and I am sure your father will come round to that way of thinking as well. You know his bark is worse than his bite and underneath he really is a dear man. I should know – I have been married to him some thirty years now. Oh, he has his ways and he can be very stubborn indeed on certain things such as being against drink and all sorts of things about religion. He just doesn't know sometimes how to show how he really feels. Him being against any of you boys going to fight in the war is not just all down to his religion, you know. Oh, it's a very big part of it of course, but mostly it's because he doesn't want anything to happen to you in just the same way as I don't. Your father will be in soon so why don't you both go and stretch your legs somewhere and by the time you come back in things will be settled. I'm sure they will.'

Indeed, their father does not prove difficult and is in fact quite reasonable about it all.

Still, Phil hardly sleeps that night. He is scared. Scared that Grace may not give him the answer that he so dearly hopes for.

# Chapter 6

Aidan and Phil receive their instructions to report for army service. They had hopes to be joining the same regiment or unit but that is not to be. Aidan is to report to Dover for almost immediate embarkation for France where he is to be a driver in the Royal Field Artillery. He may not be in the trenches and given a rifle but he will, it seems, be in the war zone, although at first it is quite unclear as to what his driving duties will involve.

If Aidan was unclear as to what his duties will involve, then Phil was even more in the dark. He is to report to Epsom Barracks where he will undertake duties as a member of the Army Service Corps. He knew enough to know what the Army Service Corps is about. No army can fight a war without food and supplies, equipment and munitions, but why should he be sent to Epsom? He is anxious to know what part he has to play.

Everyone now hated the Hun. The newspapers and certain cartoons did nothing to improve the public mood in this respect. Shops and premises owned by Germans, or bearing anything that looks like a German name, continue to be attacked, and long-established businesses owned by even naturalised Germans go out of business as no patriotic Britain is willing to be seen to be dealing with them. Many

Germans, and some Austrians, are interned and they are perhaps safer for having been so.

Events earlier in the year such as the sinking of the unarmed liner *Lusitania* off the coast of Ireland, as she was bound for Liverpool, with the loss of nearly 1,200 souls, and before that the first Zeppelin bombing of London's docks, have fanned the flames of hatred. Why, things were such that when there is an outbreak of German measles amongst some of the children at Ben's school everyone is under instruction to refer to the ailment as the 'Belgian flush' and not by the other 'unacceptable name'.

The war has brought much-needed work to the docks and to those enterprises supporting the docks. Men join up either out of economic necessity or in some cases because they have been caught up in the initial wave of patriotism. These factors have led to unemployment being less of a problem than it used to be but this did not result in Arthur's mission becoming any easier.

There was considerably less call upon Arthur's services as a master bookbinder but now he is the only one left who could bind a book in the traditional way. One of the younger women who used to cut and fold pages and make up the signatures has left just a week before, saying that she can find better money now elsewhere and support the war effort as well. Arthur spends less time at his place of employment and more time supporting his mission. Whilst his employer was supportive of Arthur's mission work, that did not extend to keeping him on the same weekly wage as he was working fewer hours and the traditional side of the bookbinding business was barely holding its own. However, the owners did not want to lose the cachet of being able to offer a bespoke bookbinding tradition.

Leaving aside the varied mixture of immigrant communities that Arthur has limited contacts with, most people in the East End are hard, rough and uncomplicated people who have a tough time in life. They see things in black and white and they see things for what they are. As Arthur had realised some time ago, they are not the sort of people who generally have the time or inclination to think about God and religion. Now with the increasing numbers of war dead and with seriously injured casualties being returned home – war wounded who may never be fit for work and employment again – Arthur's work takes on an increasingly pastoral nature. He found himself working alongside people from other religious persuasions and institutions, alongside the likes of the Salvation Army and a number of semi-formal and informal volunteer groups largely set up and run by middle- and upper-class ladies. In some parts of the country, religious observance and church attendance has increased, although from what Arthur hears from his Order, this does not mean that there is an upsurge in religious belief. Down here in the East End things seem to be going more in the opposite direction with an attitude of mind along the lines of 'If there is this all-seeing God that cares for us, then why is He letting this happen?'

Things are at a worrying stage for the British Government in Ireland. Just before the outbreak of war it looked as though there could be civil war in Ireland over the question of self-determination and the intent of the British Government to impose what is known as 'Home Rule'. The Protestants in the north of the country were prepared to fight against the prospect of Home Rule and a clash with nationalist forces demanding full independence for Ireland looked a real danger. Whilst the Westminster Parliament did pass legislation to bring into effect Home Rule, the whole process was suspended with the outbreak of war.

Irishmen of both Catholic and Protestant persuasion are volunteering and enlisting in the British Army. However, there is a determined faction on the nationalist side who are implacably opposed to aiding the British cause in any shape or form. The Government is picking up intelligence that the nationalists opposed to helping Britain and determined to stay at home were preparing to rebel against the British presence in Ireland, even to the extent of seeking Germany's assistance.

Government and military planners are looking not only in the direction of Western Europe and across into Central and Eastern Europe and into the Balkans, but also on into Asia Minor and the Middle East (where Turkey holds sway, a country which has sided with Germany and its allies). The opposing powers also have a presence in Africa as well. They also look towards Ireland – the backdoor needs to be guarded too and insurrection in Ireland could seriously jeopardise Britain's cause. This backdoor problem can only be resolved by having an enhanced military presence in what many Britons still consider to be home soil.

In his first few months in the Army Service Corps, Phil is transporting by lorry all sorts of equipment and materiel, mainly to the ports. He drives back with the more seriously injured soldiers from the front in need of hospitalisation in England as they are unlikely to be able to be simply patched up and returned to the trenches. All sorts of rumours are doing the rounds amongst the men of the Army Service Corps in Epsom Barracks, where they are but a small part of the ever-changing make-up of barracks life. One of the less exotic rumours is one that Phil thinks has been started by a fellow comrade – an Irishman from the north of that country. This rumour is that the unit will be sent across the St George's Channel into Ireland.

# Chapter 7

Emmie Prior and the two girls, or young ladies as they now prefer to be considered, board the train, having found themselves a second-class compartment. They are not aware that at the rear of the train in a third-class carriage sits a private soldier together with his mother heading for the same destination as they are and that their reasons for making the journey are the same – well, except for one major difference as far as Phil is concerned.

Emmie has bought a newspaper to glance at during the journey. The girls, as appropriate for young ladies receiving a private education, are seated opposite their mother trying not to show how excited they are about the journey and what lies ahead. The train journey itself is quite an adventure, besides being another, but still somewhat rare, opportunity to leave London behind even if only for a short period of time. With more than ten minutes to go before the train is due to pull out, Emmie starts to glance through her newspaper.

'There are far fewer pages these days,' she says to no one in particular.

There has been very little news from the front for the past few weeks. Not since the start of fighting around Verdun. Emmie's attention is drawn, though, to the leader with the headline comment:

THESE COWARDLY CRIMINALS MUST PAY

The editorial describes the inhumanity of the enemy and its pitiless use of chlorine and phosgene gas against British and Allied men. The editorial goes into some distressing detail about what happens when a man inhales phosgene gas. Upon inhalation, the gas is turned into hydrochloric acid in the lungs and this causes the lungs to start to fill up with fluid. Some unfortunate souls may die an agonising death almost straight away as the lungs become inflamed and filled with fluid and victims die from suffocation. More often than not, though, victims of these ruthless enemy gas attacks suffer severe bouts of coughing and nausea, which then subsides for just a little while. Next, as soon as the victims exert themselves, their condition worsens. As the body tries to combat the effects of gassing, it produces more fluid in the lungs and death is then caused by 'drowning'. The editorial ends with the exhortation that the whole world should rail against German evils and that it is about time that the United States of America lived up to its responsibilities to fight against tyranny and join in arms against Germany and its allies.

Emmie keeps her thoughts to herself and very nearly feels like being sick herself from what she has read. She lays the paper to one side and she is overwhelmed by a feeling of loathing for the Germans. They have killed her husband and almost every day she reads details of German atrocities. *It is so right that they have now brought in conscription for unmarried men,* she thinks to herself.

With the gentlest of double jolts the train starts to ease out of the platform at Liverpool Street on its journey to Kings Lynn. Next stop for this early-morning express service is Cambridge. When the train reaches Cambridge, Emmie and the girls alight and head for the ladies' waiting room. It is half an hour before their next train is due to leave and it is far more pleasant to be out of the cold March wind and to use the facilities before they return to the buffet room for a cup of tea.

The buffet is fairly crowded with men in uniform presumably waiting for the next train to depart for London. Emmie is looking for somewhere to sit before ordering cups of warming tea.

'How unlike the Lyons Corner House. Here you have to go to the counter to get served.'

'Let me get you all a cup of tea, Emmie. There is room over there on my table where Mother and my younger sister are sitting'.

'Phil! You must have been on the same train as us! I had no idea. I thought you must have come up yesterday.'

'I had difficulty enough getting a pass as it is, Emmie. I only have two days' leave as it is. It looks as though my unit is shipping out. Seems they are expecting some sort of trouble in Ireland and that is where I am being sent.'

'Oh Phil! Just two days! That gives you and Grace hardly any time at all together. Still you must both make the best out of what you have. Looks as though we will have a dry day, even if the wind is rather on the cold side. I am so delighted that both of you asked me to be a witness at your wedding. Grace has been such a comfort to me since I lost my dear husband. I can't tell you how much I have appreciated her companionship. Well, now that you are leaving for Ireland there is no need for her to move out. She can stay with me until you have finished with Ireland.

'Oh dear! How selfish of me! Poor Grace. Does she know that you are leaving so soon after your wedding? Now don't you worry, Phil. Grace and I will look after each other while you sort out the Irish. And the girls will, too. We will all keep Grace company and you will be back home before you know it. Now what was that you said about a cup of tea? I am feeling rather dry and we can't have that long before the train leaves for Swavesey.'

# Chapter 8

Grace looks amazing in her white bridal dress with a cream belt adorned with a flower posy around her slim waist and with her white bonnet trimmed with a red ribbon. Grace is given away by her father and St Andrew's Church is well attended by the Holmes and Carters, the bride's father's and mother's families respectively. Phil wishes that more of his family other than just his mother and young sister Elsie could have come up to Swavesey for the wedding but then it is wartime and there is the cost of the train fare to consider.

The couple pose for a formal photograph after the wedding ceremony. Grace sits in an armchair with an elbow resting on one of the arms of the chair and with her head resting on her hand.

'No smiling, if you please. This is not a family snap and I have my reputation to consider,' requests the photographer.

Much to the exasperation of the photographer and despite his pleas for the groom to look a little more relaxed, Phil stands at Grace's side looking like a wooden dummy in his soldier's uniform.

Great strides have been made in replacing the buildings burnt out in the fire but too many people's fortunes have yet to recover. It is particularly hard for the older folk who lost their homes, possessions and life's savings despite the public appeals and the fund set up to help them. Unknown to both Grace and Phil, Emmie Prior has arranged and paid for refreshments to be had at The White Horse where Grace and Phil are to spend their wedding night before Phil returns to Epsom Barracks the following day.

Caroline is amongst strangers but is made welcome. She notices though that Elsie seems to have struck up a friendly conversation with one of the boys in the wedding party.

When the chance arises Caroline asks Grace, 'Who is that boy that my daughter is talking to? They seem to be having a right old natter, don't they.'

'Why, that's my brother Henry and yes they do, don't they?'

Caroline, Elsie, Emmie and the girls are to return home to London later that afternoon and Phil the following morning. Grace, though, will stay on another two days in Swavesey before she returns to her room at Emmie Prior's.

Phil manages to secure a day pass the following Saturday and Grace meets him off the train at Victoria. As they are in a public place, Phil just kisses his wife on the cheek.

'Sorry, I am a little late, Grace. The trains these days seem to run to please themselves. So annoying when we have so little time together. I must be back at camp no later than eight o'clock this evening.'

'Oh Phil! Why so soon? Other men going off to fight seem to get two or three days' leave. Why is it you just get the one day, and not even a whole day at that? When do you leave for Ireland?'

'I think the army sees a big difference, my dear, between men going off to France, a foreign country, and the likes of me being sent to Ireland; the army still thinks it's the same as serving anywhere else in Britain. They probably think that Ireland is a soft posting compared to the poor buggers being sent to fight in the trenches. As for when we leave, well, my unit is due to leave for Kingstown on Friday. Kingstown is the nearest port to Dublin and as far as I know that is where our unit is to be based, although I guess by the very nature of the Army Service Corps we will be sent all over the place. Look, we don't have that long together so let's forget about the army and the war and Ireland for the next few hours. How have you been? Any news or new developments?'

'Quite a lot actually since I arrived back from Swavesey. It seems that Emmie has been doing a lot of thinking and wants to do something to help the war effort. I am glad in a way because it might be a sign that she is healing after the loss of her husband Robert. She has got herself involved with the setting up of the Women's Institute. It will be interesting to see what Emmie ends up doing. She is more than capable of handing out tea and sympathy to the injured men being sent back home and perhaps the WI, as Emmie calls it, can find other practical things to do as well. No chance of Emmie doing munitions work or working in a factory of course or even her becoming a clippie on the buses but at least she is now trying to do something.

'What's more, Emmie knows that our current arrangements can't go on as they are. So we have reached a decision, or rather Emmie has and I agree. We can't run the house as before as if nothing has happened. Emmie is going to be out most of the day and the girls are at day school so they don't need both me and the cook to look after just the three of them. So, Emmie is going to let us go and have a woman to come in and clean every morning except at the weekends.'

'So what are *you* going to do now then?' asks Phil.

'I'm going back home, Phil. I could not see myself working in a factory and I have told Emmie this, even though she is prepared to let me stay with them without paying for my keep. Emmie is rather upset that I will not be staying but I think the way things are I should go back home.

'The Government is telling us women that they need women to help work on the land and support food production and at least I know one end of a cow from another and I know a little about farming ways and country life. The thing is that I also know farmers and the way they think about women and women workers in particular. Some farmers think we are unable to do a man's work and they would rather use boys and old men to do the work ahead of us. One or two back in Swavesey are not quite so bad, though, so that's what I am going to do. I am going to try and find some land work. I think it's for the best, Phil, particularly as you are going over to Ireland. Mind you, at three pence an hour, or four pence if I am lucky, I won't be rushing off to buy a new hat even if I could find one in the shops. Do you know how often you will be allowed back home, darling?'

'One of the younger lads asked the sergeant that very question. He got his head right bitten off. The sergeant put him on latrine duties this weekend with no chance of a pass just for asking the question. "Not even shipped out yet,' the sergeant barked, "and you are asking when you can come back home to your mummy."'

257

I was talking later to one of the older lot who has been with the ASC longer than I have. He reckons that we should have ten days' leave every four or five months. Mind you, that ten days includes the time it takes to get home and get back again but it seems that even that is going by the by. He has a brother in France and he has not been home for nine months and doesn't know when he will next get back home to London. They are rotating the men so that they are not on the front line or in the trenches all of the time but they are only being sent a few miles back for a short rest before being sent back again. The officers, of course, are different. Bloody officers are always different! When it comes to their turn to be rotated they are allowed to go to Paris and dine out posh with a bottle of wine. We will just have to wait and see what happens, Grace. Now come on, I thought we were going to try and change the subject. Let's talk about what we might want to do once all this mess is over. Let's talk about where we'll live and start our family. Even if it's only dreams of what we want to do, let's make this our dreamtime for the few hours we have left together.'

Grace puts her arm through his and they walk off towards St James's Park with its view of Buckingham Palace. After tea and a bun in the park, it is all too soon before the couple have to make their way back to Victoria Station. As many other couples are doing, decorum is forgotten and they hold each other and kiss goodbye properly.

It is with a very heavy heart that Phil boards his train, in the knowledge that he may not see his beautiful and dearest new wife for quite some time.

# Part VI

# Across the Water to Ireland

# Chapter 1

*ASC Motor Transport Corps*
*Dublin*
*6 May 1916*

*My dearest Grace,*
*I am sorry for not writing for some little while. You find me fit and well although very tired at the moment. I am trying to write to you in my bed before going to sleep and hopefully dreaming about when we can be together again.*

*As you can imagine, things have been rather lively over here of late. Any sympathy I did have for the Irish and for the call for independence as opposed to Home Rule has gone away completely. The word going around here is that what they call the Irish Republicans opposed to a British presence in Ireland are taking arms from the Germans to use against the British Army and the police here in Ireland. It is even said that Casement was arrested because he has been negotiating with the Germans to send an expeditionary German force over to Ireland to help the Republicans fight against us. I hope they hang him for this. I assume you are already getting to hear about this back at home but we have started to execute some of the captured rebels by firing squad.*

*Now I do not want you to be alarmed. As I said, I am safe and well. I was, though, caught up in the rebellion in and around Dublin over the Easter week. Now that the British authorities over here have cracked down hard and arrested the ringleaders I hope things will be a little bit quieter around here for a while. We certainly have far more men over here following the reinforcements coming over from England and down from the barracks up in Belfast. Yet despite these reinforcements the treacherous rebels inflicted too many casualties, particularly amongst the Sherwood Foresters and the South Staffs.*

*Not just me but the entire Motor Transport Corps have been run ragged, and we catch just an hour or so sleep here and there when we can. Despite the railway, with all these men coming in to quell and secure the situation we have been running men, kit and equipment all over the place. Then when the fighting got worse our trucks were needed to move the casualties so that they could get treatment. There are not enough ambulances to deal with this sort of situation. From what I know, in the space of a week we lost over one hundred men and well over 300 and maybe getting on for 400 men have been wounded. Some of our dead and wounded are Irishmen themselves and this includes the lieutenant who I was with at the time.*

*It was the Saturday after the Monday when everything had sparked off. I had returned with three other lorries to the port of Kingstown, having earlier delivered a full load to the Portobello Barracks. While our lorries were being loaded up again, me and my mates were having a quiet smoke trying to stay out of the way and not be seen in case we were roped into loading our own lorries. Anyway, there we were when this young officer comes up to us. I did not recognise him at first in the dark but them when he stepped into partial light I could see his ASC insignia and it is then that I knew him to be my Lieutenant Purser. He told me that Major Acheson, also of the ASC and an officer I have never even seen, had taken his car and his driver and so he needed a ride back to Dublin in one of the lorries. He asked which of the lorries in our little convey would be in the lead. I told him that, because of the way we were lined up, that I would be the first to drive out. Then he told me that he would ride up in the cabin with me. Then without another word he climbs up into my cab all ready and waiting to be on his way.*

*When the loading was finally completed we started out from the docks on our way back the ten miles or so to Dublin. We had been driving for some fifteen or twenty minutes and not a word had passed between me and the lieutenant. Well, what would I say to an officer? And he certainly wouldn't want to hold any conversation with a private. It was then I could see with the aid* of the lorry lights some sort of obstruction in the road ahead. The road had been empty in both directions and I did not like what I saw. 'Sir, I'm not stopping,' I said and I put my foot down to the floor but with such a heavy load all that did was make the engine work harder and we gained no speed at all. As we got closer, I could see some men alongside the road. I just crouched down behind the wheel as best I could and kept on going. Then there was the sound of gunfire and the next thing I knew I was covered in glass. Whatever it was that they had put in the road as some sort of barricade my lorry crashed through it and I continued to keep my foot hard down on the pedal. From what I could see in my mirrors, the other lorries were still following me. 'Sir!' I shouted, 'Sir, are you hurt?' There was no answer so I reached out my left hand to touch him and he fell forward. I could not tell whether he was dead or alive. All I could do was drive as fast and as best I could and get him to a hospital.

We were later told that he died of his wound the following day. He was only twenty. At the same time we were told also that the major who had taken my lieutenant's car and driver had also been ambushed and killed. They said nothing about his driver. Evidently the major was from a well-to-do Irish family with land and a grand house down in County Cork. Anyway, that was my little adventure over and done with.

Tonight is one of the few times when I have had the time to think about how different and quiet it must be back in Swavesey. With spring coming on I can't think of anything I would like better than to be walking over the fields and down to the river and wondering at those big skies of yours before returning to what I imagine home could look like and closing the door and shutting the world and everything going on out and enjoying being together. Well, that's the last of my writing paper.

   All my love
   Phil.

*Swavesey*
*17 May 1916*

*My dear,*
*Your letter only reached me yesterday. I have been worried ever since I heard about the Irish rebellion and I have been trying to find out the latest from the newspaper but not a lot is being said. Casement's trial has started and that is taking up most of the space in the papers along with useful hints for the housewife. The latest thing now that meat is rationed is a recipe for War Time Pudding. What do these people think we do? Have meat seven days a week! All this War Time Pudding is is a suet pudding made out of vegetables and an Oxo cube. Perhaps townies and the rich do eat different from us ordinary folk but we know how to make a little go far out of years of necessity and we do not need the Government to tell us how to get by, thank you very much.*

*All is well here in Swavesey and everyone sends their love. I get the odd short note from Emmie telling me how busy she is with the new WI and her other works. I have not heard from your family so I hope Aidan is safe and well in France.*

*I am now given more work to do on the farm now that married men have been conscripted and I have to say that, although the hours are long and the work is hard, I think I do as good as most men. Yet the old skinflint still only pays me three pence an hour.*

*The Red Cross has opened up a Voluntary Aid Detachment Hospital for soldiers returning from the front at the Old Manor House here in Swavesey. You can see some of the men sometimes walking down the street. What horrors they must have seen and been through. Some are clearly so traumatised by their experience and suffer terrible fits of shaking or jump out of their skins at the slightest sound, not to mention those showing symptoms of gassing, including some who have been blinded. It may be dangerous where you are but I would rather you were there than over in France. The village has lost too many of its sons already and there is no end in sight yet.*

*I wish you were here too, my darling, but there is no point wishing for what we cannot have. Emmie has agreed that when you come home on leave that we can stay at her house and that she will use the opportunity to take Emily and Laura and go and visit her sister. What a dear friend she is. Emmie says that you would lose too much time travelling back from Ireland all the way to Swavesey and back and that, given that you will no doubt wish to see your family, it makes sense for me to come to London when you are there. How thoughtful she is to let us have the use of her house when we have spent so little time together on our own.*

*I wish that you could get some leave and come home soon. When you do, then we will have no talk of the war or of things in Ireland. Please take every care of yourself my love and come back to us all safely.*

*Your loving wife,*

*Grace.*

*ASC Motor Transport Corps*
*Dublin*
*29 May 1916*

*My dearest Grace,*

*I was so pleased to get your letter. It is still far too soon for me to guess when I may be allowed some leave back home in England but when I do staying at Emmie's house will be a delight.*

*We all sense a change here. The Government and the Commander-in-Chief cracked down hard on the rebels but the effects of the execution of the leaders of the Easter rebellion and the amount of destruction caused in the centre of Dublin seems only to have hardened the attitudes of the Irish against us being here. I am not one to go out drinking as you know but the lads that do go off barracks when off duty tell me that they feel an open hostility towards them out there on the streets.*

*Still, there are enough soldiers here now to prevent any repeat of what happened over Easter and ever since those incidents I have had a man with a rifle riding alongside me in the cab and I have a revolver in the cab as well. I feel a lot safer and in little danger so you must not worry yourself.*

*Your description of the War Pudding sounds more appealing than some of the meals we get here. What we get is of mixed quality, ranging from the just about acceptable to the inedible. We have been married over two months now and I am still waiting to try out your cooking. An ordinary married life, that is what I look forward to. Going out to work in the morning – I hope I can get my old job back – then coming home to your cooking in our own home. That is what I look forward to when all this madness in the world has come to an end.*

*All my love*
*Phil.*

*Swavesey*
*16 December 1916*
*Dearest,*

*The end of a terrible year! Months of bitter fighting at Verdun and on the Somme and now it is sinking into the ordinary man and woman just how much British, French and, yes, even German blood has been spilt and the number of lives that have been lost or ruined for just a few miles of blasted mud.*

*Christmas is upon us and we are still apart. It has been nine months since we parted. They must let you come home on leave soon surely!*

*Much love,*
*Grace.*

*ASC Motor Transport Corps*
*Dublin*
*9 January 1917*

*My dear,*
*Good news at last! I am coming home on leave and for a whole two weeks. All being well, I should arrive in London on the boat train early in the morning of the 16th January. Can you see how this fits in with Emmie and does she intend to still visit her sister in the middle of winter?*

*It has been so cold over here in Ireland for the past month. I imagine it is cold where you are up in Swavesey. I remember you telling me how cold it can be with those winds and sometimes how the pond can freeze over and people go skating on it. Much as I love the place I think I would rather wait for warmer weather before returning to Swavesey. As it seems that the trains please themselves these days, do not try and meet me off the train at Paddington. I shall make my way to Emmie's house and then we will have to start to get to know each other again after what seems such a long, long time.*

*I just can't wait to see you and for us to be together again at last.*
*All my love,*
*Phil.*

# Chapter 2

Emmie, Emily and Laura have been away for three days and are returning back home on the Saturday morning. Phil and Grace have had the house to themselves for almost three whole days. Grace can feel and see that army life and his experiences in Ireland have changed Phil to some extent, but after a few hours they became more relaxed and are able to enjoy each other's company and being on their own.

On the Friday afternoon before Emmie and the girls come back to London, Phil and Grace are visiting Phil's parents who have now moved out to Dagenham. Arthur has returned home from his mission work in the East End. Caroline, Elsie, Greg and Ben are there. Everyone is seated very close to each other around the table and Caroline is pouring the tea out from the pot. They will be eating later when Carrie returns from her shift at the munitions factory.

'How are you, Father? How are things at work and of course with your mission in the East End?'

'Good to see you home, son. It's such a long time since we were together and of course we all worry about Aidan over in France.

'I have very little to do at work these days. What with the shortage of paper, and what with so many of the professional gentlemen away fighting, I receive only the occasional commission. Things are tight but now that Carrie is working at the munitions factory and Greg is earning his first wages and with Elsie soon leaving school to find work, we are managing.

'How are things in Ireland? Whatever the rights and wrongs of us being in Ireland it disturbs me that religion seems to be the centre of all the troubles.'

Phil bridles. 'It is far more complicated than that. You can't just put it down to a matter of religion. In any case I am home for just two weeks and the last thing I want to do is talk about what I have left behind. Can we talk about something else?'

Caroline stops pouring out the last cup of tea and looks at Phil. She has never, ever heard him talk to his father in such a way before. Arthur also seems slightly taken aback but then just nods his head as if to acknowledge a change has taken place in Phil. He is now his own man and not just his father's son expected to do and run his life as his father sees fit.

It is Elsie who breaks the momentary silence.

'How are things in Swavesey, Grace? Are things still the same? How is Henry? Does he still remember me from your wedding?'

Grace smiles back.

'Nothing is the same any more, Elsie, and Swavesey is no different from anywhere else these days. I am sure that Henry remembers you. Henry is quite grown up now and he does all sorts of things. When he is not helping out on one or another of the farms or tending our vegetable patch, he does what he can at the little hospital we have to look after soldiers who have come back from France and who are hurt or not very well. Most of the hospital garden has now been turned over to growing things for people to eat and that is how he mainly spends his time there. When all this horrible business is over, Elsie, perhaps you can come up and see us all again. Would you like that?'

The conversation continues for some time with Caroline updating Phil on such family details as to how Arthur , Edith and their growing family are doing and Chris and Sarah and now their son, Chris, a nephew that Phil has yet to see.

'It would be lovely if the two of you can find the time to see them before Phil's leave is over. Both Chris and Arthur are working on making aircraft parts, you know, and are working all the hours that they can. They are the lucky ones – well I think they are – otherwise they may be on their way to the front as is happening to men who once thought they were in reserved occupations. Then they change the rules about what is a reserved occupation. Married or single, it does not matter – they have been conscripted.'

There is the sound of a massive explosion followed by a series of lesser blasts.

'What in heaven's name was that?' Caroline exclaims. 'Is it a bomb or something? Where did it come from?'

'No not a bomb and with all these buildings it is hard to

tell from which direction the sounds came from. Best to go outside and try and find out rather than just sit here and talk about it,' says Phil.

'Is that wise, son? What if there is another explosion? We might get caught up in it,' says Arthur.

'No I don't think so. It sounded to me that the explosion was some way away but a very big one. You stay indoors if you like, I am going outside.'

'I'm coming with you,' says Grace.

'And me!' says Ben.

'No, Ben!' says Caroline, 'you are staying right here.'

A number of people have had the same idea and have come out into the street to see what is happening. Arthur has followed Phil and Grace down the stairs, having thoughtfully brought Grace's coat with him to save her from the winter chill in the air. It's an act of kindness and consideration that does not register immediately with Phil.

'It will be those bloody Germans up to no good,' says a man not far from Phil. Phil ignores the remark, not wishing to get drawn into a conversation.

Then there is a fireball reaching far up into the sky that can be seen over the top of the houses in the surrounding streets. A loud roar and whooshing sound follows almost immediately.

'That came from down by the river,' says Arthur. 'It might even be near to the munitions factory but I can't understand what caused such a great fireball to happen. I must get down there. People may be hurt and in need of help or comfort. Oh heavens! Carrie! Carrie must still be down there.'

'When is her shift due to end?'

'It can vary. Sometimes she volunteers to work a little longer. The extra money is welcome but I sometimes wonder if it is because she is in no hurry to come home.'

'Whatever! I am with you, Father. Just let me get my coat.'

'My mission hall keys are on the side. Bring them down,

will you? I may need to open up tonight if things are anywhere near as bad as they look down there. Tell your mother that I may not be back tonight.'

'I am sure I can help as well,' says Grace.

'No, my dear,' Phil says gently. 'If we get separated, I do not want to be worrying about you as well as trying to find Carrie. If you don't want to stay here take the train back to Emmie's and I will join you there when I can.'

'I'll stay here then. Just be careful, both of you, and I hope you find Carrie safe and sound.'

Phil fetches his army overcoat and hands the keys to his father. The pair of them then set off down Warrington Road.

'Do you know how best to get there, Father, because I'm sure I don't.'

'We can catch the District Line from Becontree part of the way then get out at West Ham and then I guess we will have to walk the rest because the roads are bound to be busy if things are half as bad as they look. Come on, let's get a move on – Becontree is a fair old step from here as well.'

As the train gets nearer to their destination there is a glow low down in the sky down towards the river.

'Oh heavens above,' says Phil. 'Just look at that! Things must be terrible down there. It seems as though everything is alight.'

'It can only be the Millennium Mills munitions works down at Silvertown where Carrie works. They deal with TNT down there. Just look at it! There are houses right next to the place not to mention the warehouses as well. That fireball we saw earlier from back home must have been the gasometer on the other side of the river going up. If Carrie was putting in extra time when that lot went up, we have lost her to God for certain.'

As they come out from West Ham station all manner of vehicles are making their way down in the direction of Silvertown and the river. They, along with many others, make

271

their way as best they can, sometimes on the crowded pavements and sometimes in the road. As they approach the scene of devastation the spread and scale of the damage, not only to the munitions works itself, but for a very considerable distance around about, becomes all too clear. Firefighters are doing what they can to put out fires furthest away from the works but no one is going anywhere near where the works are, or what remains of them. There are already temporary barriers in place and special constables keeping people away. Phil nudges his way to the front and catches one of the special constables by the sleeve.

'We have come here to help. My father is a lay monk as well in case there are people in need of spiritual comfort. What about the people inside the works? Any news of them or where the injured have been taken? I am looking for my sister. She works there.'

'Not much you can do here, soldier, and I have orders not to let *anyone* through. From what I know, it being a Friday evening and all, there were not as many people in the works as normal. I hope you find your sister but it is these poor sods in the houses nearby that I feel sorry for. They should never have allowed a bloody munitions factory right on top of where people are living. Just look at it!'

'Do you know where they have sent the casualties or, God forbid, any bodies they have recovered?'

'No one is going near the place at the moment. There are still a few trucks in the sidings over the back and they could be loaded with explosives. We already have had one lot of trucks go up and no one knows for certain what's in those remaining ones. You can try the Royal London up in Whitechapel if you like and the Sally Ann is taking people in as is the YMCA. It's going to be a bloody cold night and people are going to need shelter and something hot to drink and something to eat.'

Phil was clearly not going to get anything more out of this

rather belligerent Special. He returns to his father and explains what he has been told.

'What do you think is best?' asks Phil.

Arthur spends a moment in thought.

'If Carrie was inside at the time of the explosion, then there is nothing that we can do about it. If they are afraid of further explosions, it may be a little while before they go in to look for any survivors, improbable as that may be, or recover what remains of those there when it all went up. Perhaps Carrie had already left if not many people work into Friday evening. She has never mentioned this to me, though. For all we know she might be back at home already, or she may have just left the works and was injured in the explosion and is up in the hospital.

'I need to open up my mission hall. It's a little further away than the Salvation Army mission but if I go there first I can ask them to send people on to me once they get full and hopefully any volunteer help that turns up. You know what some of these middle-class women are like, not much good for anything that's useful or which means them getting their dresses dirty. Well, they can make themselves useful tonight, that's for certain.'

'What about Carrie?'

'Your mother and brothers and sister will be worried enough if she is not at home by now. You going back with no news if she is not there will make matters worse. Go to the Royal first and see if she's there. If not, then come back to my mission. Do you think you can find your way from here to Whitechapel and from Whitechapel to the mission?'

'I'm not quite sure but I can always ask directions. Should we not do more to try and find Carrie?'

'And what do you propose? Walking the streets all night? Did you tell your mother that I may be opening up the mission?'

Phil nods.

'Well then. If Carrie turns up at home, your mother will

send Greg to the mission with news. If not, then we will just have to wait until the morning and find out what the authorities are doing. I will see you back at the mission.'

Arthur turns and walks away, leaving Phil standing where he is in the middle of the road. A blast from a lorry's hooter brings him up with a start and he sets off for the Royal London as instructed by his father.

Having taken a few wrong turns and asking for directions on a number of occasions, Phil at last finds himself at the Royal London. It seems that the priority is for the more seriously injured to be attended to first while those with lesser injuries have to bide their time. Phil's efforts to find someone who can tell him whether or not his sister is amongst those injured comes to nothing. Those casualties arriving unconscious can't tell anyone their names and even the names of those who are unconscious arriving with family or friends have yet to be registered; in any case everyone is so busy that they are hardly likely to have the time to give out such details. All Phil can do is to walk around the hospital in the hope of finding his sister alive, even if she is in need of attention. Phil's initial search is unrewarding. He then posts himself near to the main entrance in the hope of finding her amongst the casualties either arriving as walking wounded or on a stretcher. After around an hour of this Phil resigns himself to the fact that he is probably wasting his time. *What do I do now?* he asks himself. *Do I go back to the house in Dagenham or go to Father's mission? I wonder at what time of night the trains stop running?*

The debate he has with himself is only ever going to result in the one conclusion. He starts walking to his father's mission.

The mission hall is not particularly large and on the odd occasion when Phil has visited the place there has always been plenty of room for more people. Not tonight though. The place is crowded. Every chair is taken. Some are sitting on the floor with their backs propped up against the wall whereas others, mainly the men, are standing but leaning themselves against a wall. Phil casts his eyes around the room and can't see his father – so many people are obscuring his field of vision. As he eases his way through the room, he at last sees his father bending on one knee talking to a woman seated on the floor with her back resting on both walls in the far corner of the room.

As Phil approaches, in spite of what seems to be his father's close engagement with the woman, Arthur looks up with a semblance of a smile and nods in the direction of the other corner where there is a curtain covering the passageway that leads to the single toilet, a small kitchen with a gas stove, and the equally small room that his father uses when he has writing and other paperwork to do. Phil stands there without moving. Again his father nods in the direction of the curtain, this time accentuating the movement. Phil takes this as a message that he is needed back there in some kind of helping capacity. *Just what I need after running around all night long!* he says to himself. With a resigned shrug he makes his way across the room. He pushes back the curtain and there in the tiny kitchen with her back to him is Carrie!

After he has given her the biggest of bear hugs, Carrie explains how she was on her way to the station at West Ham when the explosion knocked her completely off her feet. When she finally gathered her wits about her, she got to her feet only to be knocked back again by a blast of hot air as the gasometer across the water went up.

'Well, I had to go back and see if any of my mates were hurt and needed help,' she blurts out and then she breaks down in tears.

'Come on, Sis. Let's get your coat and get you home before the last train goes. You've had more than enough for one night after a full shift. Let Father do what he has to do but you need a good wash, a nice hot drink and your bed.'

Over the coming days as the site of the explosion and the nearby ruined houses are searched and the newspapers declare that seventy people have lost their lives and that over four hundred people have been injured. Of these two or three people are very critically injured. It will take time, the papers said, to know the full extent of the damage but the number of properties damaged is likely to run into the thousands and in all likelihood anything between 800 and 1,000 properties closest to the former works will have to be pulled down.

The remaining days of Phil's leave pass far too quickly. Before they both know it, Grace is seeing Phil off on the train at Paddington for his journey back to Ireland before she makes her own way back to Swavesey.

Phil is not looking forward to his return to Ireland. Despite the freeing from prison of some of the Irish rebels some weeks back there is so much anti-British feeling. Some of this, Phil has to admit to himself, is as much the fault of the British response to the Easter Rising as anything else.

# Chapter 3

Events move slowly for the people back home. All too slowly for those who want to see an end to the fighting and the return of their loved ones. Of immediate consequence to those on the home front is the introduction of bread rationing. The newspapers rally public morale with reports of British victories in Baghdad and the British advance into Palestine, but what people want more than anything else is an end to the stalemate in Europe.

Aidan comes back home on leave but it is not long before he is sent for retraining as a gunner before being sent back to France.

One massive development and surely one that must at

long last tip the balance of the war in favour of the Allies is that America finally decides – some say over two years too late – to join in the fighting by declaring war on Germany.

*ASC Motor Transport Corps*
*Dublin*
*25 May 1917*

*Dearest,*
*In your last letter you talked more about events going on around you and how busy things are now that it is spring than about the thing I really want to know about – you! I hope I find you well and in good spirits and that our continued separation is not changing things in any way and how we feel for each other.*

*I dislike this place as it seems to always be wet and grey, but perhaps that is because I am missing you and I would rather be anywhere else as long as we had some time together. Things are so very much quieter here – well for the time being at least – but then with the number of soldiers we have on hand that is perhaps not surprising.*

*We are not all that cut off from developments both here in Ireland and at home. The Republicans – here called Sinn Féin – are gaining in influence and even Lloyd George is recognising that Home Rule for a large part of Ireland should happen sooner rather than later. The Republicans do not see Home Rule as an answer to their ambitions. They want complete independence for the whole of Ireland. My Protestant mates from the northern part of Ireland are spitting bullets over this idea of a separation from the rest of Britain. For my part I try not to think too much about it all. It does not pay for a soldier to dwell on such things. I am only a soldier after all and I must do what a soldier is ordered to do.*

*Please write soon. I often lie on my bed at night before going to sleep reading through your letters and trying to imagine what*

277

*things will be like when we finally manage to settle down in our own home.*

*All my love,*
*Phil.*

*Swavesey*
*30 May 1916*
*My dear,*
*Of course things are not changing because of our continued separation from each other. Quite the opposite in fact. How could I feel any differently towards the father of my forthcoming child! Yes, my love, you are going to be a father. At first I was not sure, given the little time that we have had together but there is no doubt now. It seems that I am about three months gone. I will obviously stay here in Swavesey until after our baby is born. There is no point in me going back to London until you and the army are finished.*

*I know we did not plan yet to start a family. Things will be quite difficult when it is time to set up home together but then it always has been difficult for young people in our sort of situation of just starting out. If others can do it, then so can we. I shall work as long as I can and I will pick and choose what jobs I do and what I will leave for others, for I will not put my baby at risk. The next best thing to having you here at a time like this is to be close to my dear mum and to have the rest of the family around me. If I was still in London, then I am sure that your family would be supportive and of course there is always the ever-busier Emmie, but Swavesey is where I want to be right now and with my own family.*

*If you have so much time on your hands then you can start thinking about what names you might like for our baby. If things are now quieter and stay that way in Ireland, I hope it will not be long before you can come home on leave.*

*Your loving and expecting wife,*
*Grace.*

# Chapter 4

It is a fine spring afternoon in May and Caroline is sitting with her feet up contemplating whether to venture out for an hour before it is time to start preparing for tea and Arthur's supper for later in the evening. Caroline is startled as the door, which she has left partially open together with some windows to allow fresh air to circulate around the house, opens fully and bangs against the wall as her daughter Hilda almost stumbles over the threshold.

Caroline pushes herself firmly out of the rather well-worn chair into which the occupant sinks far too easily and far more easily than it is to push oneself out of. She rushes to her daughter who is now leaning against the wall shaking.

'Hilda, Hilda, whatever is the matter? Why are you so upset?'

Upon which Hilda throws herself at her mother and buries her wet face on her mother's shoulder. Caroline knows that there can be only one cause for such distress. With one hand she guides her daughter more fully into the room and with the other hand gently pushes the door shut. As she then tries to walk her daughter over towards the table and to sit her down in one of the chairs, she sees in her daughter's hand a scrunched-up piece of paper. The tragedy of war Caroline knows has now struck at the very heart of the family. There are no words that can bring comfort and all Caroline can do is make ready the customary cup of tea that always seems to appear as a useless token of compassion in times of trouble.

When Hilda pushes the piece of paper towards her Caroline takes it and smooths the message out so that she can read it. The message is short and to the point: Hilda's husband of just two months, Rifleman C. E. Cousins of the First Battalion of the Royal Irish Rifles, is reported to have been shot and to have died of his injuries whilst serving in Belgium on 16 August 1917, just two days earlier.

Hilda's Charlie, a man whom she has known for only two months and whom Hilda has married without telling her parents, is dead. Charlie with his Irish charm swept Hilda off her feet. Caroline met him only the once after the couple married and three days before Charlie was to be posted to the front. The couple have spent just two nights together as man and wife. Arthur was furious that his daughter had married without his consent and to a man that she could hardly know.

It is not long before Ben returns home from school to be confronted by such a miserable scene. Caroline gently takes Ben to one side and briefly explains what has happened. She tells Ben to go to the mission and bring his father back home.

Hilda and her father have not been close for a long time and Arthur's fury at the marriage has made matters even worse. But Caroline thinks it best for the whole family to be together at such a sad time and to show support over Hilda's loss. She knows that her husband will do his best to support his daughter no matter what has happened in the past.

Hilda will have none of it. She needs to share her news and grief with her mother but not with her father. Despite Caroline's pleadings, Hilda leaves before her father can return home.

# Chapter 5

Arthur arrives home one evening some weeks after Hilda has come round with her tragic news. As usual, it is late into the evening and everyone else has had their supper. He spends most of his days there in the East End now as his bookbinding commissions have almost completely dried up.

Coal has been in short supply for some time, and before coal rationing was introduced it has been known for Caroline to take the old pram down to the coal merchants and queue for hours so as to bring some coal back to heat the home. With winter arriving early, the two hundredweight allowance allocated for a house of their size does not seem to go very far. Just the one fire is now lit in the sitting room and no fires are lit in any of the bedrooms. It is not down to gluttony that everyone looks on the podgy side. It is the additional layers of pullovers and cardigans that give the appearance of an overfed household.

'Good evening, my dear,' says Caroline. Greg, Elsie and Ben in turn repeat a greeting to their father.

'We have had a letter at last from Aidan,' Caroline tells him, taking a folded sheet of paper from her apron pocket and opening it up. 'He has been sent some miles back from the front for a short period of what they call rest and recuperation. The letter is short and does not make for happy reading. He writes mainly about the prolonged fighting around Ypres and Passchendaele, or what is left of those places after months of bombardment and fighting. He says that spirits are low after these months of fighting with so little to show for it all. He hopes that his hearing is not permanently damaged from the sound of the artillery firing off and then goes on to say that some of the guns are now worn out from almost continuous use.' Caroline turns the letter over and scans the scrawling handwriting.

'He seems to like the Canadians that are also resting where he is and he says that they too have lost so many men. Seems as though he gets on well with them. Brothers in arms, he calls them. That's about it really.' Caroline looks up and holds the letter out to her husband.

'Not much point in me reading it myself now that you have told me everything there is in it.'

'My, my, we are grumpy tonight! Has something upset you today?'

'Oh just the usual things and feeling so tired and with there still being no end in sight to all of this misery.'

'Arthur, you can't take *everyone*'s troubles on your own shoulders, even in those instances when you feel that people have no one else to turn to. You know it, Arthur, and I know it. There are some types that, for one reason or another, are unable to help themselves and they will just suck you dry if you let them. I can't remember when you last had a brief rest, let alone a day or two away from it all. Why, you don't even read your books anymore. You are just too tired and it is always late by the time you get home. You will make yourself ill the way you are carrying on. Take a break from it all because, if you don't, I fear you will have some sort of a collapse and where will that leave us and all those people that you are so determined to help? Just for a couple of days, Arthur, please! I for one would like to see our new granddaughter. November is not the best time of the year to travel to the country, I know, but can we not spend at least one night in Swavesey and visit Grace and the new baby? Carrie and Greg are old enough to look after the house for a couple of days and Elsie and Ben are sensible, so I have no fears there. What do you say?'

'That will be fine.'

'What did you say? Am I hearing things? You must indeed be in need of a rest if you can say yes to that straightaway. I shall write to Grace right now and post the letter first thing in the morning before you change your mind.'

'Can I please come with you?' asks Elsie.

'Elsie! You are not still thinking about Henry, are you? He is too old for you. Now would you please bring in your father's supper and please make sure that it is hot. While you are there, you can fill the hot-water bottles and put them in the beds for me as well.'

'*Please* let me come with you, Mummy.'

It is still dark when the small party of mother, father and daughter leave the house first to catch the underground railway to Liverpool Street and then make the journey up to

Swavesey. Wanting to make the most of the two days Arthur has set aside to see his daughter-in-law and the new baby, Caroline has prepared something for them to eat once on the train rather than take the time to have a breakfast before they set out. Arthur has another reason for going. He wants to see for himself the Fenland countryside even if it is, in Arthur's mind, winter, though strictly speaking winter does not start for another five weeks on the shortest day of the year.

The train eases out of Liverpool Street and it being so early in the morning they have a whole compartment to themselves. As they leave the almost featureless silhouette sprawl of back-to-back housing behind them it begins to get light and the view from the window displays grander properties with their own gardens. Caroline takes out the package of bread and cheese and the old, but still perfectly good, vacuum flask of tea. Arthur has taken this flask to work or to his mission for several years before the war and back then it had always been called the 'Thermos flask'. Arthur knew of someone who actually smashed his flask on purpose when war broke out as he would have nothing German in the house. Arthur, seeing the utility of his flask, rose above such sentiments. Granted, he stopped referring to the object as his Thermos flask and it became known as either 'the vacuum flask' or just 'the flask'. One further concession he made was to paint the outer casing so as to erase the manufacturer's name and any trace of the words 'Thermos' and 'Germany' that it previously bore.

'The train seems to be travelling slower than what I remember from last time,' says Caroline.

'Probably saving on the amount of coal used,' responded Arthur.

'We seem to be making more stops as well.'

'Probably down to there being fewer trains these days and that is why it stops at more stations and then, of course, it is still quite early in the day.'

The remainder of the journey is quite uneventful and, as this is a carriage without a corridor, they are each siting in a separate corner of the compartment content to look at the view outside under a cloud-laden sky. There is then a tiresome wait of just over an hour at Cambridge.

'Another sign of the times, I suppose,' says Caroline. 'I remember there used to be three carriages and now there are just two with that little engine to take us there. We did not have so long to wait then as now either.'

'No doubt they need all the carriages they can find for much better purposes,' Arthur responds.

Grace has taken on a small cottage of her own that she shares with her youngest sister, Jane. The arrangement suits them both nicely. Arthur, Caroline and Elsie are found room at Grace's parents Harry and Kate's house. To Elsie's delight, she is to sleep in Henry's bed with Henry consigned to the old settee downstairs. This 'sacrifice' appeals to the young girl's romantic ideas and she decides the bed smells of Henry.

Caroline spends most of her time with Grace and the baby. Arthur only some of the time. He splits the remainder of his time between taking in the wintry look and feel of the village and its immediate environs and visiting St Andrew's Church where he holds long and, to his mind, interesting and stimulating conversations with the Reverend Sharp. They discuss a wide range of issues of a theological nature, something Arthur relishes as he has little time or opportunity to enjoy such moments these days.

The Reverend Sharp is interested to hear about Arthur's mission and his work in the East End and Arthur in turn is impressed by John's –as he becomes known to Arthur – work with the fire relief fund and about his ministry to a small village community.

As for Elsie, she looks for every opportunity to be with Henry or to watch him at whatever he is doing.

'So, Grace, have you decided when to have Iris baptised?' asks Arthur.

'Not until Phil is home on leave and we will do it here in Swavesey. Would you be one of the godparents or does your being an Old Catholic monk prevent that?'

'I can't tell you how pleased I am to be asked! Of course, I will be delighted to be a godparent to my granddaughter. And, no, there's no issue to consider with me being a lay Old Catholic brother. We are in full communion with the Anglican Communion, you know, and nothing to do with the Roman Church. Did not Phil tell you this?'

'Thank you. I think Phil will be pleased. I'll be asking Emmie Prior to be the other godparent.'

Arthur and Caroline are lying awake in bed at home after the journey back.

'My dear, I can't tell you how pleased I am that you suggested going to see Grace and the baby. Just this little break has given me an opportunity to think about things in a way that I just do not seem to have the time to do nowadays. John Sharp is a remarkable man. I just wish we had more time to enjoy each other's conversation and company. When this war is at last over and Aidan is back home safe and sound I want to approach my Order and my bishop with a request that I study to be ordained as a priest.'

'Why aren't I surprised at that? I have been expecting you to arrive at this decision long before now. Then you have been so busy with your mission and that is all you seem to talk about, that and the war and Aidan and then there is Phil and Ireland. You never talk of Phil nor why he is in Ireland.

'I see Ireland as a more complicated problem and I think nothing will improve that situation until the war is over. I just hope that they don't enter into something akin to a civil war over there. No matter how bad things may get in Ireland though, it will be nothing compared with the mindless slaughter and suffering happening on the Continent and elsewhere. With the Americans coming in, though – and for all that they're coming in far too late in my mind – it's bound to tip the balance in our favour.'

'Well at last you have spoken to me about Ireland and as for the other, I can see your mind is more settled and this pleases me. What will it mean if you are granted permission to study as a priest?'

'What a remarkable woman and wife you are, my dear. Let's see about what training for the priesthood will mean *after* I have consulted the bishop and *if* I get their permission.'

'Have you noticed how Elsie seems to be attracted to Henry and he to her, despite the difference in their ages? Mind you, as they both get a little older that age difference will mean nothing. No doubt Elsie will be asking to come with us for the christening and I know she worries that Henry will soon be of an age to be called up if he isn't fool enough to volunteer himself. Young men of just eighteen and nineteen are now being sent to the front as infantry and many will not be coming back home. Anyway, enough of that. Do you remember what it was like for us when we first started walking out together?'

'Yes, of course I do. Are you tired after such a long journey?'

'Not that tired, husband, and it has been an awful long time.'

# Chapter 6

Arthur and Caroline are visiting their son Arthur and daughter-in-law Edith for a rare family get-together. Hilda has been invited but has failed to reply and it soon becomes clear that she is not intending to come over. Caroline brings with her some tea and some small cakes that she has baked herself from the family's own rations. With bread and other basics being rationed now it is the customary thing to bring something with you when calling upon other people whether they be family or just friends.

'It has been some nine months now since Hilda's husband was killed. Surely she must have got over the worst of it by now. I don't mean to sound harsh but in all fairness she couldn't have known him that long and they only spent a short time together as husband and wife before he went to fight. You would at least think she could mix with her family. Why, she has not even sent an answer to Edith's invitation to come and join us,' says Arthur.

Caroline knows differently and keeps her thoughts to herself. The truth is that Hilda does not want to suffer her father's company anymore. Hilda was always more of a free spirit than the others and resented her father's control over her life and at the same time his seeming distance and lack of affection. This is why Hilda left home early before the war and entered into service with live-in accommodation. She preferred the long hours and the hard work to remaining at home.

After a reasonable interval the children ask to be allowed outside to play in the small back garden. They are not particularly fond of their serious and sometimes – although unintentionally – formidable grandfather.

With a cheeky smile and a wink that Edith is not intended to see, Arthur says, 'Well, Father! What do you think about this plan to let women over the age of thirty have the vote?'

'Well, there might be the odd woman that is able to understand politics but I fear that it is all too much for them to comprehend the intricacies of such things. Besides, with the coalition government in place at the moment all political parties are trying to hold a common line, or at least they should be whilst our men are fighting and some are paying the ultimate sacrifice.

'Caroline has never shown any interest in politics. Her interests and abilities lie elsewhere – in raising our family and maintaining the home. This has been a matter of discussion for too many years. Granted that there are a few women who think they should have a say in how the country is run and by whom, but I just wonder how many women will actually be interested in voting and of those that do how many will understand what it is they are voting for!

'You just need to look at the Bible, which shows us just how few women of influence there have been through the ages. There have been clever women, I grant you that. There have been devious and bad women as well. Those women that have reached a position of power such as Queen Victoria and, going back even further, Queen Elizabeth, did so only by accident of birth.

'As for now, I accept that some things have changed since the start of the war and I accept also that we do have women doing jobs that previously only a man would undertake. This, though, is through a national necessity and as soon as our men return then things will revert back to how they used to be.'

Rising to the bait, as both Arthurs hoped she would, Edith responds.

'So you are one of those that firmly believes that a woman's place is in the home to wait on man hand and foot and have his babies and that she has no head to work things out for herself or to have a mind of her own? For a start it is not *all* women aged over thirty that will get the vote and why is it that men aged over twenty-one can vote and women will not? It is only those women that are householders in their own right, and by the time this war – started by *men*, I may add – is over there will be far too many of that type of woman, and those women that are married to householders that will get the vote. How many married women will be told by their husbands how to vote because their husbands think they know what's best and the poor feeble woman does not. If Arthur ever tries that trick on me, he will be in for a big surprise.'

Arthur throws up his hands as I to say: 'As if I would dare!'

'And as for you bringing the Bible into it, father-in-law, that is disingenuous of you and you know it. Your argument is weak and no longer relevant.'

It is only after they have gone that Edith realises that her husband has provoked such a discussion on purpose. She playfully admonishes him and they are in good spirits and there is a twinkle in their eyes – tonight will be an early night for them both but perhaps it will be sometime before they eventually get to sleep.

# Chapter 7

Phil is inwardly angry as he knows that he is long overdue some leave and the chance to get back home – for a short while at least. But then things in Ireland are not going the way the authorities in charge and some of the leaders in the British Government back in Westminster were hoping for. In spite of the war, which seems now to be slowly going in the Allies' favour, Lloyd George has been trying to find a solution to the Irish problem by implementing Home Rule for Ireland. It is the only solution that the British Government has to offer to Ireland.

Tensions grow when Lloyd George's initiative to smooth the way forward through what is called the Irish Convention fails through a combination of factors. There is the boycott by the ever more influential Sinn Féin party – whose Gaelic name translates as 'Ourselves' or 'We Ourselves' – which remains dedicated to complete independence from Britain for the whole of the island. Then there are the Protestants from the north-east of Ireland who insist upon remaining part of the United Kingdom and the added complication of some Unionists in the south of the country who fear what will happen to them if Ireland becomes partitioned and they find themselves as a minority in a predominantly Catholic independent republic.

Tension rises even higher when the new viceroy to Ireland, Lord French, states that he has 'uncovered' a German plot and a large number of republicans are arrested as a consequence of this 'discovery'. There is no real evidence of such a plot and a conspiracy involving Germany but this clumsy British action hands yet another welcome boost to the cause of Sinn Féin and the Republican movement. Lloyd George gives up on the task of finding a way to introduce Home Rule.

Phil and Grace can only continue to write to each other yet it is not always easy for them to find something to say in their letters. Then, after far too many months of waiting, just a fortnight after the Allies crash through the German lines at Amiens on the eighth of August, dealing Germany a heavy blow indeed, Phil is finally granted two weeks' leave at fairly short notice.

Plans are hastily made and Phil is to spend all of his leave with Grace and his baby daughter in the little cottage. Jane, needless to say, is to move back in with her parents during Phil's stay. Preparations are now made, too, for the long-awaited christening.

Back in London there is a now fifteen-year-old girl who is looking forward to a journey to go to a christening in Swavesey more than she has looked forward to anything before in her life.

Phil loses two days of his leave getting from Dublin to Swavesey and two days for his return journey, yet those ten days with Grace and the baby are the happiest in his life. On his way through London he picks up some of his civilian clothes from Ben, who has met him early in the morning off the boat train at Paddington. He relishes the prospect of being out of uniform and walking through the meadows and fields and along the riverbank in shirt sleeves away from Ireland and all its woes. It is perhaps fortunate for this young couple – who once again must go through the process of getting to know each other – that they have little or no idea what the forthcoming year or so is to bring.

It is during the middle of Phil's stay, on a Saturday afternoon, that the christening takes place. Phil's mother and father, together with Elsie, make the journey to the little Fenland village. Each in their own way is excited, though perhaps in Arthur's case 'pleased' is a better description of his emotional state. Arthur is proud to be taking the serious responsibility of being a godparent and looks forward to renewing his acquaintance with the vicar. Caroline is longing to see her son as well as enjoying the occasion, and Elsie, whilst looking forward to seeing her brother of course, is hoping that Henry has not started to take an interest in one of the girls in the village. She feels quite the young woman now that she is no longer at school and has a job running errands and small deliveries for a ladieswear shop. Later she hopes to become a member of the sales staff.

The time seems to fly by and all too soon Phil is back in his uniform and is carrying his small case as he and Grace walk slowly and sorrowfully down the road to Swavesey station. It is early morning and it looks as though it will be a bright summer's day again but their hearts are heavy.

'How many times have we wished for all this business in Europe and Ireland to go away and for us to start to have a proper life?' asks Grace.

'Almost every day but now it is harder than ever. Ireland is about as difficult to understand as I can think and it looks as though things in Europe could drag on for another year despite the Americans shipping in so many soldiers. There is nothing that we can do about it, so we just have to live each day as it comes and hope that things will turn out for the better. It is going to be a long and sad journey back to Dublin and I am missing you and this place already.'

They fall into silence for the last few hundred yards to the station platform. As they approach, Steve is standing by so as to close the crossing gates to road traffic, although it is unlikely that anyone will be about this early in the morning. Grace pulls Phil up.

'I'll be going back now, Phil. I don't want to say goodbye on the platform.'

She puts one hand to Phil's face and kisses him gently before turning away and walking back home before Phil can see her crying. Steve urgently beckons Phil to hurry up as he starts to close the crossing gates to allow the train to Cambridge to have the right of way.


# Chapter 8

Despite the German collapse at Amiens that August the German lines are holding strong and fast. That is until late September when part of the German-fortified Hindenburg Line is broken.

With the summer drawing to a close, events take an unexpected course. Germany's allies begin to lose their resolve and to crumble. First it is Bulgaria; then it is Ottoman Turkey, which has inflicted such terrible losses on the Allies at Gallipoli following the failed attempt to capture and secure Constantinople; and then it is the turn of Austria-Hungary to seek an armistice. This does not automatically mean that these countries wish to end the war – that will require complex diplomatic negotiations – but at least it does mean that these countries and powers want to stop the fighting.

Was there an end in sight at last? It does not seem so to those on the Western Front where there continues to be skirmishes and where the unfailingly accurate German sniper always finds his man. But then the ordinary soldier still stuck in his trench has no idea of what is happening back in Germany. He, the ordinary soldier, has no knowledge of the uprisings against the Kaiser in Berlin nor of the mutiny amongst the German ranks nor that the Imperial Navy is turning against their emperor.

When the news does break, both on the Western Front and on the home front, of the Kaiser's abdication and his going into exile in the Netherlands and of Germany's willingness to discuss the terms of an armistice agreement, the tidings spread like wildfire.

Back in London, Arthur and Caroline and Arthur and Edith and Chris and Sarah and their families are just like any other and celebrate either indoors or out on the streets. On that hopeful November morning, Hilda decides that she should join in the revelry and makes her way to Trafalgar Square. Despite the noise of the crowd, she can just hear Big Ben chiming noon for the first time in so many years. Her Charlie is gone – one of the casualties of war – but she, despite her sorrow and grief, is proud of her man.

At least Aidan will now be coming home – as soon as it is clear that the cessation in the fighting is permanent and Germany is no longer a military threat.

As for the Irish problem it remains a problem. No one as yet has worked out how to resolve things and certainly the British Government does not seem to have any inkling as to just how big a problem it is going to grow into.

# Chapter 9

A peace treaty has yet to be concluded and signed with Germany despite the fact that some of Germany's former allies have already taken this final step. Yet the fighting has stopped and Aidan returns home at the beginning of January; he is one of the fortunate ones to be sent back home early.

For the time being at least there is no shortage of job opportunities for a lorry driver and almost immediately Aidan secures a position. As are so many others, he tries to adjust to a normal, routine civilian life away from the horrors and memories of war.

In Ireland tensions have yet again come to the surface and Phil is resigned to knowing that he will not be coming home sometime soon. He remains conscripted to the army. The elections held the previous December have resulted in an impressive and, for the British, alarming triumph for Sinn Féin, with the exception, that is, of the Protestant-dominated part of the island known as Ulster. The fact that many of the Sinn Féin candidates were in British-run gaols did not hamper the Sinn Féin success in any way, shape or form. In fact, if anything the internment boosts the credibility of Sinn Féin over other candidates.

The elected representatives, having no truck with the Westminster Parliament, call an Irish Assembly with the result that a declaration of independence is issued and an Irish republic is declared. The mood is such amongst the new republican politicians that they press the peacemakers who are still negotiating the terms of a peace treaty with Germany in Paris to also ratify the existence of the Irish Republic. The Irish call is lost to some extent amongst other calls from colonised countries, including Ho Chi Minh's Vietnam, which is seeking independence from France and to be set free from the shackles of imperialism.

Then begins a cycle of events that is to lead to the imposition of military rule by the British and Phil's fate, for the time being at least, is sealed.

On the same day that the Irish Assembly meets and declares the formation of the Irish Republic the so-called 'Irish Volunteers' shoot and kill two middle-aged policemen on a cart delivering explosives. With the British offering no other solution than to grant Home Rule, more militant members of Sinn Féin and others are convinced that freedom must be fought for and this in turn leads to groups of Irish Volunteers being designated as the Irish Republican Army whose purpose is to wage war against the British occupiers and the Royal Irish Constabulary.

The RIC is, for the most part, comprised of Irish Catholics. It is made clear to these men that any RIC officer, Irish or not, faces lethal punishment at the point of a gun if he continues with the RIC. When the republican militancy later secures from sympathisers secret information about civil servants and individual policemen considered to be a threat to the republican cause then the newly created assassination squads created by Michael Collins are sent to liquidate these people.

Martial law is now imposed, and with there being only around 7,000 troops on active service throughout the whole of Ireland, Phil and his comrades face a terrifying prospect. Such is the strain and stress that he is under that Phil neglects to write to his wife back home in that peacefully quiet Fenland village.

Faced with the threats to themselves and their families if they continue to serve, many policemen resign from the RIC. A few RIC men set about exacting revenge by seeking out and then killing prominent IRA men or local republican politicians, but generally speaking the RIC is no longer an effective force. To replace the resigning policemen, Lloyd George, then still the British Prime Minister, recruits demobilised men and sends them over to Ireland.

295

One night Phil is lying on his bunk bed. His co-driver, George Richard, a man from south of the River Thames who was deemed unfit for active military service, is lying in the lower bunk.

'You still awake, George?'

'Of course I bloody well am. It's only nine o'clock and we are cooped up in this place with not even a sniff of a pint of beer. The mess has run out of beer and the local breweries are scared to deliver to us. Can't even go into town these days as it is so unsafe and us soldiers stick out like a sore thumb.'

'This is turning into an all-out war between us and the Irish, George, and things are getting worse all of the time. On the one side you have the IRA carrying out their assassinations of policemen and anyone with anything to do with the British way of running things over here. Just a while back the IRA sought out British officers in restaurants and hotels and just gunned them down where they sat.

'Then, on the other side, you've got the Black and Tans recruited into the RIC from the Mainland. They're supposed to be combatting the IRA but they can't find them so they are taking it out and taking revenge against any Irish man or woman who gets in their way. I feel like one of those rabbits that get stuck in my lorry headlights.'

'What's that supposed to mean?' asks George.

'Well, what I mean is that I hate the Irish for what they are doing and I hate our side, or at least the Black and Tans and the auxiliaries who are supposed to be our side, for how they are taking it out on the locals without a care as to whether they support the IRA or not. This has been going on for months now and I'm sick of it. I've been stuck out here for a year now without leave, and before you say anything I know you have as well.'

'What you going to do about it, Phil? Stick it out or try and put your papers in? Me, I've got nothing back home. Might not even be able to find myself a job. I'm gasping for a beer but at least I'm getting paid and fed. Now that compulsory military service is done away with and with you being married and with a young child, you at least have something to go back home to.'

'Well, I don't quite know how to go about getting out of the army, George, and whether the end of conscription even applies to us here in Ireland or just to those that were over fighting the Krauts and the rest of them. No point talking to the sergeant; he won't have it. Him being from up north, he hates the Irish down here with a vengeance and he's more British in his thinking than I am and that's for certain.'

'You're still putting in for leave back home, aren't you?'

'You know I am, George. Almost every other week.'

'Well, keep on asking and then when you get home see if you can get yourself out of here. Watch it! Here comes trouble!'

'Up and out of it, you two,' barks their sergeant. 'One of our convoys has been ambushed and they need us to go down and pick up the pieces. Pretty much wiped us out, those murdering Fenian bastards.'

Some three weeks later Phil at last receives welcome news – his entire unit is to be rotated with a replacement unit coming over from England. Phil is now in high spirits and writes to Grace. All that remains now is for him to get through the next few days unscathed. In addition to the incident that led to his lieutenant being shot, he has been directly involved in a number of convoy ambushes himself, although nothing like the scale of what he found when he was called out one evening a few weeks back. On that occasion not a single man was left alive and each and every truck and vehicle had been set alight. The Black and Tans took revenge the following night with further shootings and the firing of houses in the village closest to where the ambush happened. It mattered not a jot to them that the people they were hurting and killing had nothing to do with the ambush.

Phil has been lucky and just hopes that his good fortune to date will hold out and that he returns home safe and sound. For the first time in quite a while Phil finds himself praying that everything will turn out fine.

# Part VII
# Homeward Bound

# Chapter 1

Phil returns to Epsom Barracks. How much it has changed since he first went there! Desperate for hospital and invalid accommodation, they have turned part of the barracks into a hospital to accept casualties being sent home from the front.

Grace and baby Iris have come down from Swavesey and they are staying with Emmie Prior, where Grace is more than happy to do little things around the house and to help out where she can whilst enjoying Emmie's hospitality and friendship once more.

Now back at Epsom and away from Ireland, Phil seeks permission to quit the army and at the same time requests the leave that he is sure must be owing to him. His request to quit the army has to be considered and processed and things do seem promising on that front. While he awaits developments, Phil is granted the ten days' leave that he is told is owing to him.

'You not putting in for extended leave, George?' ask Phil.

'Just for next weekend, that will do. I have a married sister down Lambeth way, so I will call in on her but that's all. Most of my mates copped it, so I ain't even got me pals to go and have a beer with. I'll stick around here and see what happens. At least I can get off camp now and then and find myself a pub. What do you reckon, Phil? Do you reckon we will be sent back to Ireland again?'

'No doubt the unit will be sent back, George. Things are getting worse and worse out there. I think we should cut our losses and get out of there and let the Irish make a mess of it by themselves.'

'What about that lot up in the north like our sergeant? They'll never settle for an independent Ireland.'

'Not my problem, George. Not for the next ten days at least and then hopefully I'm out of here and out of the army and back on Civvy Street and at long last having a family life.

So, back in ten days then, George, and try and stay sober at least some of the time. Right, that's it; I'm off. See you, George!'

'Cheers, mate!'

# Chapter 2

Sitting on the train up to London and looking forward to the reunion with his wife and baby daughter whom he has not seen for such a long time, Phil thinks to himself: *So much to do, so many people to see and so little time to do it all in.*

Grace knows to expect her husband sometime in the afternoon but then as two o'clock and then three o'clock pass she gets more and more impatient and somewhat anxious. She has run out of little things to do as she tries to keep herself occupied. She dares not go out or even go into the back garden for fear that she might miss Phil or not hear him at the door. The ever resourceful and thoughtful Emmie has planned to be busy with the WI that day and she has asked the girls to join her after school to help with some small task or other that needs doing. So Grace is alone in the house with baby Iris and has nothing better to do now than clock-watching. Then at last at just gone half past three there is the sound of the front door bell. Almost to the minute the baby awakes and starts letting everyone know that she needs attention.

'Oh Iris! Could you not stay asleep for a little longer,' Grace mutters to no one in particular. 'Well, you are just going to learn to have to wait.'

Ignoring the baby's cries, Grace rushes to the front door to be greeted as she opens the door by the sight of her husband on the doorstep.

'Hello' is all Phil can say. He steps inside. 'Looks like

someone else needs your attention. It has been about a year, so a few more minutes aren't going to make that much difference and I'd like to see her for myself anyway.'

Grace and Phil take themselves off to the kitchen for a cup of tea and a bite to eat. There, they hope, they will find themselves uninterrupted should Emmie and the girls come home as they try and catch up with each other and get used once more to each other's company.

Over the next few days Phil and Grace do the rounds of Phil's family, starting off first obviously with his mother and father and those of his brothers and sisters – now including Aidan – who are still living at home. Is Phil's father at home when they call? Of course not. This time he is not at his East End mission but at the Oratory up in Haberdasher Street taking steps of preparation to enter into the priesthood. When Phil hears the reason why his father is not at home to greet him he first just shrugs his shoulders and then just moves his head from side to side as if to indicate his incomprehension, not for the first time, of his father and his father's actions. It's his first homecoming for almost a year and his father puts his church and his religion before wanting to see his son and his goddaughter.

On their way back to the underground railway station and then on to Emmie's, Phil turns to Grace.

'You think that just for once in a while my father would show some sign that he cares, but does he? No! The same old story. His church and his obsession with religion – and yes, it is definitely an obsession – you just have to look at the names I have been saddled with – always come first. I tell you what. My mother must be a saint to have put up with him and his ways for all these years. Hilda stayed away again probably because of him. I must try and see her before I go back to the barracks. I'm intrigued that mother says that Hilda is courting again and another Irishman, too!'

'Don't upset yourself, Phil. You must know very well by now

what he's like. Anyway, dear, I enjoyed the afternoon and this evening with your family. Let's just get back to Emmie's and I'll make us both a nice cup of warm milk and then we can just go up to bed. Hopefully, the little one here will stay asleep all the way back and I can just lay her down in her sleeping basket.'

# Chapter 3

There is a steady drizzle as Phil returns to Epsom and presents his pass at the gate for inspection.

'Been away for ten days, have you, Private? Going to be some changes around here. Report to your sergeant. You know the drill and no doubt he will fill you in.'

'Yes, Corporal.'

Phil makes his way to the sergeant's room, more of a broom cupboard than a room, but there is no one there. It being late Phil is pretty certain Sergeant Hughes is over at the NCOs' mess. Seeing a neatly-arranged notepad and a pencil on the tiny desk next to the sergeant's bed, Phil writes a brief note giving the time that he has arrived back. Phil then makes his way to his own hut and bunk. Apart from the single naked light bulb just inside the door, the hut is unlit and as far as Phil can tell none of the bunk beds are occupied. *Strange. What's going on? Where is everybody?* he thinks to himself.

As Phil has walked from the gate to the Sergeant's room and then on to his own hut, the rain has started to come down harder and by the time he gets into his hut it is raining very hard and Phil is quite wet. 'Be buggered if I'm going back out in this,' he says to the empty hut. Phil makes his way to his bunk and arranges his wet clothes in a way that he hopes is not going to send his sergeant berserk before settling down on his bunk. There is something not quite right. The bedding on the bunk beds is all neatly arranged, as it should be, but half of the bunks and the lockers appear to be unoccupied.

Phil lies there in the semi-darkness and after a while he hears loud voices coming closer and closer. The sort of loud voices belonging to people who have had more than a few beers. The door opens and someone switches on all the lights and Phil sees three rather wet men including his mate George.

'Phil, mate! Back at last, are you! You've missed out on what's been going on here. Then if you haven't seen that wife of yours for over a year I bet you don't care.'

The three men then burst into unnecessarily loud laughter over what George is suggesting.

'What's going on, George. Where is everyone and why are you lot out on the lash on a Wednesday night?'

George, slightly unsteadily, makes his way over and sits himself down on the bunk bed next to theirs.

'This is mine now. No more climbing over you in the middle of the night when I need a piss.'

'George! Are you going to tell me what's going on or not?'

'The unit is gone, mate. We have been amolgamated.'

'You mean amalgamated?'

'Yeah. That an' all. Some of the blokes have gone back to Civvy Street so I guess that means that you will an' all, and the rest of us are joining another unit and we are off back to Ireland in a couple of days. Bloody army! You can wait weeks or months for the simplest thing to happen like getting a plug for one of the wash basins and then bang something like this 'appens just like that. Me, Billy and Mitch over there are the only ones left now, oh and Sergeant Hughes of course. He's been unbearable over the past few days. 'Appy as Larry he is at the thought of going back to Ireland. I prefer him when he is mean and on your back all the time. At least I know what to expect.'

'Where is Sergeant Hughes, George. I tried his room but he was not there.'

'Over at the NCO mess getting plastered, I expect. The Lieutenant's gone with the rest of them so it's just the Serge and us three until we leave for Aldershot the day after tomorrow. You'd best get over to the office first thing and get yourself sorted. Jeez! My head's spinning. Must 'ave a leak first then it's hit the hay time.'

Phil lies awake for most of the night. Grace is leaving Emmie's in the morning to go back to Swavesey. Will he be able to get his old job back or will someone else take him on? Where are they going to live? Where is he going to stay until he gets things sorted? What if I'm not being released from the army after all? What if they send me back to Ireland? What if I get killed? *Oh get a grip, Phil,* he tells himself. He turns over onto his side but is still not able to get to sleep and things are not helped by George lying on his back on the bunk opposite still in his uniform and with his boots on snoring his head off.

'Oh shut up, George. Serves you dead right if there's a snap inspection or call-out, then you'll be for it.' There is no one listening. The others are as dead to the world as is George.

# Chapter 4

The next morning Phil reports to the unit office and hears the news that he wants to hear. He and the army are parting company with immediate effect. He is given a note to hand in to the pay office but not before he returns his uniform and all of his kit to the quartermaster's – if he is light on anything then the costs will be deducted from his pay. Being a rather meticulous and tidy man Phil has no worries about that happening. The army reverts to type and it takes the rest of the day before everything is settled. Phil agrees to stay the one further night and to break a habit and to go with his mates to the mess for a farewell drink. In the morning he feels that this is the worst decision he has ever made in his life. Not being used to drink it did not take Phil long to be the worse for wear. His mates had to try and get him back to the hut without being seen. Having managed this, they dumped him on his bunk before going back to the mess to continue where they left off. It is their last night as well.

The next morning a very groggy Phil makes his way to get the train into London. George, in his familiar barrack-room language, had told him that his eyes look like two piss-holes in the snow. As glad as he is to be leaving the army, Phil knows he will miss George.

First things first, when Phil reaches London he goes to see if he can have his old driving job back. That at least works out well for him. Now he needs somewhere to stay for a few days and he must write to Grace. Brother Chris seems to offer the best chance of a bed so he makes his way over to their place after going to the post office to send, what seems to Phil, a rather expensive telegram to Swavesey.

The next day Phil starts work and is happy to do so. The next step is to start looking for some rooms for him to rent for when Grace and Iris come back to London.

# Part VIII

# Priesthood and Sacraments

# Chapter 1

Grace has been down in London for almost two months. She is visiting her friend Emmie one Saturday morning while Phil is at work.

'Ah thank you, Grace, for making the tea. I am just about ready for this.'

'Where are the girls?'

'Out with friends looking at the shops no doubt. Quite the young ladies now, always interested in the latest fashions. I will have to decide what next as it won't be long now before one then the other finishes with their school. If Robert were still with us, there is no doubt that they would go on to some college or other but now I am not so sure. Oh it is not the money – well, not if they were to go on to a reasonable college that doesn't charge the earth – it's just that I do not want to be in this house on my own.'

'Have you thought about moving, Emmie?'

'No. Well, not yet anyway. I know it sounds silly but it would seem like a betrayal of Robert – after all, he put up the money for us to live here and raise the girls. Enough about me. How are things with you, Grace?'

'I'm thinking of going back to Swavesey.'

'Oh, that will be nice for you – a chance to visit the family again.'

'No, Emmie. I mean I am thinking of going to live back in Swavesey. I do not want to spend a winter in those rooms we are renting. Of late you can smell the damp and it is no place to have a baby through the winter. Those little cottages back home may not look much but once you have a fire going and with the little range on the go as well they are surprisingly snug.'

'What does Phil say to all this?'

'I have not told him yet. I'm waiting for the right moment.'

'There's nothing wrong between you two, is there?'

'No, nothing like that, but I must put Iris first.'

'Can't you find somewhere else to live to keep you in London?'

'Places to rent seem to be in short supply and certainly in the price range that we can afford with only Phil working. There is no point in leaving where we are just to end up in a similar situation.'

'What about buying?'

'Emmie! You are living in a dream world. The likes of me and Phil can't afford to buy. There is finding the deposit first and even then it might be difficult to meet the payments.'

'What if I was to lend you money for a deposit on a house? I was talking to one of my ladies on the WI just the other day and she says there are some nice places being built now just off Primrose Hill. Her husband evidently knows the builder and the way things are the houses are not selling well. Why there was one instance, so I was told, where the builder agreed to lower the price of the house if the buyer did all the painting himself. It has got to be worth a try, Grace. You can't be going back to Swavesey and leaving Phil here on his own.'

'I don't know, Emmie. It is very dear and sweet of you to offer to lend us the deposit but I'm not sure even then that Phil would go for it.'

'Look, here is what we'll do. Let me make some enquiries for you. I can find out how much a house is going for if Phil is prepared to do some painting and how much your repayments might be every week or every month, and then you can compare that with what you are paying in rent. Then you and Phil can discuss it between you. How does that sound?'

'Oh Emmie. You are the best friend I could possibly have. You are so kind and generous.'

'Enough of that! Now then, what else has been happening since we last had a natter?'

'Well, Phil's father is about to be ordained into the priesthood.'

'Old Holy Joe becoming a priest! Whatever next?' Emmie bursts into laughter.

Grace joins in with the laughing. 'I never heard you call him Holy Joe before. That is so funny! I can't wait to tell Phil what you've just said.'

'When is this meant to take place then, Grace?'

'A week on Sunday, I think, up at Holy Joe's Oratory.' Grace smirks again.

'Are *you* going?'

'You bet! I wouldn't miss it for the world. It might even be entertaining to see how my father-in-law conducts himself both before and afterwards. But apart from everything else it would be a dreadful snub if we were not to go, given that he is godfather to Iris, and Phil is his son after all!'

'You must come back and tell me all about it. Ah, that sounds like the girls are back.'

# Chapter 2

It is but just over a week since Grace visited Emmie when Emmie calls on Grace unannounced.

'Hello, Grace. I can't stop as I am on my way to meet my ladies at the WI. I have written everything down and it is here in this envelope concerning the price and repayment terms for a mortgage on a house in Angel Road, just as we discussed last week. Both of you go and have a look at the house before you make your mind up. And Grace, make sure you sound as though you mean it when you say you are going back to Swavesey rather than staying here. Nothing wrong with a little arm-bending. Oh my goodness, Grace! Even from where I am standing I can see why you don't want to stay here with Iris!

'Now you're off to Holy Joe's ordination on Sunday, aren't you? Here I've brought one of my old hats that I don't wear anymore. You can keep it but please do come and tell me all about how the day went. Right, must be away or I shall be late. Goodbye, Grace; goodbye, little one,' she says as she puts her hand to Iris's cheek.

'Bye, Emmie, and thank you!'

Grace sets Iris back down on the floor and tries the hat on and looks at herself in her hand mirror. She likes the hat.

'Now then, Iris. What we have to do is get your daddy to see this house and get him to agree that we buy it and see if he knows one end of a paintbrush from the other.'

The baby does not pay a blind bit of notice of course.

That evening Phil and Grace look at the figures given to them by Emmie. The repayment terms will exceed what they are paying in rent at the moment but at least Phil agrees to go with Grace and look at the house next Saturday afternoon after he has finished work.

# Chapter 3

The ordination ceremony is set for eleven-thirty on Sunday morning and everyone is to meet beforehand outside the Oratory in Haberdasher Street.

With the exception of Hilda, all of Arthur's children are there, as are Chris's wife, Sarah, together with baby Chris – Arthur's godson – and Grace, with Iris of course, but not Edith as two of the children have gone down with a cold. Arthur is there of course for his father's big day.

It transpires that Arthur is the only person to undergo the ordination ceremony on this particular occasion. Having waited outside on a relatively mild autumn day so that everyone can enter the building together, they are confronted with the sight of Arthur in a white surplice kneeling before the raised altar. Without a further word the family group arrange themselves, although they remain standing. After some five minutes or so another man in a white surplice enters from a side door.

'That's the bishop,' Caroline whispers to Aidan.

After genuflecting to the statue of Christ on the Holy Cross, the bishop turns to face all those assembled.

'Welcome all on this day when our beloved former Brother Arthur is to enter into the priesthood of the Old Catholic Church. Please remain standing as we say a prayer of welcome and ask for God's blessings upon this congregation.'

After a short prayer the congregation is invited to be seated.

'Ordination is the rite of entry into priesthood and is one of the seven sacraments. Entry into the priesthood is a solemn undertaking that confers the authority to administer the holy sacraments of baptism and the giving of Holy Communion.

'We are here in the sight of God to acknowledge that our beloved former Brother Arthur be recognised and confirmed as having been called by God to his ministry. We have seen over the years how he has selflessly gone about his ministry.

'As his bishop, I am satisfied and confirm that Brother Arthur has gone through the requisite period of discernment and reached a level through his training to become a fit and proper person to welcome him fully into the priesthood of the Old Catholic Church.

'Will you all now stand for the rite of ordination.'

The bishop then places both hands on the head of the still-kneeling Arthur.

'I, James McFall, by the grace of God, Regionary Bishop of the Old Catholic Church, to all whom and to all these persons present may come do make oath and declare that we on this day do during this solemn ceremony of Mass do promote the Reverend Brother Arthur Frederick Clowes to the position of Deacon of the Old Catholic Church.

'I further confirm that as a condition of entering the Sacred Order of Priesthood that the said Deacon Arthur Frederick Clowes has undergone all the rites preserved in the Roman Pontifical.

'Praise be the Lord!'

Upon which the bishop takes his hands off from Arthur's head to the top of his arms and invites him to rise. After the bishop has kissed Arthur on both cheeks, Arthur turns to face his family and, despite the solemnity of the occasion, there is the broadest of grins on his face – a sight not very often seen. If anyone other than the bishop were closer to Arthur, they would see that there are tears in his eyes.

What *is* clear for everyone to see is the tears in Caroline's eyes. Tears of joy and love for her husband. Even Phil has a lump in his throat and is filled with a strange tingling sensation. He finds himself surprised that he is so very proud of his father.

Rather than joining the family, Arthur puts up his hand as if to say he will just be a few moments. He exits via the side door that the bishop has used and as soon as the door is closed he dabs his wet eyes on his surplice. The bishop puts his hand on his shoulder.

'Come on, Arthur. Get changed and go and join your family. I will just be a minute and I will give you your Instrument of Ordination. I have already signed it and it is all ready for you.'

# Chapter 4

Having spent the winter in their new home and with spring coming, Phil and Grace have been contemplating a short visit home to Swavesey.

Grace is eagerly awaiting her husband's return home from work. Phil, on the other hand, is making his way home wondering what to say to Grace. From almost the moment that Phil enters into the sitting room, having first hung his coat on the hook on the wall by the front door, Grace can see the worried look on Phil's face.

'What is it? What is wrong?'

'I may be out of a job by this time tomorrow.'

'What do you mean? How come?'

'Things are bad, Grace, and getting worse. Men are being laid off all over the place. It is something to do with what they call a downturn. We have all been told to come to a meeting in the yard at eight-thirty tomorrow morning. That can only mean one thing. They are going to give some of us the sack. It has been coming. There are too many drivers and not enough deliveries. What are we going to do if I lose my job, Grace? We will lose the house that's for sure.'

Grace puts her arms round him in comfort. *How can I tell him I'm expecting again?*

# *Afterword*

This story relates to real people, their lives and their experiences. Much of what you have read is drawn from what is known to have happened to the characters.

The details of Josephus Clout's arrest and the charge of larceny, his trial and his sentence were found at the London Metropolitan Archives.

The family did in fact change its name from Clout to Clowes, a change that coincided with Freddy moving to Uxbridge and later back to London.

Details of the events that led up to Ann's (Susannah Ann Clowes) committal to the Colney Hatch Asylum and her case history notes were also found at the London Metropolitan Archives, as is a picture of Ann included in her medical notes. She was there at Colney Hatch on the occasion of the terrible fire that caused such a terrible loss of life.

The fire in the Fenland village of Swavesey did take place and was reported in the newspapers.

I am grateful to one of my distant cousins for providing me with both a copy of the original documents relating to Arthur's admission first into the Benedictine Order in 1905 and later the priesthood of the Old Catholic Church.

As is probably clear by now, I chose my book's title, *Signatures and Sacraments*, in part to show how on the one hand a family can have a traditional occupation for many generations (hence the reference to signatures in relation to bookbinding) and, on the other, surprising things can happen as was the case with Brother Alfred.

I hope that I have dealt with the issues surrounding the mental illness of Ann in a sensitive manner. Without access to her medical notes I do not think I could have written this part of the story with as much confidence and accuracy.